Déjà
The Jourı
By
JT Baxter

Déjà vu

Déjà vu

JT Baxter

Published by JT Baxter, 2022.

This is a work of fiction. Similarities to real people, places, or events are entirely coincidental.

DÉJÀ VU

First edition. September 9, 2022.

Copyright © 2022 JT Baxter.

ISBN: 979-8201489007

Written by JT Baxter.

Revised Edition December 2023

All that we see or seem is but a dream within a dream.

Edgar Allen Poe

As sheltered as we are, only wise men seek the truth.

Jonathan T. Baxter

A special mention to Tammy Sue, Hayley, Miles, Miranda, Monica, and Sarah.

Fond memories linger. Love ya'll.

Front cover photograph by SelfPubBookCovers.com/nishagandhi

Prologue

In less than a single beat of his heart the moment their eyes met; Travis Sage instinctively knew he had prior knowledge of this woman. In that same instant, she gasped. Suddenly, the oxygen her body so desperately needed to inhale seemed to have vanished. Her eyes searched his; his gaze rigidly fixed on hers—both questioning the possibility of what seemed impossible and yet, so familiar. The overwhelming evidence surged to the forefront of his mind as if some telepathic memory exchange was taking place. Travis became aware that she felt it too; the intensity so powerful, the sensuality uncompromising in its quest to be recognized and acknowledged. It captivated all measures of perception and sense. "Anne?" He had no idea why he said that or where that name came from.

Was it a look of shock or complete horror that instantly filled and paralyzed the features of her face? Travis watched the helpless expression of emotional overload as her eyes rolled back, which beckoned his intuitive need to step forward and catch her in his arms.

Suddenly the room was full of people just as it had been before he first saw her. Cradled in his arms Travis gently lowered her now limp body to the floor as he went down on one knee. He felt the focus drawing toward him like ripples going outward across a pond as more and more people brought their attention to his situation. But he was stuck, at least in his reasoning. His mind was still racing through the vast amount of information that had transpired between himself and .... *And who? Was her name Anne?* How could he know that? The body was unfamiliar as were her features but her eyes.... Her eyes told a completely different story which he knew and bound them together.

Chapter 1

"What do you mean Travis what are you talking about?"

"Julie I don't know how to explain it any different than I have. I know it sounds crazy but I'm telling you the truth. As incredible as it may seem I know that woman. Every part of my mind and body is telling me...."

"Travis; stop, think for a minute, how can that be possible? Steve and I have just moved here. This is the first time you've ever been in this city...."

"Sis don't you think I realize that. Before you moved here I'd never had a reason to visit this state let alone this city. I mean, apart from country singers and their fans who else comes to Nashville?"

The look in Julie's eyes indicated he was treading on thin ice. "Lots of people visit Nashville and live here for many different reasons. Nashville and the state of Tennessee have a lot to offer; just because you prefer sandy beaches and palm trees doesn't mean that any place that isn't oceanfront has no value and nothing to offer."

Travis felt frustrated, not with his sister but with this conversation. Almost forty-eight hours had passed and he was still no closer to finding out who that woman was, than when he held her in his arms.

"Steve, I'm getting close to certifiable; I need help."

"As I said before Travis when I get to the office in the morning I'll ask around. There were almost a hundred guests at the party on Friday night and honestly, I didn't know most of them, but someone should know who she is."

Julie looked caringly at her brother. He was the adventurous younger sibling who challenged the world and within which, had made his mark as one of the most sought-after oceanographers and through whom she had lived many adventures vicariously, spending hours listening to him recant his stories. Although this Travis she was unfamiliar with. Usually self-assured and passionate, this seeming instability was bordering obsession and not like him.

Travis ran his fingers through his dark hair, frustrated in his angst to find answers and discover the truth. Although, for some strange reason, he felt as though he already had the truth, and the answers lay at the end of asking the right questions. But what were the questions? Finding her was paramount in the complicated equation wreaking havoc in his head and placing a knot and hollow feeling inside his stomach.

Julie could only conclude for pity's sake that Travis had been bitten by the love bug. Slam-dunked by cupid and had fallen hard. She even felt she could find humor in the situation if he did not take it so strenuously. Her little brother was not so little anymore. Travis had grown into a man, a very handsome man and on more than one occasion, a passing glance at his facial features, broad muscular shoulders, or washboard stomach had made her catch her breath in awe. Fantasy and thought are fleeting, captured and released. Infinitesimal moments spent and passing quickly as reality struck each one down. Notions, silly notions and besides, she thought that Steve was a good-looking man and quite eye-catching when dressed in a suit. He was a kind man and only required gentle nudging to remember her birthday and their wedding anniversaries. Julie felt she couldn't complain, shouldn't complain in the overall scheme of things surrounding their relationship even though he wasn't a passionate lover.

Travis moved away from the kitchen counter; the dinner dishes were rinsed and placed in the dishwasher. He needed to find something else to do; something less domesticated would be a blessing to his confused mind, but there is only so much you can do as a guest in someone else's home leaving him nowhere to look for reprieve.

"How about a board game," Steve hesitantly suggested almost in knowing it would not win favor.

"Sorry Steve, I don't think I'd present much of a challenge," Travis responded as he took up residence on the couch and picked up the television remote.

Julie looked over at Travis and somehow felt his pain or at least sympathy for what he might be feeling. Then she turned her eyes towards Steve who, in looking at her held the look of not knowing what else to do. Julie shrugged her shoulders both to suggest understanding and agreement. "I think I would like a glass of wine, anyone else?" Julie moved towards the kitchen. There was no response. "I guess I'll be drinking alone." Still no comeback or comment either way, so she took her glass of chilled wine out onto the patio and sat on a lounger near the Jacuzzi.

A warm night breeze caressed her cheek and she sensed the fragrance of Gardenia in the air. Julie took a deep breath through her nose to inhale the intoxicating aroma, desiring to become unburdened and find some momentary relaxation. A sip of wine added more flavors to sample in simple pleasure. With her eyes closed she searched her memory for a happy place. The last two years seemed devoid and vacant of soulful happiness. Her mind did a fast rewind carrying her back beyond them quickly. Unwilling to acknowledge their so-called existence she knew she would have to confront them soon, but not now. Not in this moment, as she claimed a teenage recollection of joy. A first kiss and the emotional exhilaration of falling in love. It only lasted for what seemed like seconds before the pain of love lost clawed at her heart and snapped her back into the reality of the current circumstance, Steve.

Taking a large gulp from her glass to dispel her thoughts, Julie rose from the lounger and made her way back inside the house.

Travis was mindlessly staring at the television screen without knowing what he was watching. Thoughts whittling through the perceived information he had gathered searching for clues. It wasn't a question of who she was; it was more about what they meant to each other and how that could be. There was no reference point, not a single memory he could call to mind to give any indication or justify the things he felt were true.

Steve was sitting at the table going through some work-related papers. Travis was staring at the television. Julie's announcement that she was going to bed went unacknowledged adding to her feeling of isolation. Although accustomed to the demands of Steve's work this inattentive behavior from Travis was unfamiliar. His usual attentive affection towards her had on many occasions, provided the solace and courage to keep moving forward. Feeling hurt, Julie made her way to the bedroom.

Scrutinizing his thoughts repeatedly brought Travis to nothing but a lot of dead ends and even he was now beginning to think it was ridiculous. Why put himself and others through this torture for a lot of coincidences that didn't add up. So what if her name was Anne? She could just as easily be a Jessica or a Sue. It didn't matter; chances were he'd never see her again anyway. What was the point in worrying about it and in so doing ruining his visit with Steve and Sis? The logical conclusion had to be...... What? He didn't know that's for sure, but it had to stop. After his birthday on Wednesday, he would fly back to his home in Pensacola for a couple of days before heading off on assignment to Borneo to photograph the wall and life, as he knew it would return to normal.

Julie was his rock and his only family since the accident five years ago when both parents were killed in an automobile pile-up on the interstate. It had been a difficult time for Travis and if it hadn't been for his sister and Steve, who knows where he would have ended up because he sure as heck didn't. He'd gone through a wild patch consuming alcohol and partying as if there was no tomorrow. And, if it hadn't been for the hardline Julie took with him, there was a good chance he wouldn't be breathing now. But things change, they had to in his case and he was well aware that he owed his life to her. Although, when he arrived last week he sensed something different about Julie. Maybe it had been the move and relocation to another city, the third since she and Steve had been married. All work-related as Steve climbed the corporate ladder. Maybe that had to take a toll on his sister, leaving friends behind and finding new ones fitting into a new community and finding her way around a new city. All good reasons to consider because Travis couldn't put his finger on anything else. And then, with this fiasco on Friday night his attention had been drawn inwards.

******

When Travis made his way from the guest bedroom into the kitchen, the sun had well and truly risen. He couldn't believe the noise that was puking out of the radio. "Oh, heck no Sis, don't tell me you've converted. Some lonely cowboy and his dog, horse or truck broke down. Or he got ditched by some woman with more sense than he's got. When did you start listening to that type of music?"

Julie stood staring out the window above the sink and was taken by surprise. Quickly she tried to wipe the tears from her face. Travis froze for a moment to absorb the scene before walking over to her.

"Sis what's wrong?"

Julie tried to raise a smile as she turned to face him. "Nothing is wrong I'm just being a bit silly, that's all." She took note of the concerned look on his face and tried again to smile more convincingly.

"Sorry Sis I'm not buying it. Come, sit at the table and tell me what is happening."

Julie knew that if she began to let it out there would be no stopping it. "Travis it's nothing. I'm missing old friends, just haven't got settled yet, that's all." She found it challenging to meet his gaze, he would know she wasn't telling the truth if she did. "Please Travis, I'm a mess. Stop staring at me and fix yourself a cup of coffee or something."

"Okay Sis, but only if you're sure there's nothing you want to share with me; you know I love you, and if you need...."

"I'm fine, really I am." Julie could feel his eyes watching her suspiciously as she moved busily about the kitchen achieving almost nothing. "I think I had better get dressed. Will you come with me to the store? I need to get some things and we can get lunch while we're out."

"Sounds like a plan Sis. Give me an hour to get cleaned up."

With that said Julie was gone and securely cocooned in her bedroom. Travis stood by the sink, coffee mug in hand mulling over what had just taken place.

Chapter 2

It had been a complicated weekend for Samantha. Concerned parents had only been part of the problem. Sam was an only child, the daughter of two highly intellectual parents. Her father a Doctor of Medicine, and her mother is a psychiatrist. So, both physically and mentally she had been well cared for and raised in a loving, although in many ways hectic home full of schedules and work-related demands. Privileged but not spoiled and although she knew they meant well, their caring attention felt smothering amid the thousand times they had asked if she was feeling okay. Or how she was feeling just because she had 'fainted.' Even to the point where her dad had blundered around the inquiry to discover if she thought she might be pregnant. *Wow*, she had expressed sheer amazement and found herself speechless when she had finally figured out what he was hinting toward and knowing *she would need to have had sex for that to happen*. Something that hadn't happened in almost eighteen months. Not since... *That was not a good memory, and she willed herself not to revisit it.*

So absurd, and Sam would have been more offended if her thoughts were not centrally convened on a totally unrelated issue. *That man, just what the hell had happened?* A confusing dilemma plagued her thoughts. Her entire being had been uprooted, shaken and replanted inside another body. But even weirder, if that was possible she had sensed the same in reverse and his residue was still inside her. In a light-hearted moment of reprieve of which there had been few, she toyed with the idea that it had been the best sex she'd ever experienced and wanted more.

Her dad, a great physician and knight in shining armor had rushed to her rescue. Thanking the stranger for his assistance, he had scooped her up in his arms and carried her to a quiet room. And having conducted a quick assessment of her condition he suggested to mom that they should take her home. For Sam, the party was over before it even got started. Then the questions began, *was she eating properly, getting enough sleep? Had her finals been too strenuous? Had she taken any medication and worse still, was she using illegal drugs?* All parental concerns were invoked to give some justification for whatever she had succumbed to. The interrogation, though subtle was comprehensive. *Welcome home Sam.* Yes, it had been an exhausting year but she had achieved what she set out to do, a double major in Archaeology and History the two passions of her life. Now that graduation was over her dad had promised, the following year was hers to do with as she pleased. Although it needed to be stated, *if only for the record.* That the promise came with the usual *within reason clause.*

******

Without warning the picture painted in a time long past mounted in a plain wooden frame, suddenly drew her attention as she slipped a tee-shirt over her head and noticed it. What was it about that painting that flaunted a knowledge of something she could not grasp? Found in a secondhand store several years ago and purchased for five dollars. She sensed then it had something important to share with her. No one else seemed to see or feel it but the old brick arch that joined two buildings over a narrow-cobbled street seemed familiar to Sam. The artist's signature, O'Connell was barely legible in the bottom right corner and even that name seemed to mean something. So many hours had been spent looking at that painting on her bedroom wall.

A shiver rushed through her body at lightning speed; she felt both chilled and hot. A flash of memory which seemed long forgotten yet vividly, she sensed his presence. There in the picture his deep, dark eyes gazed out at her from beneath the arch. A warm feeling emanated inside her, and Sam sensed her desire to rush toward him. And just as suddenly as thought and feeling had emerged, it vanished. *"No,"* she whispered, although she wanted to scream. To move so quickly from the emotional high of imagined connection to the despair of total loss overwhelmed Sam and dropped her to her knees, unable to comprehend what had just taken place. *It was him again she was sure of it.* She would never forget those eyes, their memory deep, dark, haunting and mysteriously searching her mind. Delving into her soul exhuming knowledge and exchanging information which held her transfixed and breathless in their grasp. She couldn't let go, felt no desire to be free from the man she......*loved? Had loved? Would love?* Sam didn't have all the answers but the agony felt real. With tear-filled eyes she bowed her head, consumed by what she could only perceive as a broken heart.

It made no sense and offered no clarity as unsubstantiated thoughts gave way to reason. Sam felt lost in a quagmire of self-doubt. Too many thoughts so many questions and nowhere to turn for answers. It didn't help that she had no idea who he was, how to find him, and did she want to see him again? *He could be dangerous. Hell, yes he was dangerous; look at what he's already done to me.* Even so if her questions went unanswered would she, could she, live with that? And it didn't help to remember the name he had called out to her, Anne. The why and how had proved unnerving and even now taunted her mind with disbelief.

Sam kept a journal. She always had for as long as she could remember. Notebooks full of thoughts, dreams and drawings; all stored in a box on the shelf in her closet. It wasn't with an easy feeling she was reminded of them or the one thing that had so perplexed her those many years ago at the age of eleven. A time when little girls stop being little girls and begin to change. Where dolls and playhouses seemed less meaningful and silly schoolyard topics turned her attention to boys. Where the style of the clothes she wore became all-important amongst her peers, and her behavior in mixed company was more closely monitored.

Sam brought down the box from the closet shelf and placed it on her bed with some trepidation. Almost in a ritualistic ceremony, she carefully removed the lid and gazed at the hidden contents. A slight hesitation preceded her hand entering the box and moved her finger along the book spines. It was an unnecessary act of reverence because she knew precisely which journal contained what she was looking for. Flipping through it, she once again found the page. So many times, Sam thought she had imagined it and then, just like today was given cause to check. Her eyes were now transfixed on the words she had written so long ago. '*Anne. My name is Anne.*'

Chapter 3

Travis had no idea *shopping* involved purchasing a dress. Julie must have picked out and tried on at least a dozen. *Hanging around* in the ladies' clothing department held little appeal and probably he thought, there were few distractions because it was mid-morning on Monday. Although, when Julie walked out of the dressing room to seek his approval his awareness of how lovely his sister was as a woman was undeniable. *Funny,* he thought, *how you can look at someone and not really see them. Especially when they're your sister,* and in an inspired moment he wished he had one of his cameras to capture the images as she presented them.

And then they came to the shoe department where Travis thought how fortunate he was to have been born a man. It was quite an expedition and one he had not prepared for, no survival kit. When they finally sat down to have lunch at three-thirty his stomach was convinced his throat must have been cut. He lacked nourishment and felt starved and why would anyone, especially his sister *who said she loved him,* put him through such an ordeal?

On the flip side of that coin, *yes, there is always a flip side.* Julie had enjoyed the morning and as it turned out, the first part of the afternoon as well in having a man's opinion readily available to her as she shopped. It was priceless, even if it was her kid brother. Through inquiry, what started as ordinary conversation during that time had somehow initiated an idea. And although the thought process was not yet complete, she decided now was as good a time as any to act upon it.

"How would you feel about me staying at your house in Pensacola while you're away on your next assignment?"

The response came quickly. "Sure, why not." Travis didn't even look up from the menu he was studying.

"Are you ready to order?" The waitress had arrived and stood between them.

"I'd like the Philly-beefsteak sandwich and fries, large fries please. What are you having Sis?"

Julie was still looking at him, thinking the penny hadn't dropped and wondered if he'd really heard what she had asked. Having dismissed the menu Travis closed it and laid it on the table. Only then did he meet his sister's gaze and she became aware of the urgency to place her order. Diverting her eyes quickly towards the waitress, "Could I have the soup and salad please?"

"Yes, ma'am and to drink?"

Travis was thinking as Julie replied. "Tea please."

"And you Sir, what would you like to drink?"

Momentarily pulled from his thoughts, "I'll take a Dr. Pepper."

"Thank you. I'll be right back with your drinks."

Julie felt his eyes searching her face as she pretended to read the menu, a pretense without a sensible explanation considering she had just placed her order.

"Sis, did you just ask if you can stay at my place. Is something wrong?"

She felt like she had no choice but to look at him. The thing was, was she going to lie or tell the truth? "Would you believe me if I simply told you I need a vacation?"

A moment of tension was expressed in her eyes. Travis caught it. "That depends on whether it's the truth."

"Travis I......." Tears appeared in her eyes. Her bottom lip quivered as she reached into her bag for a tissue.

"Sis, take a moment and then tell me what's going on, okay?"

Julie nodded.

The drinks arrived.

Julie discreetly wiped the tears from her eyes and gently blew her nose. "If I told you I feel invisible in a marriage where the predictability of each day offers no more than the day that preceded it, could you even begin to understand?"

Travis was confused but did his best not to show it.

"Travis, you have a life. You go places and do things, breathe life in every day. I doubt if you could even imagine what it would be like to wake up each morning knowing it would be the same as the day before and it will be the same thing again tomorrow. I need a break, some time away to think. I'm not saying anything bad about Steve. This is about me and what I feel I need."

He sensed desperation in her voice as he covered her hand with his.

******

"Happy Birthday."

Once again, Travis had not risen at the crack of dawn. It was almost nine-thirty when he made his way into the kitchen. "Thanks Sis."

Julie walked over and kissed his cheek. "Coffee? Freshly brewed, I heard the shower stop running. Your breakfast is almost ready."

"Wow, you're spoiling me."

"Take a seat. I'll pour your coffee."

Travis perched himself on a stool at the kitchen bar. A nicely decorated package with a blue ribbon and a card was placed before him. "Sis you didn't have to."

"Shush, I wanted to, and besides it's from Steve and me."

"Well thanks and thank Steve for me."

"You're welcome. Go on; you can open it."

He had to smile, more so at Julie's enthusiasm than anything else. She had always been the 'master of ceremonies,' orchestrating the events even when they were kids, always his big sister.

Travis began to pull carefully at the ribbon. "Sis I've been thinking. Staying at my place while I'm gone. I'm not so sure that it's a good idea."

Julie swung around from facing the stove to look at him. The smile had evaporated from her face. "What? Why? I thought that was settled and Steve is okay with it. So why on earth would you change your mind now? We're supposed to fly down there tomorrow morning. Travis, don't do this to me, please."

"Sis I don't think it's a good idea, you would be alone and you don't know anyone down there."

"Travis please. I'm a grown woman. I can take care of myself."

"No, Sis my mind is made up."

Julie turned back to face the stove. There was no way she wanted him to see her tears or know how much he had just hurt her.

"No, a much better idea in my opinion would be to invite you to join me on my next assignment."

It took a few seconds to register and even then, Julie wasn't certain she had heard correctly. "What?" She was almost too afraid to turn around in case she had only imagined him saying what she thought he just might have said.

"What do you think?" Travis casually inquired.

Mortified at the thought that she might not have heard him correctly and ecstatic in the belief that she might have. She turned; Travis was admiring the diving knife.

"Thanks Sis, this is fantastic."

Julie felt uncertain about everything. "What did you just say?"

Travis looked confused, "The knife Sis, it's fantastic. Thanks."

"No Travis, before that."

He drew his attention away from the knife and looked straight at her. She had a lost deer in the headlights look about her. "Do you mean about coming with me to Borneo?"

"Seriously, you mean it?"

"As long as you've got a passport."

Julie rushed around the kitchen bar and wrapped him in her arms. "Really? I can't believe it, I'm so happy. You'd think it was my birthday instead of yours." She could hardly stand still as she kissed both of his cheeks.

"Sis, I think I smell something burning."

"Oh shit. Oops, sorry." Her hand covered her mouth as she rushed toward the stove to rescue the sausage patties. So delighted in her excitement, trying to regain some remnant of composure and focus on the task at hand. Yet, at the same time, take in the explosion of thoughts. "I have a passport; *I'm not sure where it is. Steve will know.* What will I wear?"

Her rush of thoughts was apparent in the speed at which the food items found their way onto the plate and were tossed in front of him. In watching Julie and hearing that last question his thought was, *PLEASE, don't suggest we need to go shopping again.*

******

To Steve, it didn't appear to make a lot of difference. Pensacola or Borneo, Julie would only be gone for about three weeks and with this new plan she would be with Travis. So, when they arrived at the restaurant for dinner Julie was still flying high in her excitement and a thousand thoughts. And once the drink order had been placed and delivered, Travis excused himself from the table to go and wash his hands. He too, was excited about taking his sister with him, but one of them had to remain calm and calibrated, which was something he was used to doing. Because death in the depths of the ocean was always only one miscalculation away.

******

Opening the restroom door to leave; the door to the ladies' restroom across the passageway opened simultaneously and Travis stood in disbelief as she stepped out from behind it.

"Anne?"

Shock and sheer amazement locked in their expressions although she averted her eyes almost instantly. "What are you doing here?"

He could ask her the same question.

"And my name is not Anne."

"Samantha; there you are, we were getting worried." Her mother walked closer as Sam and Travis stood facing each other. She inquisitively looked at Travis. "Sam, do you know this man?"

There was a brief hesitation before she answered. "Mom, this is the man from the party who caught me when I fainted."

Travis took note that Sam refrained from looking directly into his eyes. *Sam, Samantha, not Anne?* Boy, had he got that wrong. Even so, she was beautiful and he was sure he could not have forgotten her if they had known each other at some point in his past.

"Well, Sam, are you going to introduce me to this young man?"

"Sorry, mom, this is......." *Who the hell are you?*

The hesitation again. Travis suddenly realized she didn't know who he was and picked up where she left off. "Travis; Travis Sage. It's wonderful to finally meet you although I have to admit Sam hasn't really told me much about her parents." *Why did I say that? It seemed polite but totally uncalled for.*

Sam shot him a glance that implied, *what the heck, what are you talking about?* Maybe it was something worse than that and if so, he didn't want to know.

"We can remedy that can't we Sam. Would you care to join us for dinner Mr. Sage, I'm sure Sam would love to have someone closer to her age to help celebrate her birthday."

If looks could kill, he felt certain the look Sam fired off should have dropped him where he stood. But then again, he was still standing and it might prove interesting to pursue this a little further. "I'm sure I'd be delighted. Wait, Sam. Is it your birthday? I didn't know that and what a coincidence, today is my birthday also."

"How fascinating Mr. Sage, so you'll join us for dinner?"

There was that look again from Sam.

Okay girl, I get the message. I'll let you off the hook.

"As I was saying Mrs........?"

"Oh! how impolite of me. Helen, Dr. Helen Sanders."

"Dr. Sanders, it's wonderful to meet you finally. Unfortunately, I'm here to celebrate my birthday with my sister and her husband. Otherwise it would be an honor to join you and learn more about Sam's parents. Sam, I can't believe you never told me how beautiful your mother is?" Sam opened her mouth to say something. Her surprised and stern expression forewarned him that he would not like what she wanted to say. Fortunately, she didn't get the chance.

"Nonsense Mr. Sage, it would give me pleasure if you and your party would join us to celebrate your birthdays together."

"But...." *What the heck and why was Sam now smiling?*

"No, Mr. Sage I insist. Allow me to take Sam away from you for a short time and arrange for a larger table. When my mission is complete, I'll send a waiter over to collect you and your party."

Travis wasn't sure why he was smiling as they parted company. But using the back of Sam as his reference point he had to admit to himself that she sure looked fine from head to toe. *Well, that's a fine mess I just got myself into, better rally the troops.*

******

As soon as he sat down beside Sam, he felt her hand on his thigh, and her nails dug in hard against his jeans. *Thank God I'm not wearing shorts*, he thought while taking hold of her hand to extract it.

Something passed right through him when he touched her, some strong emotional force. Her sigh indicated she felt it too and instinctively he let go in fear that she might pass out again. *What the heck?* They glanced at each other; Sam withdrew her hand and quickly looked away. She sat to his left. His sister sat to his right, then Steve, seated next to Sam's father Richard, Dr. Richard Sanders then Helen and back around to Sam. Travis had experienced the same strange feeling of connection again and the questions came flooding back.

"We need to talk." Spoken quietly and directed toward Sam.

"You're right about that."

Steve, it seemed, had taken up a conversation with Richard. Julie and Helen were talking to each other across the table.

"What's going on Sam?" Again, Travis addressed her quietly.

Sam turned toward him, "That's what I'd like you to tell me."

Their food arrived. Travis felt he could have been knocked over with a feather when he saw that Sam's plate, the meal she had ordered was identical to his. No one else at the table had ordered this just him and Sam. *Coincidence, another coincidence.*

He picked up his knife, transferred it to his left hand and waited. Then felt a sense of relief that Sam didn't do the same thing. *Something different, good.*

"Why did you call me Anne on Friday and again tonight?"

"I don't know. I just felt that that was your name."

"You felt? So, you felt something too?"

"Yes, a feeling as if I......."

"Had intimate knowledge?" Sam finished his sentence.

"Yes, how did you know?"

"I felt it as well, on Friday and again tonight when you touched my hand."

"But how?"

"You're asking me? I don't know."

They both became aware that Helen and perhaps Julie were eavesdropping and decided it was better to postpone the investigation, for now at least.

******

It was almost time for the *surprise* birthday cake, which appeared every year at this time. *Sam couldn't wait.* During a lighter conversation Travis concluded that he liked Sam, although they had pretty much avoided direct eye contact. Even so, he understood her unspoken request not to look at her eye-to-eye whenever anyone else was around. Although he had to wonder how she got that message inside his head. And in thinking about it, it wouldn't matter much after tonight anyway. Tomorrow he'd be on a plane with Julie, heading home.

"Can I show you a picture?" Sam was fiddling around with her smartphone.

"Sure."

She found it and handed her phone to Travis.

He looked at a picture, probably a painting, he thought it looked old and.......? "I feel like I know this place."

That statement took Sam by surprise. "Where is it? I mean, do you know where this picture was painted?"

"No, not really but I think I should. Something about it seems very familiar. Beyond the arch over to the right is a church. Although you can't see it in this picture and to the left, beyond the arch is a redbrick building, I feel certain about it."

"How do you know that?"

"I don't know; I somehow sense it, as if I've been there. But in reality, I don't think I have."

"How odd?" Sam felt confused.

Then it hit him; powerful thoughts collided in the front of his mind. He sensed Anne; no, Sam. No, it was Anne standing beneath the arch in the picture. She was smiling, waiting for him to reach out and......... And what? He couldn't let it go........ Needing to pursue it further he saw the affection in her eyes and felt loved. It disappeared without warning and was gone.

Sam glanced towards him, "Are you alright? Travis......Travis?"

"Huh, yeah. I mean, yes, I'm all right."

"Would you like to step outside with me and get some air?"

"Sure, good idea."

"Are you okay?" Julie inquired.

"Sure Sis, I think Sam might have put a spell on me."

Julie smiled, as did the rest of the dinner companions.

"We'll be back shortly." He informed everyone as he and Sam rose from their seats.

Sam linked her arm through his with the idea of offering support, but one flex of his firm muscular arm offered no credibility to her thought. She would be as much use as a fly sitting on a cow's ass if Travis toppled over. Outside, they stood both facing the street. Both feeling the urge and neither willing to risk looking into each other's eyes.

"What did you see?"

"I saw you. Not you, as you are now. I saw Anne. You and Anne are the same? I know that sounds crazy; I can't explain it."

"You don't have to. When I looked at the picture on Monday, I saw you. Not Travis but your eyes. They are known to me as if I have looked into them a thousand times before."

"Can we try holding hands again?"

Sam looked down at his hand as he held it open for her to take hold.

"Promise me Travis, if it gets crazy you will let go."

He didn't say a word. The trust was a foregone conclusion as Sam carefully placed her hand in his.

Chapter 4

"Okay Travis, wake up. We need to be at the airport in four hours."

"Wau, Sis. Morning, you sound.... Cheerful."

In anticipation of her drawing back the drapes and opening the blinds just like their mother had always done, he pulled a pillow over his head and sure enough, she did it.

"Come on, the coffee is brewed and I want to get these sheets washed and dried before we leave."

It was a hard choice to have no choice, and even though he felt drained he had to comply. Such is life when you don't live alone he reminded himself.

It was a struggle, like ...... Like he had? He had to think about that on his way to the kitchen. Like he had been making love.... *All night long?* Coffee, even the first sip offered some much-needed life-giving nourishment and stimulation. So why did his head hurt? He hadn't consumed that much alcohol and it wasn't that late when they arrived home. And Sam, he hoped she was in better shape than he was. Hoped no one had gone into her room threw back the drapes and opened her blinds. If she had one or both of them, he had no idea. But he sure as heck knew a lot more than he did at this time yesterday.

******

"Well Sis we should be home in about four hours maybe four and a half depending on traffic after we leave the airport."

"Now that I've got you all to myself tell me about Sam. Is it love at first sight?"

"I don't know Sis, it's something."

"Really? Tell me more, like what went on between the two of you last night. You were as thick as thieves."

Travis smiled; they had been somewhat covert for reasons he was still struggling with and she was beautiful. But, and the 'but' is something he didn't quite understand. Impossible as it seems, there are two of her. One he appears to know intimately and one he has yet to discover. The trouble is, they are wrapped in the same body and he won't get one without the other.

"Honestly, I think it's too early to tell, we've connected so maybe it's better to wait and see where it goes from here."

Julie felt somewhat disappointed. Travis didn't know how to explain what had taken place last night. Trying to explain what happened last Friday night at the party had been difficult enough and he could get away with sounding like a raving lunatic once. But sounding like a raving lunatic twice might raise some eyebrows and find him in need of psychiatric assistance. And the picture Sam had shown him, how could he explain that? Or the things he had sensed seeing in it and beyond it? Holding hands had seemed unreal and concerned him even more. Making love? No, maybe making love wasn't the best way to describe it, although it sure had been emotional. The thing was the picture bothered him more than anything else. That was an inanimate object or at least the image of one. That was hard to explain and the birthday kiss; that everyone at the table so enthusiastically seemed to think he and Sam should engage in, after they had blown the candles out. It had been a moment of trepidation for both of them especially after holding hands outside. And yet when they did it, nothing happened which surprised them both.

******

Travis by nature was organized; his cameras and dive equipment were already packed in two large watertight containers before he went to visit his sister. And having taken Julie to a local dive shop; the day after they had arrived in Pensacola, all he needed to do now was find room inside them to fit the wetsuit, fins, snorkel and mask he had purchased for her. The containers would be shipped via Fed-Ex International tomorrow and received by Mac before he and Julie arrived at their destination.

Mac. Mackenzie Adams and Travis had been working together for the better part of three years. Mac by trade was a divemaster whose origins appeared to be Australian, but considering he'd lived in many places, his home was wherever he was and right now he was in Semporna, chartering a boat and gathering supplies. He had already been there a week, frequenting local bars and socializing with any available women. Mac was a lady's man, tall, handsome, and as he put it, built like a brick shithouse. It was true that Mac was the embodiment of a woman's dreams; several years older than Travis, but their physiques gave no indication of an age difference when they stood side by side.

Unfortunately for Mac, tourist season wouldn't start for another month and Semporna wasn't your typical tourist destination. So, it was slim pickings on the female front, although he had found a young dive instructor and she looked promising. Tourists came to Semporna for one reason, to dive the wall. The wall is one of those unique wonders of nature in which man has played no part and leave all who see her breathless and in awe.

The third team member was Deb, a relative newcomer considering this was only her fifth time with Travis and Mac on assignment. Deb, a marine biologist from the UK adds her own flavor to this otherwise two-man team, and even with her own agenda they fit together like three peas in a pod. At thirty-four years of age, she is very accomplished academically, and Deb had determined she fit right in the middle and was the best part of the sandwich. So, the plan was that Deb would fly out from the UK to meet with Travis in Kuala Lumpur Malaysia. And after a good night's sleep in a hotel, they would continue their journey to Borneo to meet up with Mac. And Mac had just received an email from Travis informing him that someone called Julie would be traveling with them.

******

Sam was finishing breakfast, unsure whether she felt angry or sad. It was the start of day three since she and Travis had celebrated their birthdays and not a peep. Not a word. No phone call, email or text message. It was like he'd just up and dropped off the edge of the world, her world at least. She was displeased. *What was the point of swapping contact information if he had no intention of using it?* Sam was quickly running out of things to distract her, and too predisposed to think of anything new. And with so much going on that night, she wasn't sure when he said he was flying to Borneo. *He could very well be halfway around the world by now.* A tear seeped from the corner of her eye. That was the sad part. The not-so-sure if she should be angry part quickly wiped it away with her fingers.

True love never runs smooth. She couldn't cope with that concept; not for her and Travis. He was the man of her dreams; there could be no question of that, not after.... She sighed almost painfully. Everything she had felt; all the feelings that passed between them, transferred heart to heart. The warmth and wonder of it sent tremors rushing through her body even now at a fantastic speed and with such intimacy, she could.... *Augh. Ahh.* She sensed it, almost did, but managed to pull it back. If he had been there, to share this moment...... It was unbearable. Sam desperately needed to see him, touch him and have him touch her.

******

Like any great sister, Julie felt duty-bound to give Travis's house a good cleaning, contrary to being asked not to.

"Sis have you seen my phone?" "Sis did you move my laptop?" "Sis, I can't find my keys, I always leave them on the kitchen counter." Travis knew she meant well even in this new chaos and his frustration. "Sis stop; I'll do anything. Even go shopping with you or listen to country music; but, please, I'm losing track of where everything is and there's nothing wrong with harboring a bit of dust here and there. It's manly!"

Julie smiled as she placed her hands on her hips. "Well now Travis." She brought her hands forward and removed the rubber glove from her left hand. "Come to think of it." Julie pulled the glove off her right hand. "I would like to take one last trip out to look for swimsuits. You said it's what you all wear, most of the time while out on the boat."

Why did Travis feel like he walked right into that one? But at least she would stop faffing around with his stuff, and tomorrow they would get on a plane.

An exasperated "Okay.... Help me find my keys."

******

For Julie, the adventure she had just embarked upon was, in many ways, surreal. Never in her life could she have imagined such a thing, doing such a thing and yet here she was preparing to get on a plane and fly to exotic places. The very sound of the name Kuala Lumpur presented her imagination with unthought-of mystery and excitement. Keeping herself busy was all she could think of doing to stop herself from bursting at the seams or squealing like a silly schoolgirl. *It was happening, it's really happening* and there was a lot of energy to burn up if she was going to get any sleep tonight.

She had always tried to be the perfect daughter, the perfect big sister and the perfect wife. She catered to whatever needed to be done to maintain harmony and order amid the busyness of those who surrounded her. A role in which she had unconsciously placed herself and her needs last. It felt like the right thing to do for many years, but these past two years had proven difficult to come to terms with. Steve had a life, a life separate from the one he....... Shared....... With her. That was the problem; Steve had stopped sharing a life with her. Sure, he still came home. They slept in the same bed and every morning he would go back to his other life. Leaving her right where he usually found her, in the kitchen preparing his meals. On the weekends, he still seemed consumed with his other life and the mountains of paperwork he brought home. If anything needed to be done around the house she did it or arranged for someone to come in and fix it.

Steve called it teamwork; only Julie couldn't figure out whose team he was playing for. It had gotten so bad during the last two years that Julie had thought more than once, to heck with making love, she would be content if Steve would have sex with her. But a year passed and then two and Julie gave up hope. She tried talking with him, enticing him all to no avail. He was tired, stressed, had a headache, or had to get up early for a special meeting. Which, of course he had to prepare for and even though Julie knew it would break all the rules she had considered having an affair. But who with? There was a sampling of males but always too many reasons not to venture into that arena. Steve was a lucky man, even if he didn't seem to realize it.

Chapter 5

The flight to Bangkok was long and uneventful with a two-hour layover, which turned into three before their next plane took off. The airport itself was a busy hive of activity. Julie marveled at the sights and sounds—eavesdropping in on conversations and not understanding a word being spoken, as her mind reeled in the excited confusion. She was in a foreign country for only the second time in her life. That is if you count her honeymoon to Mexico, and the confines of the resort where she and Steve stayed. The staff there spoke English, even if it was sometimes a little broken. But this, this was the real deal; she was now believably the foreigner standing head and shoulders above most of the beautiful people that surrounded her. Placing their hands together in a prayer-like manner and bowing their heads as they came towards her made Julie wonder if they had mistaken her for someone of importance.

"It's a sign of respect Sis," Travis had informed her. "Just do the same and smile. Thai's love to smile. They are a very gracious people."

The bubble burst when she saw the McDonald's sign above the entrance to the fast-food restaurant and Travis insisted they go in.

******

It was late afternoon as they made their way toward the baggage claim. In contrast, the airport in Kuala Lumpur seemed somewhat sterile and calm, or so she had presumed until they got to the arrival's reception area where a multitude of people waited noisily. Taxi drivers were hurriedly touting for customers, trying to take possession of their luggage and steer the traveler towards their waiting vehicles. Friends and family members were anxiously waiting to recognize the face of the person or persons they had come to meet. Street vendors were selling all manner of items. Hotel minibus drivers were holding up signs, all jockeying for position. "Hey, Sis, grab my hand and don't let go." The size of Travis must have looked like a bulldozer as he worked his way through the crowd pulling Julie behind him.

"Finally Sage, you managed to get your arse here. You took your bloody time about it."

"Hi Deb, it's good to see you too."

Travis dropped his bag and scooped Deb up in his arms. Julie stood and watched, sensing affection.

Deb opened her eyes and took note she was being observed. "Okay Sage, this isn't a bloody love affair. Put me down."

"Sorry Deb, the plane was late taking off. Oh, Deb this is my sister Julie, Julie this is Deb."

"Pleased to meet you Deb."

Deb took a long look at Julie, "Likewise, I'm sure.... Sister?"

To Julie, it sounded like Deb was asking a question, so she smiled and nodded.

"Does Wicket know about her?"

Julie felt sure she didn't know the answer to that, having no idea who Wicket was or could be. So she assumed the inquiry must have been directed to Travis and unless she missed something, he didn't answer, just said, "Come on, let's get out of here."

As soon as the sliding glass doors opened the extreme heat and humidity engulfed them. Julie felt like she had just stepped into a steam boiler and toyed with the notion of turning around and going back inside the airport. But Travis and Deb kept moving towards a taxicab as if they were unaware of the change. Already she felt the sweat oozing out of every pore and her clothing sticking against her body. It was like heating the oven to four hundred and fifty degrees, opening the door and sticking your head in it. Every step was an extreme effort. Why she wondered, had she packed so many clothes? Her bag felt heavier than she was and threatened to crush her beneath its weight. Why had Travis insisted she packed her things in this oversized, olive drab canvas monstrosity now strapped to her back when she had a perfectly good nest of three suitcases with wheels? Why are Travis and Deb now standing beside the taxicab smiling at her?

All good questions to Julie's way of thinking although, in this heat she wasn't about to stand around and ask them. Travis took a couple of steps back toward her to help remove the shoulder straps from her body. Deb took a seat up front next to the cab driver as Travis threw Julie's bag in the trunk alongside his own and Deb's before closing the lid. "Okay Sis, climb in, it's hot out here." *Oh, he noticed!*

Thank God for air conditioning. Julie was trying to get comfortable as the cab sped along a beautiful multi-lane highway that could rival any back home. The city skyline was ultra-modern with the sun glistening off the glass on the tall buildings. Pockets of tropical vegetation, lush and green obscured the angular structures at ground level and palm trees dotted the landscape. It all looked pleasingly different from what she was used to and had imagined.

"Hey Deb, what's your assignment?" Travis inquired.

"To assess the health of the coral reef. The Department of Tourism and interested businesses are trying to get the government to issue more dive permits."

"That should be interesting!"

"Okay Sage, it's the best I could come up with and get the funding quickly."

"Whatever works Deb, happy you could come along but you do realize it's political?"

"Don't go all sissy on me Sage, just because your sister is riding with us."

Deb appeared to be an interesting woman, Julie thought. Her accent sounded real British, like on Downton Abby and some of the other shows she'd watched on the BBC America and PBS channels.

"So, does Wicket know?"

"I'm sorry, who?"

"It's okay Sis, I've got this. Yes, I sent him an email."

"This is going to be fun, watching Wicket when there's a beautiful woman on board."

"Deb, she's my sister. I think Mac can handle it."

"I'm confused?"

"Don't worry Sis, this is just Deb being Deb."

"But who is Wicket?"

Deb turned in her seat with a devious smile lighting up her face. "Wicket is..."

Travis cut her off, "Wicket is Mac, and they are one and the same; Deb calls him Wicket, and I call him Mac. In fact, Deb is the only person to refer to Mac as Wicket."

"Want to know why I call him Wicket Julie?"

"No Deb, I don't think Julie needs to know why you call Mac, Wicket."

"Okay Sage, but she's going to find out soon anyway."

******

Three bodies, two beds. Two females, one man? "Julie, it's no big deal and besides it's only for one night." Julie couldn't understand why Travis hadn't booked more than one room and now because the hotel was booked solid it wasn't an option. And if this had been the original plan; before he'd invited her…. Did he and Deb have something going on? Was she an intruder? A little embarrassed she caught Deb's eye; she was smiling.

"It's okay Julie. You can bunk with me if you……."

"I don't think so Deb, Travis interrupted, you girls take the beds and I'll sleep on the floor."

"It's okay Travis. I don't mind; Deb and I can take one bed and you can have the other."

"Sis," it was a perplexing moment as Travis looked at his sister and then over toward Deb. "Deb, help me out?"

Deb took great pleasure in the awkwardness strung about Travis's expression and decided to taunt him. "Sorry Sage, I need to take a shower." With that she quickly stripped out of her street clothes and flew towards the bathroom in her underwear. Only looking back before pulling the door shut behind her to say, "I do believe we're in for a lot of fun on this trip."

Julie thought for a minute before saying, "Travis, if you and Deb want to sleep together, I can sleep facing the window in the other bed."

******

Another long day of travel was almost at an end once the plane touched down on the runway. Deb went off to find Mac, while Travis and Julie collected their luggage.

"Wicket!" Deb's voice sounded shrill as she called out through the movement of human bodies when she caught sight of him. Mac, in instant recognition scanned the area where the voice emanated from and there she was, and seeing her petite frame rushing towards him, smiling excitedly, he opened his muscular arms to catch her.

"Ouch, Wicket I think you've just ruptured my tits."

"Awe, Deb it's good to see ya; need me to kiss them better?" Then, still holding her up against his chest with his left arm he gently cupped her left breast in his right hand.

"Put me down, you silly sod and get your hand off my tit."

With her feet back on the floor, she looked up affectionately into the face of this mountain of a man. "Hello Wicket." Their close bond of friendship bid him bend forward and Deb planted a big wet kiss on his cheek.

Wicket's heart melted. Deb was his mermaid, who he'd literally scooped up from the ocean eighteen months ago, when he and Travis came upon her quite by chance. She had been wreck-diving; became entangled in the old rigging and had just about run out of air. He and Travis fought like crazy men to break her free; taking turns to force air from their mouths into her lungs, keeping her alive when she had given up and accepted her fate. Wicket knew he would not let that happen; captivated by her peaceful beauty even at that moment as her long flowing blonde hair moved gently with the current. Working feverishly, they were using up their much-needed oxygen from their tanks. At a hundred and twenty feet below sea level there were perilous challenges even in their ascent. They didn't talk about how they had done it, they just both knew that they had to. And now Wicket's mermaid stood before him once more, all five feet four inches of her looking as beautiful as the day he'd first found her. Deb traced her fingers along his angular jaw and smiled knowingly.

Their greeting complete and in knowing the spell had to be broken, Wicket asked, "Where's Travis and who's this Sheila he's bringing along?" That broke the spell for Deb as she warmed her thoughts to think curiously about what would happen when....

"Mac." Travis shot out his hand to meet that of his friend.

"G' day, mate."

Two muscular, powerful forces came together in a bear hug as Deb instinctively moved out of the way. The clash of two titans filled the immediate area and dominated the scene as Deb, and now Julie looked on.

Even then in that first moment with Travis's back blocking some of her view, Julie felt palpitations in her chest at the sight of his face as she caught her first glimpse of the man with two names and felt bemused at the size of the hand that lay on her brother's shoulder. But that was just the prelude to how she felt when Travis stepped to one side and introduced her to him.

"Mac, I'd like you to meet Julie...."

Mac was stunned and stuck to the spot; both feet nailed firmly to the floor. The rich dark hair and piercing deep brown eyes seared forever in his mind with instant recognition that she was the most beautiful woman he had ever seen in his life. And her lips challenged every sinew and muscle in his body to resist. ".... My sister." It took Mac a few seconds for it to register. "Your sister?" He had to think quickly. *'Sister......'* He reached out his hand with his mind still in confused angst. "Nice to meet ya, Julie." Deb watched as, metaphorically, the gentle giant was brought to his knees and conquered without a single blow.

******

In the early predawn hours the small windowpane shattered, and a hand reached through the void where the glass had been to unlock the bolt that secured the door. Stepping on the glass as she entered then closing the door behind her, she waited with bated breath before flipping the light switch on. Taking only seconds to acclimate herself she moved quickly and quietly towards the door she assumed would lead to the garage. After raising the outer garage door she drove her BMW inside and pressed the button to lower it again. With the first part of her mission accomplished Sam smiled and breathed a sigh of relief.

Chapter 6

Voices echoed from somewhere close by. The movement was apparent with the cling-clang sound of metal and the thud of things tossed on the deck not two feet above her head. Highlighting the bodily sense of motion as she stirred from her sleep, realizing just where she was and what she had done last night. Julie brought her hands out from under the sheet and covered her face in disbelief. *'Oh God,'* she felt the pain. *How much did I drink?* Her mouth felt as dry as a sandbox, and a jackhammer played its way across her temporal lobes. Pitifully she drew her hands away from her eyes and delicately surveyed her.... Her what? It wasn't big enough to be considered a room, *a broom closet, maybe.*

Three hard thumps on the door and the bellowing sound of Travis's voice startled and caused her to sit up fast. (*Thud*), her head met the ceiling. "Ouch?"

"Julie.... Sis, come on Sis. We've almost finished stowing the gear and we'll be casting off in about an hour. If you want coffee better get to it."

Of course, Travis had felt similar effects three hours ago, when he got out of his bunk but strong black coffee and hard physical labor had brought him through the worst part of the recovery. It was time to go through the navigation charts and check the long-range weather forecast while Deb studied the satellite communications. Mac finished stowing the dive gear and Julie fell out of her bunk (*THUD*). "*Ouch!*"

As Julie came out of her closet, Deb had just descended the ladder into the main cabin. "Morning Julie." Spoken in a jubilant tone, it sounded far too happy to Julie and the best response she could manage was a pathetic "hi."

"Oh dear!" Taking note of Julie's expression, Deb offered. "I think you need the morning-after tonic."

The half-hearted look on Julie's face gave little indication of any interest. She stood forlorn almost, in her housecoat and PJs, clutching her toiletries bag and smartphone. Deb pulled a cold bottle of water from the icebox and placed it on the small table.

"Come and sit-down and drink this, it will help rehydrate you and I'll fix us some fresh coffee."

Julie sidled onto the bench seat and after placing her things on the table, she unscrewed the bottle cap and took a long drink.

"The boys certainly know how to party, don't they? But you can't blame them really. They were just celebrating getting together again." Deb was trying to make conversation while getting the coffee organized. "And now that's over with; they will be all business once we leave port."

"I think I'll feel a lot better after I've taken a shower."

Deb turned and looked at her thoughtfully, then returned her attention to what she was doing. "You've never done this before have you? And I'm guessing Travis omitted to tell you what to expect."

"What, about drinking? I have been drunk before but it was a long time ago and...."

"No, not drinking." Deb carried two mugs of coffee to the table set them down and sat.

"No, I'm talking about showers."

Julie swallowed the last of the water and as if a question lingered in her thoughts, she placed the empty bottle on the table.

"Julie we don't do showers, at least we don't while onboard. There's not enough water storage so, as far as pits, tits, and you know where, a soapy facecloth is about as good as it gets until we get back on dry land."

Julie's expression said it all and needed no interpretation.

"Think of it as primitive camping." Deb offered. While in thought she condemned Travis. "Did Travis tell you anything about living on a boat? Did he warn you about no room for modesty or that you can't fart without everyone knowing about it?"

Julie's unsurprising blank look placed a caring concern on Deb's next words. "Here, drink your coffee then I'll get you a bowl of water to freshen up with and show you how to operate the Jon. But remember you don't flush the loo unless you do a number two.

Up on deck in the wheelhouse, Mac joined Travis. "Everything's stowed mate."

"Thanks Mac. The weather looks good, might hit a rough spot in about four days though."

"Well she ain't much to look at but she'll float, and we came out here to get wet."

Travis smiled, "Mac it's great to see you again."

"Same here mate."

"Ready to cast off in about thirty?"

"You've got it skipper. Think I'll go check on the ladies."

"Hey Mac?" Mac had turned away but stopped and looked back. "Try to remember she's my sister."

It had been a fitful sleep; restless in that wave after wave of emotional desire played with his mind. Mac was besotted the moment he'd laid eyes on Julie and damned in the same instant when he heard the word, 'Sister.' She was the reason he had drunk so much, tried to pulverize every natural instinct to sweep her up into his arms and……. Feel her kiss on his lips. Now, like a bug drawn helplessly to the light, he had to get back to her. To look at her again and gaze into her beautiful deep, brown eyes. Experience the breathless wonder of ………… His heart ached so much worse than his head, but thoughts about how this would work, how this could work without challenging his friendship with Travis remained obscure.

******

Half a world away Sam woke peacefully in his bed and once again; just as she had done when she first slipped between the covers, she inhaled his scent on the pillow deeply and smiled. Then excitedly she threw back the covers with vigor to begin this first day. There was unpacking to do; familiarize herself with where he kept things, arrange to have the glass replaced in the backdoor window and make herself comfortable. But first things first, she thought. Get cleaned up, dressed and find a grocery store. Sam had already noticed how clean and tidy the house was last night and although somewhat surprised, she found it endearing and disappointing that the refrigerator was empty.

******

Deb was just through showing Julie the mechanics of the loo when Mac announced he was coming below decks.

"I'm not dressed. He can't see me like this."

Deb stood bemused for a second with Julie's panicked statement. "Hold up there Wicket. Can you give us a minute?" Poking her head out of the door, Deb wanted to scream with laughter and fought hard to contain it. Mac had stopped on the ladder in limbo, two steps above the cabin deck.

"Keep him out Deb; please send him away."

The look of horror on Julie's face was priceless as Deb battled even harder to stay composed.

We're on a forty-foot boat; where the hell am I supposed to tell him to go?

"Hey Wicket, we've got a girl thing going on; a bit of privacy if you please."

"I guess?" Although not sure what Deb meant exactly by 'girl thing.' Mac kinda figured out he wasn't welcome. Even if he liked 'girl things,' maybe in this instance he wouldn't. So he ascended the ladder back to the main deck.

"That was fast Mac. How are the girls. Are they ready?"

Mac looked at Travis blankly and said, "Maybe give them a few minutes." Before he moved towards the bow.

Deb flew by Travis without a word, leaped onto the dock and ran for cover after giving Julie a bowl of water, facecloth and towel. Her urgency to bust her gut laughing could be contained no longer. Travis said, "Hi Deb," as she passed by. Then stood and wondered as she raced along the dock. He turned to look at Mac, who looked back at him and shrugged his shoulders before saying, "It's a girl thing skipper."

Deb walked back along the dock about ten minutes later, smiling. Her entire face was alive with excitement. Travis watched her hair dance as she moved and felt the full force of the love he held in his heart. He sighed gently, had fleeting thoughts he hoped would pass quickly, *if only she*....... And even if....... He knew Mac held some deep feelings towards her and there was no way he would risk their friendship.

"Hey guys," Deb called out, "this is promising to be the best trip ever. I wouldn't have missed it for the world. Are we ready to go?"

Travis still caught up in his thoughts as Deb came up beside him and took hold of his arm and even in that, he wished for something he knew he couldn't have.

"Okay Mac, cast off the bow line, Travis ordered as he turned the key and the engine came to life.

Chapter 7

Travis managed to keep most thoughts about Sam separated from his plans which were already in place, with determined effort. The only part of his life that he considered had been unfocused was after his parents had died and the self-recrimination of his stupidity still haunted his memories of it. But feelings towards Sam at times were confusing. There was something very special about....... About the experience of her or through her he wasn't sure which, bonding them in some strange and beautiful way. And now with the boat at anchor and thousands of miles between them, Travis stared up at the moon and felt the desire to hold her hand again.

"Sage are you okay?" Deb's inquiry pulled him back from distraction.

"Hi Deb, yes sure. I was just thinking.

"Brought you a mug of hot cocoa."

"Great thanks. Want to sit with me for a while?"

She snuggled in beside Travis on the cushioned bench and rested her head against his arm.

"First dive tomorrow. Are you coming with us?"

"I was planning on it, but who will look out for Julie?"

"How do you mean?"

"She doesn't know much about living on a boat."

"You're right, she doesn't and honestly I should've talked to her about that before I invited her. But it was a spur-of-the-moment thing and 'that talk' seems to keep getting pushed forward behind everything else. How is she doing so far?"

"Hmm, there have been a few surprises, nothing I can't handle. But can I ask, why is she here?"

"Honestly Deb, I think Sis just needs a break from her routine; at least I hope that's all it is, and I'd appreciate you showing her the ropes. You know, girl to girl."

"Not a problem, by the way. Can I sleep with you tonight?"

Travis turned and kissed her forehead.

"Wicket's gone all gooey-eyed over your sister and it's better not to tempt participation in his dreams."

Travis understood. Deb's anxiety before a first dive was a remnant of the tragedy she had survived. Her dive buddy and lover Christine, had not. After discovering a weak pulse, fighting for Deb's survival had filled his thoughts, motivated their actions and Christine had perished trapped inside the wreck. The manufactured thoughts of 'what if', could have and should have, gave birth to many unfounded remnants of guilt, and bound them each to her.

******

"Morning Sis, sleep well?" Julie had just stepped up on deck holding a mug of coffee. Travis was sitting near the stern checking his cameras.

"Much better than the night before, no hangover. Morning Mac."

Mac was mid-ships checking diving equipment. "G'day Julie." The smile that passed between them was equally strong in both directions.

"Sis, I should tell you, make sure you coat yourself well with sunblock the reflected light off the water gets fierce." Whether she heard him or not, Travis wasn't sure. She and Mac were still locked in their smile until the disturbance in the water at the stern caught Julie's attention. And as she turned in that direction Deb appeared on the ladder climbing back on board naked as the day she was born.

"Morning Julie. Just taking a bath."

Julie looked shocked.

Deb picked up a towel and wrapped herself in it.

Julie looked at Travis who hadn't seemed to notice. Then at Mac who also appeared unconcerned and almost oblivious to what had just taken place.

"Okay, your turn Wicket, here's the soap. Deb tossed the bar of soap in his direction. Mac pulled off his shirt and just as he removed his shorts, Julie turned away and diverted her eyes. Although embarrassed, she heard the splash and found herself amused and curious.

"Want to give it a go Julie?" Deb asked playfully.

Travis looked up with an awkward expression.

Deb continued, "Better to bathe in the morning, the sharks get a bit hungry at dusk."

"I think I'll just enjoy my coffee for now but thank you for asking." Glancing over the side Julie observed Mac, who seemed perfectly content with this bathing ritual and she tried to imagine herself being free willed enough to try it.

******

Mac and Travis stood on the dive platform, geared up and ready to go. Deb had elected to stay onboard and readied herself to hand off the camera to Travis. Julie watched in quiet excitement, thinking about the adventure stories her brother had relayed and trying to imagine what it looked like below the surface of the water. And Mac, her thoughts were or should have been unthinkable but she was thinking them all the same. He looked....... Hmm, so indescribable for a married woman to even contemplate, but her body was mesmerized by the impulses derived in her mind. "Ready Mac?" He gave Travis the thumbs-up and stepped off the platform. Travis lowered his face mask and followed him in. Then taking the camera from Deb, Travis and Mac disappeared from view, leaving air bubbles to rise in their wake.

******

"Okay Julie, you've got forty minutes max before the boys get back, maybe a little less." Deb held out a towel and a bar of soap. "So now's the time to get on with it."

Julie understood, although feeling nervous.

"The thing is Julie, you're on a boat. We left modesty back at the dock."

Sheepishly Julie took the towel and soap. "Can I have a little privacy?"

"Americans, you have so many inhibitions. Julie, the rule is no one in the water unless someone is on the deck. It keeps everyone safe. Just do it."

******

In a peaceful world with only the sound of their breathing resonating in their ears, Travis and Mac moved serenely through the water a few feet off the surface of the coral reef. Intermittently pausing to communicate between themselves using hand and finger gestures. They were back in the environment they loved and the element they seemed naturally acclimated to. Diving deeper into the depths, they passed through a thermocline at sixty feet; and the water felt cooler. Stopping periodically to investigate and take photographs of the magnificent colors and the diversity they were surrounded by. Perfectly coordinated in their movements, Travis and Mac presented no disturbance to the abundance of marine life which at times, appeared to interact with them out of curiosity.

******

Fresh off the boat or in Julie's case feeling fresher when finally, she climbed back on board. She stood for a few minutes and allowed the warm ocean breeze to touch all parts of her body, a sensation she had never experienced before. Mischievously devilish in her exposure and curiously fascinated in the way it made her feel. She desired to embrace this moment of her newfound liberation.

"Here's your towel. The boys will be back any minute. Nice bod Julie. Better get some sunblock on it though, or you'll be hurting tonight."

Julie needed to think about that. *Nice bod.* The compliment felt real and coming from Deb who had such a beautiful body herself made her feel……

"I see their bubbles; they're almost here."

Julie wrapped the towel around herself quickly and scurried towards the main cabin in haste.

******

During the lunchtime break Travis asked Mac to step down from the afternoon dive. He would go down with Deb instead, and perhaps Mac might be interested in giving Julie some diving instruction. Somewhere in the back of his mind he knew he couldn't babysit either of them, although judging by the enthusiastic response he found it hard to determine which of them was the most excited, Julie or Mac. And it gave little comfort when Deb sarcastically whispered in his ear. "Damn Sage, you've just put the fox in the hen house and the farmer is going out of town."

******

Sam sat on the couch and looked admiringly at the wall full of pictures Travis had accumulated from his work worldwide, and tried to imagine what it must be like to dive deep into the ocean. The photography was amazing and captivated her senses about the man behind the lens and in the visualization of what he wanted his audience to feel. She got it, felt it and her love for him grew deeper, as did her anguish in not hearing from him. *He's got to come up for air sometime, maybe then.......* Then she might hear something or get a text or email. *Please Travis, I love you so much.*

Her phone rang and in her longing, she rushed to grab it off the table and to her disappointment saw it wasn't from Travis. "Hi mom." "Yes mom, I'm fine." "It's a dig mom. Indian burial mounds." That's right the Porch Creek tribe. There are sites all over the Florida panhandle." "It's interesting." "Yes I'm bunking with three other girls from the dig." "Yes mom I'll call you every other day. Give my love to dad." "Yes mom, I love you too. Bye." *Maybe.* She thought. *If I email a copy of the picture, will it remind him?* Sam opened up her laptop.

******

"There's nothing better than a fresh catch."

"You're right Wicket, this is good. If you ever get around to opening a restaurant I'll be your best patron."

"Thanks Deb, I can always count on ya."

"Now hold up a minute you two. Admittedly this is good, but you can't beat a good slab of prime beef steak. So you're going to serve that too, right Mac?"

"Who wants to eat a dead cow when you can eat this? Oh, that's right, Sage."

"Hey Deb, just because you don't eat red meat just means there's more for the...."

"Cavemen Sage. What about you Julie? Do you subscribe to eating a dead cow, or have you evolved?"

"Hey Deb, I'm the newcomer here, don't make me choose sides this early in the game, but Mac this is excellent."

Mac paused to look at Julie before responding. "Thank ya Julie."

Travis and Deb looked across the table at each other knowing that sounded different? Overly sincere?

"So Sis, how did your first dive go?"

"She's a natural Travis, swims like a fish. I wouldn't be surprised if she's hiding gills behind those pretty ears."

"Well thank you Mac, but I'll admit I was a bit nervous Travis, but Mac stuck with me and......."

"Wicket does tend to stick Julie. What's that expression? Sticky Wicket. Cricket anyone? Who's up to bat first?" The friendly banter was gushing out of Deb faster than Mac or Julie could keep up with her. Travis was laughing so hard he excused himself from the table and went up on deck, which is where, a few minutes later Julie came to join him.

"Hey, Sis. How's it going?"

"Honestly Travis, I'm having the time of my life. Thank you for bringing me along."

"Really." He put his arm around her shoulders. "That makes me happy."

"Me too Travis, me too. That's why I want to talk to you, alone."

"Well Sis. Unfortunately, I can't make those millions of stars vanish or make that big moon stop shining but other than that, I'm all yours."

Julie reached up, kissed his cheek and nestled her head against his shoulder. "This sky is beautiful." She was silent for a moment as if gathering her thoughts. "Travis, I know you think highly of Steve and so do I. He was there for us both when we lost mom and dad and he was there to help you through the rough patch you went through. So whatever I tell you, I don't want it to affect how you feel towards him. He is a good man with many fine qualities, works hard, provides a good home and as far as I know, he's faithful. So please remember those things, but they are not everything it takes to have a good marriage."

Travis sensed a hammer was about to fall, and he wasn't sure if it was something he was equipped to deal with. Julie and Steve were his family, and he had an ominous feeling rising in his chest. "Sis, are you sure you want to tell me?"

"Yes. I've been carrying this for a long time, and it will be good for me to get it out in the open and get your thoughts about it."

Another moment of silence. "Steve and I...... As a woman, Steve hasn't shown any interest in me in more than two years. I've tried and I've heard all the excuses. I've blamed myself; his work, and I've tried to be understanding. Honestly Travis, I know you will probably hate this, but I even considered having an affair rather than giving up on my marriage. Stupid, right?"

"Yes, no, I mean yes. Stupid. Sis, I'm not sure what to say. I mean, the spectrum of relationships covers so many facets. But there has to be trust for it to work, right?"

"Travis, I don't know what to do. Think of it like this. In the last week I've experienced more adventure and felt more alive than I have at any time in my marriage. And guess what? Steve isn't involved in it. I've done things, seen and felt things I never thought I would. I'm hungry, starving and I need to be fed. But I'm also married and as I said, I don't know what to do?"

Chapter 8

Either subconsciously or unconsciously Deb had divided her life into two parts. Before and after the incident. The before had in many ways become little more than a dream she once had. Like any loving relationship, her life with Christine had its ups and downs although now the downs gave no significance to the deep bond of love they shared. Had shared, and Deb sometimes got a bit confused between memory and fact. Christine was gone, but the strong feelings stayed tethering Deb to a lifeline of incomplete emotions that had become the after.

Life for Deb as it is for everyone moves forward, uncaring of the heart's desire. Unconcerned about anything left undone or unresolved. Perpetually moving us forward and away from the place where we longed to remain, the time before the incident. A lover's kiss, a warm embrace, the shared joy, and the feeling of belonging to someone other than herself. The now impossible dream.

The sheer terror of that day was relived a thousand times and still leaves room for doubt. Christine was trapped beneath the iron beam deep within the bowels of the wreck. The unrelenting struggle to get her free and Christine's awareness that she had to send her lover away or they would both perish. The agony of those few precious minutes where words could not be exchanged and the hard thump of Christine's fist made Deb realize what she had to do to survive. And now these two amazing men who risked their lives to save hers. Had saved her when she had no desire to be saved. Breathed life into her body and stood beside her as she wept. Love blooms in many ways and her heart recognizes them even though her body has not. But love is love and although its fashion is not always in sync it will not be denied. The lover and the loved.

******

Deb woke to the sound of water lapping against the side of the boat. Nestled comfortably beside Travis and all the warm assurance his body had to offer. She turned to face him and lovingly kissed his cheek. Light poured in through the porthole; the morning had begun. She adored this man and all the qualities he possessed and for a brief moment mused a desire to know him completely. But it passed quickly and in that realization she ambled out of the berth.

Julie sat reading a book up on deck as Deb exited the steps leading from the cabin.

"Morning, is it interesting?"

"Not sure yet, still on the first chapter."

"Seen Wicket yet? Sage is still sleeping."

"Wicket? He's in the bathtub."

There was an engaging almost conspiratorial tone in Julie's voice.

"Can I get you a mug of coffee?"

"Thanks Julie."

She folded the corner of the page before laying the book aside and making her way down to the cabin just as Wicket climbed back onboard.

"Morning Wicket; I've talked with you before about bringing that dangerous weapon onboard the boat. That thing could start a bloody war."

"Hey Deb, don't knock it till ya tried it."

"Try it? I'd be ruined for life. So, you just keep that thing at a safe distance, or I'll report you to the Department of Defense."

Mac grabbed a towel and secured it around his waist.

"Thanks Julie. You just missed Wicket's solo performance. One of the rudimentary elements in the game of cricket."

That whole concept appeared to fly straight over Julie's head.

"Well Wicket's out, so I'm going in unless you want to go first?"

Julie looked hesitant.

"Tell you what Julie, better idea. We can go in together, come on." Deb pulled Julie up before she could object and walked her over to the dive platform.

"The quicker you do it, the less it will be noticed." Deb stripped quickly, and just as Julie removed her panties, Deb called out to Wicket. "Hey Wicket, over here on the arse-end. Julie and I are going in." She waved to make sure she had his complete attention. "You're on watch." With that, she pushed Julie and followed her into the water.

They came up laughing and splashed each other in play.

"Sometimes Julie, you just have to dive right in and not be concerned about who's watching."

Julie glanced up and saw Mac standing on the stern, smiling broadly.

Deb sensed a familiarity in the unfamiliarity of her present company and for just a second, felt the desire to touch playfully. Then as if scolding herself and the infidelity of her thought, she drew back a little. Deb sunk below the surface and moments later reappeared and called out.

"Wicket?"

He turned and looked in her direction.

"Wicket quick! Hand down facemasks and fins." Deb swam towards the dive platform and Julie followed. Wicket passed a pair of fins and facemask to each of them.

"I've got a surprise for you Julie; we have visitors. Put your fins on quickly, follow me and stay calm."

A few yards from the boat Deb submerged, Julie hung back in uncertainty and lowered her head below the surface to see where Deb was leading her. She didn't see anything at first except Deb, when suddenly out of nowhere, the giant shape came into view. Panicked at first, Julie surfaced and took a deep breath and out of concern for Deb, she went under again. To her astonishment three giant shapes were moving gracefully through the water and one passed between her and Deb. It was fearsomely spectacular and Julie was afraid to move as it seemed to look directly at her as it sailed by.

Julie resurfaced and inhaled the deepest breath she could manage before going under for the third time. Deb was about twenty feet away and she determined to join her. They met, and Deb took Julie's hand in hers as the giants of the deep flaunted themselves around them. Their size and shape were incredible and the blue marking on their backs seemed almost iridescent as beams of sunlight captured the majesty of these gentle creatures. And as quickly as they had appeared they vanished behind the curtains of turquoise water.

Breaking the surface they both inhaled a fresh supply of air.

"That was the most amazing thing I've ever seen."

The excitement was evident in Julie's voice.

"It's certainly something to write home about."

Julie laughed at Deb's comment.

"What the heck were they, Deb."

"Whale sharks. The big one looked to be about twenty feet in length."

"Sharks?" The smile and enthusiasm dropped out of Julie's voice.

"Whale sharks Julie. Whale sharks. They're vegetarian. They were as curious to see you as you were to see them."

Julie got her smile back. "Yes, one looked right at me, unbelievably beautiful."

Without a second thought, Julie followed Deb to the dive platform. They removed their fins and facemasks and climbed onboard. "Wow, Deb, I still can't believe what happened. That was amazing." And turning slightly, she realized Mac was close, holding a towel and she was fully exposed. Instinct baited her to grab the towel. Nervously she fought to resist the urge. Deb was standing right beside her and she found strength in numbers. Politely she thanked Mac, reached for the towel and walked by him with it still in her hand, and Deb followed her in like manner.

******

Travis came up on deck clutching several sheets of paper and called everyone together.

"The forecast has changed, and it's been upgraded to a tropical storm and could get even worse. So, I think we can get a couple of dives in before mid-afternoon, and then we should weigh anchor and head back to port to ride it out. Take a look Mac. What do you think?"

Mac eyed the information. "Better safe than sorry skipper."

"Right. You and Deb take the first dive and Mac, how would you feel if you and I took Julie on the second. We can do a shallow dive; keep it above twenty meters."

"She's ready skipper, and I'll stay right beside her all the way."

"Okay, you and Deb get suited up and while you're gone, Julie and I will stow what we don't need."

It didn't take long before Mac and Deb were in the water.

"Okay Julie, see what you can rustle up for lunch, aim at 11am and see what you can put together for an evening meal. It could get a bit rough heading back to Semporna. Then stow anything in the galley that might get thrown around. I'll start on the main deck and work my way down."

"Travis, is this serious?"

"Let's just say I like to prepare for the worst-case scenario. You get fewer surprises that way. But I don't want to worry you."

******

The sun was shining and the ocean had a light chop to it when Mac, Julie, and Travis went down. Taking it slow, Mac as promised, stuck beside Julie while Travis led the way. Introducing Julie to his world had been something he'd thought about several times over the past few years, although never foreseeing how it would happen. A deep-sea adventure is a far cry from the life of a suburban housewife. But as his sister is proving, you just never know. Travis turned to look back and shot several pictures of the woman he was proud of.

The taste Julie had yesterday paled in comparison to the wonderland she had just dropped into. Breathtaking, vibrant, alive, even those words didn't do justice to the spectacular arena she had entered and was weightlessly drifting through. Her brother paused by a giant sea turtle resting on a ledge and waited for her to catch up. Then on through schools and shoals of brightly colored fish, along with intricate formations of coral. It was the most beautiful place she had ever seen, a paradise just beneath the ocean waves. The movement was stunning wherever she looked, and even the sharks seemed unperturbed with their presence. How, Julie thought, could she go home and leave all this behind.

The presence of Mac offered another tantalizing flavor to her adventure, he'd seen her, seen her in her entire nakedness, and she hoped he had appreciated all that he saw. The pleasure of it enticed her to imagine his hands touching her, searching her body, and navigating a course to discover her deepest desires by possessing her completely. The how, when, and where she didn't care, in the euphoria of her imagination. Although in reality, she knew it couldn't happen as long as she was married. But the freedom to think, feel, and experiment gave rise to a woman who has been subdued, long discarded, and too stifled in mere existence without validity, which was a volatile combination.

Chapter 9

Images, images, more than he could count. Thoughts punctuated only by the limitations of reason and the reasons seemed to exile his desire to have her. The sweet ensemble played carelessly with his heart, taunting his mind and Mac found no amusement in that. The turmoil of these past seven long years halted in one unrelenting moment when Julie's eyes met his and the wall of self-preservation surrounding his heart crumbled.

For Mac there had been no resolution, or if there was he had failed to find it and so, in conclusion the unwelcome truth had to be acknowledged. Maggie had betrayed him. Leaving him devoid of feeling anything other than resentment and anger. His heart, hopes, and dreams shattered instantly as the window of his life turned into a million shards of glass and tore him apart. And so one day, without further provocation or conclusion of thought, he turned his back on the life he had known and got on a plane. And from the ashes of his life the vagabond had emerged.

******

Julie's long, lean, shapely body moved gracefully through the water just below him. Travis, three meters lower still and in front. Mac monitored the theatrics of everything that moved, surveyed the terrain, and glanced at his dive computer periodically to coordinate their performance in the underwater world he had adopted as his own. Catching the attention of Travis, Mac pointed at his wrist, then held his hands up and open. Travis held up his thumb to acknowledge he understood. They would end the dive in ten minutes and make their way back to the boat.

******

A wind came out of nowhere, the ocean swell had increased and the sky looked threatening as Deb downloaded the latest meteorological weather update. An ominous sound vibrated along the anchor line and continued to resonate through the boat's hull. The anchor had broken free of its hold and was dragging; then suddenly, it caught again. The report indicated the storm had been upgraded to category one and increased its speed as the boat became restless and unsteady. Deb methodically closed air vents and battened hatches in anticipation of a rough ride back to port. Then she double-checked the lashing, which secured equipment up on deck and prepared to assist the divers as they came back on board. She checked her dive watch and knew they would be back in fifteen minutes or less. The haunting sound of the anchor dragging resonated again. *One thousand and one, one thousand and two, one thousand and three, one thousand and four*, then stopped. It had caught again. The reef was fifty feet off the port side and would get closer every time the anchor broke free. She quickly checked to ensure the key was in the ignition, then fastened her hair back in a ponytail to get it out of her face before grabbing a rope to rig a 'jack line' from bow to stern.

******

Mac looked up to search for the boat's hull as they made their ascent and saw the turbulence in the water. Touching Travis's arm Mac pointed, and Travis became aware of the situation above. They both looked for the hull and when Travis saw it, he touched Mac's shoulder and pointed toward it. Mac indicated he would go up first with the camera and Travis should surface with Julie away from the boat. A bouncing boat could be a deathtrap waiting to smash someone's skull if they were to get dragged beneath it. Travis and Mac knew this and were aware of the danger it posed, but Julie didn't and they did not want to alarm her.

Deb held on tightly as she climbed down onto the dive platform. The water swelled over her ankles, then drained and raised her two feet above the waterline only to drop down again. She tied a strap around her waist. Once she had gained her balance, she secured the other end to a stanchion bolted to the hull. *Any time now guys, come on?* There was little point in looking for air bubbles amid the turbulence, but she looked anyway. The vibration registered through her feet; the anchor was slipping again. *One, two, three*, out of nowhere Mac appeared six feet off the stern removed the breather from his mouth, and gave an okay sign to Deb.

Mac waited and watched the swell, preparing to make his approach. There were few second chances and if he miscalculated he would get dragged under the hull. Travis and Julie surfaced about four meters away, bobbing like two corks. Deb had lost count, but the vibration had stopped as she retrieved the camera from the grab-net. Then she threw a line towards Mac once he snapped open the buckles securing his buoyancy control vest and removed it. He attached the line tightly and as her feet felt the water rise she hauled it up onto the dive platform. Then moved it out of the way quickly as the swell crested and carried her high above Mac's body.

The fins came next one right after the other, hurled above Deb's head and landing on the main deck. This was it; the moment had arrived. Deb readied herself to grab hold of him; he was too precious to lose. The vibration started again; but she could not allow herself to be distracted. Mac lunged forward with force, caught tight hold of the handrail, and propelled himself onto the dive platform knocking Deb on her arse. She didn't care; she held on to him with all her strength. He was safe and that's all that mattered. *One down, two to go.* They both got up; Mac picked up his equipment, Deb gave him a quick kiss and climbed onto the main deck.

Mac turned his attention to Travis and Julie.

"Mac, we've got a bigger problem. The anchor is dragging. I'd guess we're fifty percent closer to the reef now than we were this morning."

"Shit!" He rushed into the wheelhouse, looked at the navigation screen, made a mental note and then rushed back out onto the deck. Deb took Mac's gear and stowed it quickly.

A series of hand signals were exchanged between Travis and Mac.

"Okay Sis, we're going to be here for a short time while Mac and Deb re-secure the anchor. You don't happen to have a deck of cards on you, do you?"

Julie could see the ocean was rough and understood it would take a little effort to get back on board. But she had no concept of the real danger it presented. Travis knew the longer it took to get them aboard, the harder it would be. This was just the beginning of the storm as Travis felt the first drops of rain on his face.

Moving quickly, Mac tossed a lifebuoy towards Travis and told Deb to fire up the engine while he went forward to operate the winch. His thoughts focused; he had to get this done fast. The boat would be moving away from two people he cared deeply about and the dark clouds looming overhead threatened to make this bad situation even worse by the minute. Deb understood. She knew what she had to do. Part of her heart was still out there in the water and she was just now beginning to realize the depth of her love. *Travis I love you. Oh, God.* Tears filled her eyes. *Please!* She had felt it this morning. *Why didn't I make love to you?* She needed another chance. *Christine, I will always love you but I want Travis. Help me. I love him so much.*

"Hey Sis, if all else fails there's an island about two miles over that way." He pointed. "It's called Sipadan, tropical paradise, white sand, palm trees, the works. So, if we have to swim for it that's the way to go." Julie looked concerned. "I'm joking Sis." They silently

DÉJÀ VU

watched the boat moving away, and the rain was stinging their faces as the wind drove it hard into them.

"What time did Deb say the sharks get hungry?" Travis looked at her, now understanding her concern.

"Sis, you've been watching too many movies." He pulled Julie into his arms and kissed her cheek. "And besides, we've got this." He produced the dive knife with its twelve-inch blade which she and Steve had given him as a birthday present. Julie didn't appear comforted.

Slowly the boat seemed to draw towards them stern first.

"Okay, I know what they're doing. They've secured the anchor and they're keeping the line tight as they come back for us. Good thinking." Julie looked relieved. "Now, Sis, when they get here, you saw what Mac had to do? He watched the boat to time his approach so that just as it was about to go low in the water he leaped forward, took hold and used the downward motion of the boat to help lift him onto the platform. Try to visualize it, watch the boat, determine how high it rises and see the mid-point as it comes down. That is when you make your move, grab the handrail and don't let go." Even as Travis spoke, he could see the boats' rise and fall had increased and if there were any other option he would have gladly taken it, and not placed his sister in harm's way.

The boat stopped. Deb had cut the engine and Travis moved towards it with Julie. Mac climbed down onto the platform. Travis unclipped the buckles on Julie's vest and helped her remove it once she had taken off her fins. Mac threw the line; Travis secured the equipment and Mac yanked it on board and passed it up to Deb. The boat was rising four feet, the prop visible at its peak as Travis prepared Julie to leap. "You go on two." Pause. "One. Tw"

"I can't do it." She turned and grabbed Travis. "I'm sorry, I can't do it." Through fear-filled eyes, she wanted to cry.

"Sis it's okay."

Travis and Mac looked at each other. They both knew this had to happen.

Mac climbed down onto the dive ladder. At the rise, his entire body was out of the water. On the bottom of the low he was submerged up to his chest. It was a dangerous move but hell, in his mind if he had to swim out and get her he'd do it. Travis saw the determination in Mac's eyes.

"Okay Sis, Mac is there. He is going to catch hold of you and keep you safe. So, let's watch the movement again and when I say go, jump into his arms. Alright?"

Julie looked at Mac she kind of wanted to jump into his arms but she hadn't thought about it under these conditions. She nodded and turned to face Mac. He tried to issue a reassuring smile. Travis watched; Mac waited. They had one shot at this and they both sensed Julie wouldn't be up to trying it a third time.

"GO." Julie lunged forward catapulted from Travis's arms toward Mac. Mac reached but she slipped as their wetsuits met. She locked her fingers between the platform boards and her head went below the water's surface. Mac grappled to hold her in place and in the sheer thought he might lose her he put all protocols aside. Reaching down, he forced his hand between her legs, laid his hand firmly against her pelvic bone and heaved her up onto the platform. "Julie.... Julie." She looked up at Mac uncertain if the ordeal was over. "I love ya. But right now I need ya to climb onboard. Deb's there." He pointed and as if numbed by the experience Julie got up, grabbed the rail and climbed on board without any expression on her face.

Mac turned back towards Travis and held out his hand. They looked at each other for a moment. "Mac, you're like a brother to me and I know you mean well, but we both know the ladder won't take the weight of both of us. So, if we're doing this, I need you to go up on the platform." Lightning bolt close by, one, two, boom. It was deafening across the open water. Travis unclipped his vest.

Mac climbed onto the platform and threw the line out. There was a thick heavy feel to the air as the black clouds tried to block out the light. Another lightning bolt, followed quickly by a third and then a fourth, the booms directly overhead echoing out in all directions.

Travis decided to keep his fins on, hoping they might provide extra momentum. The rain felt like small pebbles pelting his face and he'd been in the water for a long time. Deb took Julie below decks, stripped her out of her wetsuit and wrapped her in a blanket. She wanted to do more, fix a hot drink or something but she was drawn back to the stern of the boat. Travis lunged forward; the ladder snapped out from its slots.

"SKIPPER!"

"TRAVIS!"

Chapter 10

Sam was cuddled between the sheets sleeping peacefully when suddenly she screamed in agony as the pain surged through her right shoulder. She couldn't move, couldn't breathe, or catch her breath. The feeling of being underwater overwhelmed her. Again she cried out as the pain snapped at her forearm and contorted her face. Air shot into her lungs and almost instantly there was no more. She gasped again to find more air and cried out through pain-filled tears. *Was it real? Was it a nightmare?* Was someone attacking her hidden from view in the darkness of the night? It was real; she could feel it, although everything seemed normal when she examined herself with her hand. And just as quickly as the pain had arrived, it dissipated and after turning on the bedside light all trace of it had vanished.

Sam got out of bed carefully, uncertain about what had just happened but knowing something had. She stood motionless for a few seconds, then decided a warm glass of milk might calm her down. She glanced at the bedside clock before leaving the room and had the strangest feeling that she should be aware of something, something about herself but she couldn't seem to take hold of it. *Damn, where did that come from?* Sam was warming her milk in the kitchen. Her bag was on the counter so she reached inside, pulled out a small diary and opened it. *Period's not due for another week. Ouch?* She had a headache, so she poured her milk into a glass and went to the bathroom cabinet to search for pills.

******

"TRAVIS." The scream wailed out into the storm. If there was any divinity, she demanded their attention. Deb dived into the water with only one thought, one concise determined instinct. Her life was worth nothing without the man she loved and if fate wanted him, it had to take her as well.

******

Travis woke slowly in a long room full of beds, most of which were occupied by men. It didn't take many seconds for him to realize why he was there. His shoulder hurt like hell, as did his arm and his head.

"Ha, good. You are awake. I'm Doctor Rasheed. Do you remember anything about your accident?"

"Do you mean on the boat?"

"Yes, but I believe you were not on the boat exactly. Am I correct?"

"Right Doc; I was in the water trying to get on the boat."

"Good. What else do you remember?"

"Do you have anything I can drink?"

Dr. Rasheed called out to someone and they left the ward. About a minute later Mac walked in with a bottle of water. "G'day Skipper, ya damn near scared me to death."

"Hi Mac."

"I bloody well need to teach ya how to jump. How are you feeling Skipper?"

"I've had better days. How are the girls?"

"They're fine, a bit worried about ya though."

"Are they here? Can you bring them in?"

"They're back at the boat waiting. They're not allowed in here. It's men only."

Dr. Rasheed had remained silent until Travis looked at him.

"Mr. Sage, you hit your head, no skull fracture and required eight sutures. Your shoulder was dislocated and has been reset. The bone in your right forearm is broken and will heal, but I advise you to have your doctor in the United States look at it within the next six days. You appear to know where you are and you are aware of the events that brought you here. Unless you develop new symptoms you may leave."

Having said that Dr. Rasheed turned and left the room.

"Damn, Mac, what would I have to do to earn two days in here?"

"It's okay Skipper. I think they feel a bit strange about having us non-religious types in their midst. Deb booked a hotel room; ya can rest up there till we decide what to do. Let me help ya get ya shirt on."

Travis tried to raise his right arm and almost instantly changed his mind.

"Mac, I think we can get the left arm in the sleeve but the right side, better just go over the shoulder and I think I might need some pain medication."

"I'll see what I can rustle up for ya mate."

"Mac. Thank you."

"Come on Skipper, let's get ya out of here."

******

Travis felt certain he'd just experienced 'the ride in hell' by the time they got to the hotel. The taxi driver must have searched for every pothole he could find and probably taken many detours to do it.

"Okay Skipper, I'll get ya settled then head back to the boat. I'm guessing the girls are anxious to see ya."

"Thanks Mac."

About an hour later Deb and Julie arrived. Travis hadn't moved off the bed. He was happy to see them both and even happier to see they'd brought medication and food with them.

"Let's get you medicated."

"Thanks Deb. I don't remember much about the boat trip or how you all managed to get me on board."

"You have to thank Mac for that."

"What did the doctor say?"

"Well, as you can see Sis, I'm pretty banged-up. He thinks I need to have my doctor back home check out my arm."

"Then that's what we're going to do."

"Hold on a minute Sis. I don't want to ruin your trip; you stay here. I mean, I'm not going to be diving for a while and I'm pretty sure I can manage to get myself home okay."

"Don't be silly and besides, who's going to take care of you once you get there?"

"You stink!"

"Thanks Deb. I'll stop and put deodorant on after my next surgery just for you."

"Come on, into the bathroom. We'll get you stripped off and clean in no time."

"Hold on a minute Deb. We, as in you and me? OR WE, as in you and Sis?"

"My, oh my Travis Sage, you're a prude? What if Julie was the only person here with you? What would you do then? This is a whole new side of you that I don't know anything about. What do you think Julie? Does he stink?"

"He sure does Deb."

"Would you care to help me, help Travis get over this inhibition?"

"I'm with you Deb."

"Wait a minute girls. Girls! Ouch, OUCH. Gently, please."

******

"Mac, I need a favor."

"Name it skipper."

"Julie is insistent on flying back to the States with me. I don't want her to leave here thinking about how the trip ended the way it did. So, before you and Deb set out to finish up her project, would you consider taking Sis out for a couple more dives, like a day trip type of deal?"

"Consider it done skipper. But I need to talk to ya about something first, then ya can decide."

Travis could see that Mac was setting a serious tone.

"What is it Mac?"

"Truth is, you're me best mate. I've never had a mate I care for more than ya. And I'd be damned lucky to ever find another mate like ya and that makes ya important to me. But I have to tell ya I've got feelings. Feelings for Julie, and I know you've seen me with a lot of women but I gotta tell ya skipper, this is different. Julie's different and that makes me wanna be different. That's all I'm gonna say about it. Just wanted ya to know that skipper."

"Mac, I love you like a brother you know that and I don't want this to come between us, and besides, Julie is married. In a few days she'll fly back to the States and eventually back to her husband and Mac; I'm happy you have feelings for her because I love her too. She's a good woman, and the best sister a brother could ask for. So be careful you don't get your feelings hurt."

******

"Julie's packing up all your stuff and Mac will bring it by later. Here's your laptop. I've already logged into the Wi-Fi while I was in the lobby so it's good to go."

"Thanks Deb. I hate bailing out on you like this."

"Come on Sage, knock it off with the teary-eyed drama."

"Deb...."

"What?"

"Never mind. Let me take a look at who's been trying to reach me. I'm pretty sure my assignment is up shit-creek and probably the next two, as well."

Travis scrolled down the list of emails. Most weren't that important and could wait. Then he noticed he'd got an email from Sam, so he clicked on it. There was no message just an attachment, so he clicked on that and the picture came up full screen. He felt something and turned the screen away from himself with almost no hesitation.

"What's that?" Deb moved in for a closer look. "Hmm, looks familiar. What are you doing with a picture like that?"

"Like what, Deb?"

"Like a picture from an old English town. You've never been to England, have you?"

"No I can't say that I have. Wait a minute. What makes you think it's a picture of an old English town?"

"Well, I can't be a hundred percent certain but if it's where I think it is, then I can say I've walked under that arch on quite a few occasions."

"What you're kidding, right?"

"No, well, I'm fairly sure I'm right. There's a marketplace beyond the arch and I've shopped there. Yes, I'm sure that's it."

"Turn the laptop off for me Deb."

"Good, now I have your full attention. Mac's taking Julie diving tomorrow, probably making an early start in the morning and so I was thinking, I could sleep here tonight and take care of you tomorrow."

Travis looked surprised. "I thought you were going with them?"

"No, that was never discussed and besides, I have no idea when I'm going to see you again."

"But do you think it's safe to leave Mac and my sister alone overnight?"

"What? What the hell are you thinking? They're both adults."

"My point exactly, Mac is sweet on Julie and she's having some relationship issues back home."

"I don't believe you Sage, so what are you, some sort of judge who gets to decide who should be with whom?"

"Deb, she's my sister and Mac is my friend."

"Newsflash Sage, that doesn't mean diddly squat. You need to butt out and mind your own business. If they want to have a romantic fling that's their choice. As I said they're adults, so butt out."

That wasn't the conversation Deb wanted to have with Travis, and it certainly didn't put any notion of romance in the air.

******

For what felt like the first time, alone with Julie seemed awkward to Mac.

"All done." Julie appeared from Travis's cabin. "His bag is packed and mine is kind of, sort of, except for what I am wearing tomorrow and the outfit I'll be wearing on the plane."

Mac was a crumpled mess inside; the love, yes he knew it was love. Real love, the kind you know you're damned lucky to find and you'll fight like hell to hold onto, but she'd be gone in a couple of days. *What then?* What the hell was he supposed to do then?

Something had changed inside him and he didn't want the 'old him' back. What he wanted, what the 'new him' wanted was Julie and the 'happy ever after' story. But he was stuck on the 'once upon a time' part where they first met and he knew he'd fulfilled his part; he'd fallen in love. But what about Julie; she's a married woman, how does he feel about that? The storybook never mentioned that part. *How do I feel?* How was he supposed to feel? Knowing that his heart will be ripped from his chest and fly off with her when she steps onto the plane.

Julie is a lady; he'd almost forgotten what one of those was. She wasn't the one-night-stand type of woman he'd become accustomed to. Mac felt so ashamed and embarrassed by his own doing. *Damn,* he'd fallen a long way down that hole. The old him, 'the really old him' was respectable, recognized and highly thought of. *What the hell happened to me?* He knew the answer to that question. *Maggie?* Maggie had ripped his world apart. *How long ago was that? Really, had it been that long?*

******

Was the reflection she saw in the mirror the same woman she knew back in Nashville? It seems almost translucent and vague in comparison. Julie nibbled at the tidbits of information as they passed through her thoughts, uncertain of finding any resolve. Finally she closed her eyes and sighed deeply; *it wasn't supposed to be like this.* Those thoughts about her life, marriage and mainly Steve disturbed and unsettled her knowing she was going back. *How can I go back? Do I want to go back?* Back seemed to be the operative word and having moved forward, she found her thoughts hard to digest.

******

"Hi Deb."

"Julie. That brother of yours is driving me crazy."

"Why, what has he done?"

"Nothing really; he just has some weird ideas. I wanted to talk to him but he got off on a tangent and completely ruined the moment. Julie, can I ask you something?"

"Sure Deb."

"It's going to sound stupid and I'm amazed that I'd even consider asking you."

"What is it? Hold on, why don't we pour ourselves a glass of wine and sit down first. Then we can talk. I can't believe we've spent all this time together and not found time to chat?"

"Good idea, I like the way you think."

"Deb, I think you're the most amazing woman I've ever met."

"No, I'm just a working woman trying to make ends meet. You know, house, car, mortgage, the usual stuff, nothing amazing really."

"But that's it, your choice of work, the travel, the adventure...."

"Really? That's the superficial stuff. Don't get me wrong, I love what I do but you're looking at it from the outside. You only see the travel and adventure. From the inside the picture is quite different. I'm away from home a lot. I miss out on socializing with family and friends. I miss important events and then there's who will watch my cat, 'this time.' I swear I think my cat is more familiar with some of my friends than she is with me. So really, I don't get included in a lot of things because I never know if I'll be home or not."

"Wow, I hadn't thought about it like that," Julie concluded. "They always say there are two sides to everything. But what was it you wanted to ask me?"

Deb was quiet for a few moments. "I'm not sure how to say it without seeming like I'm prying into something that's none of my business."

"Well, Deb, we're not going to know that until you say it?"

"Okay then. Does Travis.... Does he have a steady girlfriend, someone with whom he might have plans?"

Julie pondered the question carefully. "That's a surprising question, an honest question and a curious question. Let me see. First-of-all, surprising in that you probably spend more time with him than I do. Honest in that, if you are interested in him it is something you would want to know and should know. And being curious about that, I would be drawn to think that you do."

Deb laughed. "Okay so now you've analyzed the question, what's the answer?"

Chapter 11

Discovering that Deb was planning to spend the night at the hotel with her brother. Julie wanted tonight to be special, perhaps very special. Because tomorrow would be her last day with Mac and she was very aware of the life that waited for her in Nashville. Julie was content and at peace with her decision and now, as she finished the final touches to her make-up, the rest would be up to him. Julie would place herself in his hands, literally and their night would officially begin.

******

Mac knew he couldn't take back the rambunctious lifestyle he'd carelessly adopted. The countless women and the drunken nights where nothing mattered. The debauchery in search of self-satisfaction and the nothingness of any emotional ties. The revolving door of repetition had suddenly smacked him in the face and demanded some accountability and Maggie no longer justified the reason. He had to face himself. The rude awakening daggered his conscience in realizing how far he had fallen down the hole and if any reformation were to be had, he had to confront his past. Surprised in his recollection of the numbers, he tapped them into the satellite phone and listened for the connection. "Dad?"
"Mackenzie? Son?"

******

Stunned in her amazement and heart-pounding delight, Julie caught sight of the most gorgeous man on the face of the planet as she stepped out onto the deck. "Mac?"

He smiled; his entire face radiated the warmth of his heart and Julie stood captivated.

"How?" She had never imagined this, couldn't have imagined it in her wildest dreams: Mac, the man. Dressed in a crisp white cotton shirt and navy-blue slacks and in all fairness, she could easily forgive the sneakers considering the size of his feet.

"You look beautiful." They both said it at the same time to each other.

Mac, too felt his heart melt as he gazed longingly at the woman he loved. Her pale green dress emphasized the perfection of her body and the elegance of her movements. The depth of her deep brown eyes pulled him towards her like a magnet and warranted the exchange of their first kiss.

******

Limited wasn't a good place for Travis and being stuck in a hotel room was definitely not his idea of a good time. He was feeling restless, in need of fresh air and was almost willing to suffer 'the ride in hell' to get it.

"I'm sorry Deb, I always thought I'd make a terrible patient and look at me. I was right.

"It's okay, I understand. You're like a fish out of water. Is there anything I can do?"

"It's exhausting Deb and to think I've still got tomorrow to get through."

"TRAVIS, you should be thankful that you have tomorrow." Deb hated herself for the scolding tone in her voice but it was true. She had almost lost him and why shouldn't he be thankful to be alive? It startled him. He was used to her English sense of humor and being the butt of her wit. But this was neither of those.

"I'm sorry Deb."

"Please stop saying you're sorry it doesn't help." Her bottom lip quivered and Travis saw it before she turned and ran into the bathroom.

"Deb I'm sorry."
"STOP SAYING THAT."
He could hear Deb crying behind the locked door.

******

Julie sighed as the sweet gentle kiss lingered in the warm night air offering the promise of more and the sweeping sensations urgently awakened the woman who had been kept dormant too long.

******

Travis leaned against the bathroom door and listened as Deb cried. She was right; *of course,* he should be thankful he was alive. And at the sound of her crying, he really was sorry but afraid to say the words. "Deb, please unlock the door. I feel terrible that I've made you cry. If you only knew how much I care about you. Deb, I love you, and right now my heart is breaking knowing that I've hurt you. Want to know a secret? I fell in love with you the very first day I saw you. I remember how I felt even then, and in getting to know you I've grown to love you even more. The irony of that is, so does Mac. We both love you; I've watched the way he looks at you and I know how he feels, and I can't fault him for it. Because in faulting him I'd be faulting myself.

You have two men who love you deeply, and the consequence of that is we both know we're stuck and must accept things the way they are. So maybe it's better this way for Mac and for me, in that you choose neither of us as long as you know just how much you are loved. But I've got to tell you Deb, there have been so many times when I've fought off the urge to wrap my arm around you and felt the desire to.... Kiss you passionately... Make love with you... Even just holding your hand the way two lovers do. I've imagined doing everything with you."

Lost in his emotional confession, Travis was unaware she had stopped crying. Quietly, Deb listened with all her heart and fought back emotional tears of joy.

"I'm your lovesick fool, so please unlock the door and tell me how crazy I am. Forgive me for being so thoughtless because the truth is, I am thankful to be alive and for all the wonderful feelings of love I feel for you."

Deb could hold back no longer. *'Click.'*

******

Four hearts yearned painfully; torn in their need to say goodbye and their desire to have no part in it. Four hearts interwoven in their longing for inseparability. Each trying to find acceptance in the inevitable ending of this, their chapter. Four hearts full of hope in their sadness; full of joy in their discovery, and the anticipation of another day. In their quiet displeasure, Julie and Travis said their goodbyes to Mac and Deb and boarded the plane. Four hearts stilled in their urgency to scream.

Chapter 12

"All I know Sis; is I owe my life to Mac."

"Yes, that's probably true, but what about Deb?"

"How do you mean?"

"She was in the water with you."

"What? No, she was on deck."

"No Travis, Deb was in the water. Let's see. I was in the cabin when I heard her scream your name, so I rushed up on deck and ran to the back of the boat. Mac was on the platform holding onto your arm; Deb was in the water with her arm around your neck, there was blood on your face and she was fighting to keep you from being pulled under the boat. I was terrified and screamed. Mac told me to stay back. They fought like crazy to get you up on the platform. It was like a nightmare, twice over. Mac had Deb then lost hold of her, she went under several times and came back up. Finally Mac got a good grip and literally ripped her from the ocean, as if he had super-human strength and he'd be damned if he was going to let Davy Jones take her. I took care of both of you while Mac got us back to port."

How could he not have known?

If there were any way he could get the plane turned around, Travis would have ordered it. Right now, at this very moment he could only think of holding Deb in his arms. Heck, he'd been thinking that since they left the hotel this morning, but the desire was even more vivid now knowing she had risked her life to save his. It didn't take anything away from how thankful he was to Mac; it just increased the close bond he shared with both of them and within that, there was pain at the thought of how Mac would handle finding out that Deb had made her choice.

It still seemed like a dream he'd dreamed many times over during the last eighteen months, and now the dream was real. Deb loved him and her admission of it had caught him by surprise. He could still hear her saying it for the first time and what seemed like a hundred times since she stepped out of the bathroom. What a fool he had been; why hadn't he known that too? *Am I that dumb?* There must have been signs and if there were, why had he missed seeing them?

******

"I've been meaning to ask you Travis; although it's a moot point now, and I don't want to seem ungrateful but how come you and Mac had decent-sized cabins, and I got a broom closet?"

"Huh? Well, Sis, when Mac leased the boat he didn't know you were invited. In fact you weren't at that time so he leased the boat thinking there would just be three of us on board. Mac, me, and Deb, so we just had to do a bit of reshuffling. You got Deb's cabin."

Julie thought about that and.... "So where did Deb sleep?"

"She just bunked in with Mac or me."

"What? Are you saying Deb just climbed into bed with you? Mac? Willy-Nilly? She just randomly picked one of you to sleep with. Did she sleep with Mac?"

"Yes, why? Is that a problem?"

"And you slept with her?"

"What are you driving at Sis? Deb has slept with one of us many times. No harm done."

Julie was furious and fought hard to stay composed. Mac was a bastard and how could she have believed otherwise. The pain hurt badly and in her embarrassment his words had been nothing but lies. She had trusted him and now felt violated in her own foolishness. He was probably laughing at the memory of his deception right now. She wanted to cry. Scream. The betrayal had been complete. *But why?* That question would eat away at her and she felt trapped in the deceitful compromise of a secret.

******

"Wicket you seem quiet, is everything alright?"

Even the look in his eyes appeared distant, as if he was somewhere other than on the boat.

"Aye Deb, I'm just thinking......."

"What Wicket, what are you thinking? I'm starting to feel like I'm alone."

"Huh. Sorry Deb. We should be dropping anchor soon."

"You look bloody morbid. You'd tell me if something's wrong, wouldn't you?"

Mac didn't say anything, he just stared at the horizon and continued to steer the boat.

The happiness in Deb's heart refused to be stifled. Her life had just done a complete turnabout and for the first time in more than a year she had something to focus on other than her work, Travis. He loved her and she loved him, and apart from geography and a million little details she felt they were together. And as soon as this assignment was completed she was going to America. Well, after she had flown back home first and taken care of her cat. That was a detail. The geography would take care of itself.

******

His lips touching hers, *softly she moaned*. Hands felt warm and gentle against her skin, the memory of which ignited a tormenting pleasure unlike anything she had ever experienced.

'*Ah..............Hmm*'

"Hey Sis, are you alright? Are you awake?"

"Huh? What?............ What?"

"Just checking Sis, I think you were having a dream or something. You were making some funny noises. Anyway we'll be landing in Honolulu in about twenty minutes."

'Damn that man!'

Safely behind the locked door of the restroom, her heartbeat still raced as the heat of her emotions threatened to consume her. *Damn you Mac.* Tears filled her eyes and ran down her cheeks, and even in her anger she felt the yearning deep inside. *Goddamn you. Why did I think....* The 'return to your seat signal sounded and a small sign illuminated, indicating she had best hurry. Julie moistened several paper towels with cold water and did her best to freshen up quickly.

******

"Wicket does it have anything to do with Julie?" Almost immediately she could tell from his cow-eyed expression, it did. "Okay then, I'm not going to spend the next two weeks putting up with your bloody moping. So, you better tell me what's got you all arse-about-face."

"It's complicated Deb."

"What's complicated? You didn't bonk her, did you?"

Mac turned away.

"No? You bonked her? You bonked Julie? What the hell were you thinking Wicket?"

"Deb, it's not what ya think...."

"It doesn't matter what I think. What do you think will happen when Sage finds out you bonked his bloody sister? For God's sake Wicket, I told Sage it was none of his business. I didn't think the two of you needed a chaperone. He will blame me for not staying on board to keep an eye on you. Damn it, Wicket." Deb threw her hands in the air and stomped off below decks.

Chapter 13

With immediate surprise Travis knew something wasn't right when he pressed the remote button on the transmitter inside his vehicle. And after a long and tiresome journey it was the last thing he had expected to find. As the light inside came on, through the line of windows built into the door he saw the top of a car, and as the garage door raised, the back of a maroon BMW came into full view.

"What the......?" He looked at the house wondering if he'd made a mistake and realized he hadn't.

"Who does that car belong to Travis?"

"I haven't got a clue Sis. Wait here a minute."

"Travis what are you doing?" Julie asked as he opened the passenger side door.

"What do you think I'm doing Sis? I'm going to see if there is someone in the house. Wait here and lock the doors behind me."

"Shouldn't you call the police first?"

"What? And sit out here and wait?"

"Yes Travis."

He was out of the vehicle and closed the door.

Julie watched anxiously as he stepped into the garage and examined the BMW before moving towards the door which led into the house. Grabbing her bag she pulled out her phone and hesitated, uncertain what to do watching Travis disappear through the door into the house. The clock on the dash indicated 11.30 pm just before all the instrument illumination went off after she remembered to press the door-lock button. Julie looked around; most of the houses along the street were in darkness.

Travis listened intently while standing still in the dark before making any further movement. The distant sound of running water drew his attention towards the master bedroom, so quietly he moved in that direction. A lambent light source filtered out along the passage through the slightly open door and a sweet floral fragrance filled the air. As he slowly pushed the door open and looked in a sense of femininity sparked in his mind. The soft glow of candlelight bathed the dimly lit room and the bathroom door was closed.

"Travis," Julie whispered. She had crept up behind him.

"Sis, you were supposed to wait in the car." He whispered back at her while trying to hide the fact that she'd startled him.

"What, and wait while you get knocked over the head by some burglar? No way."

He looked down and saw the pipe wrench in her hand. "Okay then."

The sound of the shower water still emulated from inside the bathroom.

"Just stay behind me." Mentally Travis counted to three and on three he burst into the bathroom and drew the shower curtain back with force. The SCREAM instantly resonated throughout the house.

The sheer mass of Travis's body, even with his right arm in a sling was imposing and struck terror into his would-be victim. The registering of which was plain to see on her face, and seeing how small and insignificant his quarry was, made Travis feel apologetic. But the fact remained she was an intruder although at that moment, he somehow felt intrusive.

"It's okay, Travis; I've got this, you go and fix us a drink."

Leaving the traumatized girl to Julie, Travis thought she looked somewhat vaguely familiar as he made his way to the kitchen. She looked like a drowned rat, a cornered, blonde-haired, pretty, drowned rat. *Yes, definitely blonde* he reminded himself.

******

Dressed in a bathrobe, his bathrobe he noted. The drowned rat was escorted into the kitchen by Julie. Her eyes looked towards the floor.

"Travis, meet Sam. You remember Sam don't you? Although, what she is doing here in your house she has yet to divulge."

"Sam? What the heck.... I mean, what's going on? I don't understand?" Now he recognized her, although the wet straggly hair didn't help. She raised her hands to cover her face and said in a teary voice. "It wasn't supposed to be like this?" Then, lowering her hands slightly she turned her head and looked directly into his eyes soulfully. Travis instantly felt the link but forced himself to look away. "Sam, no." He then realized Sis had followed her gaze. "I mean, no tears Sam. We've got to talk about this like adults. You broke into my house; at least I think you did. How did you get in? How long have you been here and most importantly, why are you here?"

Sam tried again to connect; Travis diverted his eyes. How she thought, was she going to explain everything in front of Julie and not sound like a raving lunatic? Especially when Travis was avoiding eye contact. "I'm sorry, I.... I know it seems impulsive. Absurd even, but I was so attracted to you that night at dinner I couldn't get you out of my mind, and yes, I remember you telling me you were going away. And yes, this might sound crazy. And it is, but my feelings were so strong. And if I couldn't be with you to explore them, I figured I could at least surround myself with the things that make up your life and somehow come to know you better. So, call me crazy, but before you call the cops, look around, nothing is missing and nothing is broken. Well, the back-door window was but I've had that replaced."

Travis didn't know what to say. He looked at Julie and shrugged his shoulders, or at least he tried but was instantly reminded that was not a good idea. Julie thought about it for a moment before softening her temperament. In doing so, she realized this was more of a cupid issue than anything harmful and Sam had acted very unwisely. Julie was unpleasantly reminded just how unwisely one could act when the emotional attraction is strong. "Sam, why don't you go back into the bedroom, dry your hair and put something on. It's late, I'm sure we're all very tired and we can talk again in the morning. But, considering Travis is injured I think you should let him have his bed and I'll get you a pillow and blanket, and we can make up a bed on the couch."

******

Travis followed Julie into the guest bedroom carrying her bag. "Sis, I'm not sure what to make of it?"

"Travis, it's easy. Think about it? She's in love with you." Julie gave him an all-knowing smile.

"But Sis...."

"But nothing, that girl has got it bad can't you tell? But that doesn't give you the right to take advantage of her. Remember that because I'll be watching you." While Julie was talking, she was unpacking things from her bag.

"This is crazy Sis; Sam broke into my house."

"Travis, have you never done anything foolish? But I will admit that breaking into someone's house is a little extreme." Julie sorted her PJs, a two-piece swimsuit and laid them on the bed.

Travis followed her back to the kitchen where Julie pulled a trash bag from the pantry and tucked it under her arm.

"So, what are we going to do with her?"

"Do with her, Travis?"

"I mean...."

"Why not wait until the morning? We can have a good talk and then decide what's best." Julie went to the linen closet and pulled out fresh towels.

"Hi Sam, there, you look much better. Doesn't she Travis?"

Travis had to admit, dressed in her PJ bottoms and a tee-type top with her hair dried and flowing. She looked better. *Much better.*

"Travis, you take Sam into the living room. First, I'll get your bathroom ready; then I'll bring some bedding out for Sam."

Always the organizer. My big sister. "Come on Sam, I'm sorry I scared you. I could say I scared the pants off you, but as it turns out you weren't wearing any."

"Very funny.... What did you do to your arm?"

"Boating accident. So, as you can see I had to cut my trip short."

"Is it broken?"

"Huh, yes."

"Does it hurt?"

"Only when I try to move it."

"Here you are Sam, two pillows okay? Travis, if you're ready I'll be in to help you bathe in a few minutes. Just take off what clothing you can, I'll help you with the rest."

Travis realized he had been dismissed. "Goodnight Sam."

After getting Sam settled Julie picked up her PJs and bathing suit from the guest room and headed into the master bedroom. She helped Travis finish getting his remaining clothes off and put the trash bag over his cast. "I need something to secure this, to stop the water from getting inside. Any ideas?"

"Not really, but I've got some neckties."

Julie opened his closet and found them. "Which one do you like the least?"

"All of them, take your pick."

"Okay, give me a couple of minutes to change into my bathing suit and start the shower. Then come in."

My Sis would make a great mother. I think she's enjoying this.

******

"Good morning. Pancakes?" Julie had just stepped into the kitchen to make a pot of coffee. Sam was busy cooking breakfast; the coffee was already brewed.

"This is a nice surprise. Good morning Sam. Did you sleep okay?"

"Like a baby, now I know Travis is safe."

"What do you mean, safe?"

"Well, I felt he'd been hurt...."

"How do you mean Sam felt?"

"When he was in pain I felt it. First in my shoulder, then my arm and after I got out of bed I had a terrible headache. I felt his injuries."

"When, last night?"

"No, six nights ago when he got hurt."

Julie didn't know what to think. She contemplated the possibility of a mental disorder.

"I'm not sure I understand Sam. It's easy to imagine something like that; especially now you've seen Travis, his injuries...."

"No, Julie. I knew before you got home that he'd been hurt. But seriously, Travis told me he'd been in a boating accident last night but he wasn't. He was in the water; I felt him in the water, I couldn't breathe."

"Is this some kind of game Sam? Because if it is, it's not very funny." *There is no way she could know that, unless Travis mentioned it.*

"Julie, I swear I'm telling the truth. I don't understand how it happened but since the first night Travis and I met, we've had a connection."

"Sam, I understand 'connection,' really, I do. Falling in love makes people behave differently and imagine all sorts of wonderful things. So maybe seeing Travis with his arm in a sling sparked some type of sympathetic empathy."

"Okay, you don't believe me, I understand. Why would anyone believe me?"

"Look, Sam, you're right. I don't understand how any of what you're saying is even possible. But, let me think about it. There must be some rational explanation for what you say you experienced. But at the moment I just don't have any idea what that could be. Okay?"

******

"Morning Travis, I've brought you a cup of coffee and Sam is cooking pancakes."

But, of course, Travis's first thought as soon as he became cognizant was to pull a pillow over his head. And sure enough Sis pulled back the curtains and opened the blinds.

"Come on sleepyhead, what time do we have to be at the hospital for the x-rays?"

"Sis ask me when I'm awake."

"Then wake up. You wouldn't want to disappoint Sam would you? Not after she's gone to the trouble of cooking breakfast for you and besides, I have something I want to ask you?"

"Any other reasons why I need to wake up?"

"No, that just about covers it. Question, breakfast, and appointment."

Travis struggled to sit up, and Julie rearranged the pillow behind him.

"What did you tell Sam last night about the accident?"

"How do you mean?"

"Well, I'm sure it came up in conversation, so what did you tell her."

"Not much. I just told her I'd been involved in a boating accident. Why?"

"You're sure, that's all you said? You didn't say anything about being in the water or which day it happened?"

"No, I don't have any reason to give her the details. So why.... Is she asking questions?"

"Not exactly, but she knows when it happened and that you were in the water. She said she felt it happening."

"Sounds crazy to me Sis, like breaking and entering. Huh, maybe we should call her parents, I wonder if they know she's here."

"That seems a bit odd Travis?"

"What?"

"You sound like you don't care about her. When only three weeks ago, you drove me and Steve crazy to find out who she was. Don't you remember?"

"A lot has happened since then Sis."

"Travis, that sounds a bit flakey. Really are you that type of guy?"

"What do you want me to say? I came home, tired and busted up and found her in my house. I don't think I'm being flaky; I should be pissed and even if I think I know her, really I don't."

******

"Come on Deb, this silent treatment is killing me."

"What? I'm speaking to you."

"Aye, about the dives an the boat but ya ain't speaking to me like ya normally do."

"What else am I supposed to speak to you about?"

"Please Deb, ya know I love ya and this not talking stuff...."

"You love me? Wicket, I think you're a bloody arsehole and you don't know the first thing about love. Love isn't bonking your best friend's sister...."

"Deb, it's not like that and besides, I didn't bonk her."

"That's rich. Now you're going to sit there and lie to me."

"I ain't lying Deb. I'm not saying I didn't want to and I thought I was going to...."

"Wicket? Either you did or you didn't. Which is it?"

"Deb, I love Julie...."

"Oh great? First you say you love me, and now you say you love Julie. As I said, you don't know the first thing about love."

Mac cringed. How could Deb not know how much he loved her? How could he explain the way he felt about Julie when inside, his emotions were ripping him apart?

Deb felt so angry she needed to distance herself from Mac. But where the hell was she supposed to go on a forty-foot boat out on the ocean? It was her fault and she knew it. *If I'd stayed on the boat* like Travis had assumed she would, *this would've never have happened.* And when he finds out it will be the first thing he remembers.

("I thought you were going with them. Do you think it's safe to leave Mac and my sister alone overnight?" "What the hell are you thinking? They're both adults. I don't believe you Sage, so what are you, some sort of judge who gets to decide who should be with whom? Newsflash Sage, you need to butt out and mind your own business. If they want to have a romantic fling that's their choice.")

Yes she thought, in hindsight, Travis had been right and even though there was a choice, it was a bad choice. And that choice would not have been available to them if she had been on the boat. Deb stared out across an endless mass of water as the tears trickled down her cheeks.

******

Sam was still trying to come to grips with last night, it had been such a shock and she sensed the distance Travis had put between them. *If only he would look at me or take hold of my hand.* But somehow she knew she couldn't force it, and she felt Julie's skeptical eye watching her as they sat across from each other in the hospital waiting area.

******

"I've looked at your MRI Mr. Sage and everything looks good. So, you were in Borneo?"

"Yes Doctor."

"I'm not exactly sure where that is?"

"Malaysia Doctor. It's part of Asia."

"Sounds very oriental. Fine stitchwork, so I don't think you're going to have much of a scar. Arrange with your primary physician to remove the stitches in about a week. The x-rays of your forearm would suggest that whoever set the bone, did an excellent job and it's knit together nicely. Unfortunately there are some torn ligaments in the tissue surrounding the shoulder and upper arm. So I suggest you keep it rested and not try to do anything strenuous. A heating pad should help with any discomfort and I will prescribe pain medication to use as needed. Any questions?"

"How long?"

"I'll have the nurse set an appointment for you. Then run another set of x-rays of your forearm. After that, if everything still looks good there's no need for me to see you again. Any other questions?"

"No, thanks Doctor."

"Okay, sit tight and I'll have a nurse come in and put a cast on your forearm. It was nice meeting you Mr. Sage. Have a good day."

"Same to you Doc."

"Travis smiled as the doctor left the room. He remembered Dr. Rasheed and how he too, wanted to be done with him quickly.

******

Julie's thoughts were far away, enraptured in memories of passion as the feelings washed over her entire body. She hated him and fought hard to resist but the experience of him could not be extinguished and would not allow expulsion from her mind as the waves of immersion carried her back to that night. His lips, his tongue, and his fingers now owned her and the indescribable crescendo of pleasure that dominated her desire. Although in a strange moment of thought; abrupt in its appearance, a question was suddenly posed. *Why did he stop when he could have completely humiliated me, or because he stopped did that, in fact, make the humiliation more complete?* And at that moment the reminiscent spell was broken.

******

Travis entered the waiting area smiling and in a moment where his guard was down, he caught sight of the beautiful young woman who smiled back at him and their eyes locked. He felt the surge of connection and their emotions interchanged. He tried to resist but the knowledge of affection was ignited, it was too late. Sam rose from her seat.

"Travis, you're back." Julie had risen from her seat and stood in front of Sam, which severed the connection. The look in Travis's eyes seemed to stare right through Julie as if she wasn't even there, and the color had drained from his face.

"Travis?" He remained motionless for a few seconds before inhaling a deep breath.

"Travis? Are you okay?"

Seeming like he had been somewhere else, he suddenly realized where he was.

"Yes, Sis. Yes I'm okay."

"Are you sure? You look like you've just seen a ghost."

"No. No I'm fine."

"How did it go? What did the doctor say?"

"Everything's good. The doctor said he wants another set of x-rays in three weeks. Other than that, I'm mending okay."

Sam felt a bit wobbly on her feet and took hold of Julie's arm for support. "Sam, you look a bit pale. What is it with you two?"

"Maybe hunger Sis, we've been here for over two hours and it's way past lunchtime."

"Are you hungry Sam?" Julie inquired but didn't wait for a response. "Well let's go get something to eat, the last thing I need is two invalids to take care of." Julie linked arms with Sam, and Travis followed them to his vehicle.

******

Later that afternoon Travis went into his room to lay down for an hour before dinner. Sam and Julie decided to go to the grocery store to pick up a few things. Travis was already on his bed when he caught sight of what he could only presume to be Sam's backpack by the side of his dresser. He tried to ignore it at first but the more he tried the greater the impulse was to look inside. After all, he thought, hadn't Sam herself said that being amongst his things would help her get to know him better?

It didn't take him more than a couple of minutes to hit pay dirt. If he could consider two hard-covered notebooks that appeared to be journals as pay dirt that is? There were quite a few things in the bag, mostly girlie stuff, essential to a woman may be but of no significance otherwise. And of the two notebooks one looked like it was current. The other confused him at first. *Why would Sam have an old journal?* The dates written on the spine indicated a time in her preteen years. Why he wondered, did she deem it important enough to bring with her on this trip? His curiosity was aroused and he decided to look through that one first.

******

"Deb, I know ya don't want to talk to me, but maybe ya could just listen and at least let me try to explain."

Deb remained quiet and tried hard not to look interested. Mac felt like he had to give it a shot anyway. But where should he start? There was just so much stuff to sort through.

"Deb. Back seven or eight years ago I had a life; a good life and if ya told me I'd be where I am now, I'd have laughed at ya and told ya, ya were crazy. But here I am anyway so the jokes on me. Back then, I worked hard. I did well and was in love with a beautiful woman named Maggie. I gotta tell ya Deb, Maggie was my world, we were gonna get married and have us a bunch of kids and live happily ever after. But it didn't work out that way and she busted me up into little pieces. So one day I just turned away from everything, got on a plane and never looked back and that's where I've been ever since. The easy life, no obligations, livin one day to the next. But then Julie came along an.... It forced me to look at myself and I didn't like what I saw."

Deb gave him a sympathetic look but chose to say nothing.

"Julie's a lady just like you. She lives in a world I used to belong in; but Deb, Julie made me feel things and want to be somebody she could count on, and that got me to thinkin I had to change. I love her and if changing might bring me into her life, I'm gonna do it. So honestly Deb, I give ya my word I didn't bonk her. Came pretty damn close but I couldn't do it; not to her, I love her too much to not treat her like a lady."

Deb looked at Mac and somehow knew he was telling her the truth.

"Wicket, I'd like to wring your bloody neck. Do you have any idea of the grief you've put me through? But it still doesn't change the fact that Julie is a married woman, and I'm glad that you didn't just up and bonk her. That makes me feel good about you, you silly sod."

Mac smiled for the first time since.... *Saying goodbye at the airport, even though that hadn't really been a happy smile.* And although Deb felt the relief wash over her briefly as she contemplated Wicket's dilemma, she knew she had a confession of her own to deliver.

******

Travis admired Sam's artistic ability while looking at her drawings in the journal. Took heart in the simplistic ideas of a preteen girl and ached emotionally at some of her written concerns. It was a tough age to be. Although his childhood memories were few and perhaps faded he wished he had kept a journal to have better insight. The notions of youth were lost except perhaps in this opportunity to see it again through Sam's eyes. Sam's eyes? His thoughts turned to the emotional entanglement earlier at the hospital.

There was so much love. He felt overwhelmed again, just thinking about it. He could easily lose himself in the power of that love if only......... That was it; that was the problem? The 'if only,' and if that wasn't complicated enough, he loves Deb. *I need to have a good talk with Sam before this all gets out of hand.* Which would be a great idea 'if' it wasn't already out of hand? Travis continued reading through the pages of the journal.

Chapter 14

As usual at 7 am, Julie rose and went to the kitchen to brew a pot of coffee. The house was quiet and peaceful as her thoughts meandered routinely through the simple tasks of making coffee, taking her shower, getting dressed and preparing breakfast. And if for no other reason than to reaffirm all was well she looked in on Sam, but Sam wasn't there. The blanket and sheet were pulled back and the indentation on the pillow gave confirmation she had been there. *Sam's awake,* she thought, and somehow slipped past her and into the bathroom.

Moving back towards the guest bedroom she saw the hall bathroom was empty, and with a suspecting eye, Julie turned and looked at the master bedroom door. Perplexed in her thought and uncertain how she felt about that. Caught in a momentary memory of flesh touching flesh bothered her as quickly she peeled it from her mind.

But the thoughts seemed unrelenting as the warm water cascaded over her body and her transgression hauntingly pursued her conscious awareness of how it made her feel. *Damn you Mac.* Her hands had become his hands as they caressed her breasts, and the fingers rippled over her nipples. She couldn't stand the delightful agony of its persecution, knowing it had all been a lie. Beguiled by his sweet, tender kisses and misguided in her desire, she had abandoned all reason.... And no she suddenly thought; she had no desire to be tormented by the silly smiles and adoring looks Travis and Sam would surely share in front of her.

Toweling herself off quickly, Julie dressed and picked up her phone. There was a flight at noon, and she called for a cab after making a reservation. And so, with her nest of wheeled suitcases she hurriedly packed and waited by the front living room window for it to arrive. Julie was aggravated in her own humiliation and thankful that the two love birds had remained in their nest. Then, with quiet displeasure she pondered the life she was going back to.

******

Travis sensed the lateness of the hour when he eventually woke up, and although wondering why Julie had not disturbed him, he was thankful she had left him to rest. It had been a rough night as he wrestled with his thoughts about what he had found in Sam's journal. It had spooked him and kept him awake. Unintelligible thoughts with no answers congregated in his mind and filled him with concern. But finally, and with his sensing of the pre-dawn, he had reached a decision.

Almost with a childlike thought of self-protection he had donned a pair of dark sunglasses and gloved his hand with a white cotton sock before making his way to the living room. Sam looked peaceful in a beautiful sort of way, and he almost had second thoughts about waking her, but he had determined he had to put distance between them.

"Sam," he whispered. She did not stir. "Sam, wake up." Travis shook her shoulder lightly.

"Hmm."

"Sam, wake up."

Slowly she opened her eyes and caught her first sight of him, panicked, and readied herself to scream and in quick response, Travis covered her mouth with his socked hand.

Fortunately for Sam it was a clean sock.

"Sam it's me, don't scream; everything is okay, we need to talk."

Gathering her thoughts quickly she reached up and removed his hand.

"What's with the sunglasses?' Then upon inspecting his hand. "And the sock?"

"Sam, I don't want you to take this the wrong way but I'm going to ask you to leave."

"Why? Travis, I love you. Have I done something wrong?"

"Do you mean apart from breaking into my house? No."

"Then why do you want me to leave?"

"Sam it's complicated. We've both experienced some very unusual feelings."

"Wonderful feelings Travis."

"Okay Sam, wonderful feelings. I'll even go as far as amazing, but there's something strange about them as well."

"Travis, please don't make me leave; I belong with you, can't you see? We are meant to be together."

"That may be true Sam, but I want some time to figure everything out and I feel certain I'm not going to be able to do that while you're here. So please, for both our sakes, give me the time I'm asking for and leave quietly."

Sam wanted to cry and beg, but she sensed creating a scene and getting into a no-win situation wouldn't keep them together either.

"Travis, are you sure? Is there nothing I can say to change your mind?"

"Sam, I have very strong feelings about this. We still don't know much about each other except what we feel we've experienced. Just give me some time."

******

Later that morning Travis looked at his bedside clock as he struggled to get out of bed. It was almost noon and as he wandered into the kitchen. The full, now cold pot of coffee seemed odd but gave no cause for concern. He surmised Julie might have gone shopping until he opened the connecting door to the garage and saw his vehicle? The front doorbell rang and he assumed Julie had forgotten to take a key, but the Fed-Ex van belayed that notion. "I have two large containers for you, sign here please?" After signing, he opened the garage door and had the driver bring them inside. *Maybe,* he thought, *she was taking a nap?*

The guest bedroom was devoid of anything which might indicate that his sister inhabited the space, as he looked around and checked the closet. *What the....* Travis couldn't imagine that Julie would be offended because he'd asked Sam to leave, or that she would take off without saying a word. He walked swiftly back to his bedroom and picked up his phone; speed-dialed her number and listened to it ring. No answer. He was connected to her voicemail. "Sis where are you? Why did you leave? Call me; we need to talk.... Love you."

Chapter 15

A hundred miles from Travis's house, unable to hold on to her emotions any longer Sam guided her Maroon BMW into an empty parking lot. It hadn't taken her more than a few minutes, as she quietly gathered up her belongings to figure out why Travis was wearing sunglasses and covered his hand with a sock. He'd placed a barrier between them; there was no opportunity to look into his eyes or take hold of his hand. She had been offered no reprieve to his decision and now her heart cried out mournfully in the soulful devastation of this still new day.

******

This day had to come; even as unmarked as it was on any calendar, Julie always knew she would be returning to her old life as a suburban housewife. Yet, she felt stifled in thinking about it as the plane carried her ever closer to her home in Nashville. Even thinking Nashville in her mind seemed grim and uninviting compared to Bangkok's exotic sound, Kuala Lumpur, or Borneo. She was now a woman of the world although in one respect, the world, or her experience of it had shown her to be a fool. The burden of which she was now forced to bear.

******

Out of the clear blue ocean; the mermaid broke to the surface and climbed onto the dive platform, as the morning sun glistened amid the droplets of water as they danced downward along the full length of her naked body.

"Here, Wicket." Deb tossed the soap bar to Mac, whose tall, muscular, tanned body stood waiting for her arrival.

"Thanks Deb; I was beginning to think ya were gonna stay in there all bloody day?" And with a huge splash, he had jumped over the side and into the water.

Things onboard were back to normal; or as Deb had concluded, as normal as they could be under the circumstances. Wicket still pined for Julie; he didn't say much but Deb could tell he was well and truly besotted and as far as she herself concerned; Deb still had a date with a confession which she feared might just break his heart even more than it ached right now, and if that wasn't enough to contend with, her heart ached for Travis and the love they had acknowledged.

Her work was going well; testing and analyzing the samples of coral she had carefully collected and on dives, collecting photographic data to substantiate her conclusions. All that, and in the evenings keyboarding reports into her laptop computer. And because she didn't have to share Wicket with Travis she was getting ahead of her schedule. This could prompt an earlier end to the project, but things could turn on a dime as Deb knew only too well. A few days of bad weather and rough water could quickly put her behind.

******

Sam was traveling North on I-65 after traveling west on I-10. It had not been an easy decision to return home to Nashville. She had toyed with the idea of finding a motel in Pensacola and sticking around but realized she might run the risk of annoying Travis. No, she had determined; if she wanted Travis to trust her, she first had to allow him to trust himself and the feelings they shared and the only way to do that, was to give him the time and space he'd asked for. In hindsight she had been wrong to invade his sanctuary, but nothing had been severed and she had to find the strength in what she believed to be the truth. Although, no reason or conclusion could lessen the ever-deepening heaviness she felt as she moved further away from the man she loved.

******

Travis had to force himself through the dull throbbing pain in his shoulder to get dressed in a button-up shirt. Fastening his pants proved to be quite a chore, but what choice did he have? He was alone now; his sister's two-piece bathing suit still hung in his bathroom goading him in his incapacity to perform the most basic of functions, he was not having a good day.

******

Julie checked her messages during the cab ride from the airport and decided she just wasn't ready to talk to Travis yet. Steve would arrive home from work in less than two hours and already she was thinking about what to cook for their evening meal. She couldn't believe how easily she was slipping back into her old routine as the dutiful wife.

Chapter 16

Paranormal Psychological Anomalies. The three words rolled around in Travis's mind as he opened his laptop in his quest for answers, and his search revealed a wide variety of information. Finally, he came across something called Retro-cognitions which referenced the déjà vu phenomenon, a recollection of periods between one human life and another. Having no idea what he was getting himself into or where it might lead, discovering the subject had been written about piqued his interest. And besides he thought, *what else am I going to do?* Reduced as he was to microwave meals and finding something to fill in the spaces between them.

He had unpacked the two large containers in the garage. Washed and rinsed the wetsuits and other dive equipment in the bathtub and hung everything up to dry. But when it came to his cameras, he quickly realized there was no way he could manage to get them out of the waterproof cases with one hand. He still didn't understand why Julie had left the way she had. He couldn't think of anything he'd said or done to provoke her to leave. *Women!* Although, even in thinking that, he knew he loved her as he turned his thoughts toward Deb.

She would be arriving in about ten to fourteen days and then……? A tentative plan was in place; there was no 'then?' It was more of a continuation of all the thoughts and feelings he held in his heart and bound by loyalty, had felt unable to express. Travis was torn between his friendship with Mac, his love for Deb and knowing how Mac felt about her. *Deb?* His thoughts ran deep and raced through his mind. After acknowledging her love for him the emotional desire that had been harnessed for so long could not be contained; although in the complicated complicity of his mind, he also felt drawn toward Anne. *Sam,* he had to remind himself. *Her name is Sam.* But that did little more than add to his confusion of knowing one and not knowing the other. Travis felt confronted with a complex riddle that offered few clues and no promised results.

******

With the washing machine in full motion, Julie scrubbed hard at the shower walls in the master bathroom. Subdued anger filled her determination to decontaminate every vestibule of the space she had called home. The time for crying had passed; gone with the darkness of the previous night, and now she was consumed with the pain of having her world turned upside down. The confrontation had seemed surreal, even more so when he did not attempt to deny it. But the cruelty hit hardest when he confessed who it was and that it had been going on for almost three years.

******

The déjà vu phenomenon is the awareness and familiarity of a previous encounter with a person or place for which no rational explanation exists to quantify the emotional experience. Travis could buy into that concept and it was precisely what he had felt, but as he read more the idea of reincarnation seemed a little far-fetched. Although, when he thought about it, his opinions and reasoning couldn't provide the answers so he continued to read.

******

Three years; almost three years, how could she not have known? The question hung over Julie like a storm cloud challenging her memory and yet the 'why' didn't seem that important compared to the 'how,' 'when,' and 'where,' Stacy had slithered into her marriage or the 'what,' Julie herself had done wrong?

******

He read about ESP, PSI, and telepathic transference of thought. Altered states of conscious awareness, dreams, a spirit world in a parallel dimension, and hauntings, but he kept finding his way back to the déjà vu theory. It seemed like a logical choice although its logic required some imagination and accepting the possibility of a different reality. *But,* he thought, *I'm already part of a different reality.* It was time to look at the picture again.

The emotional recognition of the scene held a familiar sense of belonging, home? And he felt the certainty of knowing he'd passed beneath that archway many times and knew what buildings lay beyond it. He sensed the existence of a door to the left and wondered why it wasn't shown in the painting. Yes, he vividly remembered a wooden door there; he felt sure of it. But where was Anne? She wasn't there waiting for him. Travis felt disappointed and continued to investigate the picture for several minutes hoping she would appear.

The distraction was abrupt when his phone rang.

"Hello."

"Sage, is that you?"

"Deb?" He was delightfully surprised. "How are you? Is everything okay?"

"Yes, everything is fine. I just wanted to hear your voice; I miss you."

"I miss you too Deb. I love you."

"I love you too. We should be able to wrap things up in a few days."

"How is Mac?"

"He's taking his bath. That's why I thought I'd take this opportunity to call you. Travis, I really do love you; it's like a dream come true and I'm looking forward to being with you, I wish it were today."

"Deb, you know how I feel; it's a dream come true for me as well, you've been my dream for a very long time."

"Travis, I haven't said anything to Wicket yet...."

"No, Deb, don't say anything, I think I should be the one to talk to him about it...." Travis looked at the picture on the laptop screen. "Deb? How would you feel about me flying over to meet you in the UK?"

"Oh, you're an eager beaver; I guess you want to get into my knickers, how's your arm?"

"The doc says I'm mending just fine; still some pain but I'm dealing with it."

"Travis, you do know I've never been with a man?"

"Are you scared?"

"No, not scared exactly, well a little bit maybe?"

"We can take it slow. I love you, and we have all the time in the world. The last thing I want is for you to feel afraid."

"Oops, Wicket's swimming toward the dive platform. I'll call you in a few days. I love you. Bye"

He heard the disconnect sound before he could say anything else and if ever he needed a tonic to pick him up and make him feel good, he just received a full dose. But, *Deb, Deb, Deb,* he wished it was today also. A change of plans; he would fly over to the UK in about a week, and he would get to see this arch if Deb was correct in her assertion of knowing where it is.

******

"What are you doing here?"

Steve's face looked drawn and pale. "Julie, I'm sorry. I never meant to hurt you."

Julie scoffed. "Steve, you hurt me the minute you decided to sleep with her and every time you chose to be with her. You've hurt me for three years; how dare you stand there and tell me anything different? Why are you here?"

"Julie I...."

"If you're going to say you love me then don't. You brought that woman into this house and slept with her in our bed. So don't you dare say you love me."

Steve hung his head; he knew this had to happen. Julie had every right to berate him.

Julie trembled with anger. Part of her wanted her life back; but knew it couldn't happen, not now, not ever, Steve had defiled her trust in their relationship.

"Why... How was Stacy here? She was your secretary in Charleston?"

"Look, Julie..."

"No, Steve, I have a right to know how she got here."

"I arranged for her transfer."

"You bastard. So you had a young piece of tail that you couldn't leave behind. Do you know how worthless that makes me feel?" She could feel the tears welling up in her eyes, and she was determined not to let him see her cry.

"Steve, get whatever it is you came to get and leave." She turned her back toward him and started to walk away. "And before you leave I want your key to the house."

******

And so, there was Julie alone in a city where she had no friends, and her only family was Travis who she had walked away from. She contemplated that for a few minutes. Travis was no better than Steve; after he slept with Deb he turned right around and took Sam to his bed, and Deb, she reminded herself, was also sleeping with Mac. Had the whole world gone mad? Or had it changed so much that she was an oddball who just didn't understand the new order of things? And why had Mac rejected her? More tears filled her eyes.

******

Julie imprisoned herself in the house unable to move forward; two days and nights of soul searching, wrestling with bitterness and mournfully shedding tears only to conclude, it would have been easier if Steve had just died. She could have lived with that loss more easily than accepting the fact that he was alive and screwing a younger woman. In the last two years there had been times when she had all but begged him to.... To what? Screw her? The fricking irony of it smashed at her insensibility.

But now, the walls were starting to close in on her, and she did need bread and milk. And she was beginning to remember the last two years had not been happy. And although she was frightened by the rapid change, it might eventually be a change for the better. She just had to accept what was and keep putting one foot in front of the other. Julie took a deep breath and prepared herself mentally to get into her car and face the world. And when she did, she drove straight past the grocery store heading towards the mall.

******

Sam couldn't believe her eyes and thought she must be mistaken. "Julie?"

"Sam? What are you doing here?"

"Shopping; bored really, but why are you here? I thought you were looking after Travis?"

"No I thought you were looking after him?"

"That doesn't make sense, he asked me to leave so I thought you would be...."

"When did Travis ask you to leave?"

"Four, maybe five days ago but you should know that, you were there?"

"Sam, I think I need to sit down, is there a coffee shop close by?"

"Sure, are you alright, you look a bit off?"

Julie managed to collect her thoughts together while talking with Sam and fished the details out of her. She hadn't slept with Travis. Sam had already left the house by the time she woke up, so Travis was alone and had been forced to fend for himself. Inside, Julie was beside herself with worry; poor Travis, she had acted out the role in one of those country and western classics. Somebody did somebody wrong songs, and all fingers were pointing at her.

******

"Hey, Travis."

"Hi Sis, finally you've got around to returning one of my many calls."

"Travis I'm so sorry, I need to explain?"

"I'm just glad to hear your voice; how's Steve? I bet he's happy to have you back?"

"Long story, but first, let me explain?"

"Sounds serious Sis are you okay?"

"Yes, I think so but Travis I'm sorry I left the way I did. I was wrong and it was stupid of me to behave like that."

"Why did you leave like that, without saying a word?"

"I thought...now don't laugh at me.... I thought you and Sam were in bed together."

"And you had a problem with that notion?"

"Well yes, obviously I must have."

"Hmm, and why's that Sis?"

"You know why Travis; you had been sleeping with Deb, you and Mac both had been sleeping with her, and it just didn't seem right that you'd use Sam like that."

"Now hold on a minute Sis. I think you've got the wrong end of the stick. You do know Deb is gay, right?"

"What do you mean?"

"Why do you think I was against the two of you getting in bed together at the hotel in Kuala Lumpur? Deb prefers women, or at least she did."

"I'm confused. Why would she go to bed with you, and Mac, if she's gay?"

"That's a whole other story Sis. Deb was involved in a diving accident where her partner Christine died. Since then, Deb gets a bit nervous before a first dive and needs the comfort of a warm body every once in a while. So, she would sleep next to Mac or me, and I mean sleep, that's all. Nothing else. Mac and I look out for her, and on this last assignment she gave her cabin up for you. So she just bunked with me most of the time."

Julie thought about that for a few seconds. "What did you mean when you said, Deb did prefer women?"

"Again, a whole other story. When Deb stayed at the hotel to look after me; the night before Mac took you out diving, Deb and I had a long talk. I've had feelings for her for a long time and well, as it turns out, Deb has strong feelings for me. We love each other."

"So, you have slept with her?"

"Not in the biblical sense Sis. Can you picture me making love to Deb with a broken arm and torn shoulder ligaments? No, on second thoughts, don't. I'm your brother."

"So you haven't made love to Deb?"

"Of course not Sis, and besides, there's another complication. Mac cares about her and it might not go over too well when he finds out."

"What about Sam? Where does she fit into all of this? You know she's in love with you, right?"

"I'm very aware of that, but the complication is it's very spooky and I'd prefer not to get into it over the phone, you might think I was crazy. But I decided the best thing to do was send her home while I get my thoughts straight."

"I know; I bumped into her at the mall today, that's when I found out I'd left you all alone."

"It's okay Sis; I'm surviving."

"No. I mean, I want to come back and take care of you."

"Don't worry about it Sis, you're home now, and as I said, I'm sure Steve is happy to have you back. I can manage...."

"Travis?"

"What?"

Julie took a deep breath and prepared herself to deliver the news.

"Travis; Steve and I are not together anymore."

"What the heck are you talking about?"

"I don't want to talk about it over the phone. Please let me come back and take care of you. I need this Travis."

He paused to digest what she had just said. "Sis, are you sure you are alright? Do you need me to come up to Nashville?"

"No Travis. What I need right now is distance, and you're it."

"Sis I'm so sorry; of course you can come back, my house is your house for as long as you need it to be, and I could sure use your help. But I've arranged to meet with Deb in England in a few days, so if you come down you will be on your own for a while."

"I don't mind that Travis, really, I don't. It will give me time to think."

"So, are you flying down?"

"No, I would prefer to have my car. I'll drive down tomorrow."

"Sounds like a plan. I'll see you sometime late afternoon; early evening tomorrow then and Sis, I love you."

"I'll see you tomorrow. Love you too and thanks."

Chapter 17

The following morning a package arrived via UPS and when he managed to get it open, Travis found it was the original painting of the arch. There was a note from Sam that read. *'This is something we share, and I'd like you to have it. I love you. Sam.'* Again; Travis sensed the familiarity with the scene but Anne was missing and he felt anxious, because she wasn't there beneath the arch. His heart began to ache with worry. "Anne; where are you, has something happened?" Suddenly realizing he was talking to an inanimate object; he slid the painting back into the box in which it had arrived. But the feelings he felt were real, and his concern for Anne's well-being tugged at his emotions. He couldn't understand any of it. Had something happened to Anne? Or was it Sam he should be worrying about? Quickly he picked up his phone, then hesitated. Did he want to talk to Sam? Again, he felt uncertain and in that uncertainty, opted to send her a text message instead. *'Sam, I received the painting. Thank you.'* If she didn't respond, he decided then he would think about calling.

Why, he thought, when he was near Sam looking into her eyes or touching her, did he feel so totally connected emotionally? And now, with the distance between them, it confused him as to exactly what he was connected to. He remembered the deep feelings and understood their implication. It's love, he has no doubt, but there is a weariness contained in the aftermath of each exposure which, as of yet, he can't seem to pinpoint its cause.

******

Sam perused through the letter inviting her to join Dr. Samuels and his team at a Mayan dig in southern Mexico. Dr. Samuels was a renowned archeologist, and she realized the gravity of the invitation and the impact that working alongside him would have on her future career. It was an awesome opportunity, and if it were not for the fact that it would carry her further away from Travis, she would pack her bags immediately. But therein lay the quandary of her thoughts.

******

Turning his thoughts towards Julie and Steve, Travis couldn't come to grips with what his sister had said, *'Steve and I are not together anymore?'* Her tone had a permanency sound that he hoped wasn't true. *Maybe*, he thought, *they'd had a big argument and needed time to cool off?* In which case, separation was probably a good thing, giving them both space to reconsider their differences and realize their insignificance. *All couples have disagreements. It's not the end of the world,* he concluded, finding some consolation in that thought.

He looked over at his laptop sitting on the table and wasn't sure if he wanted to continue reading more about paranormal anomalies. His brain felt overloaded with all the information he'd tried to absorb, and some of it didn't make sense. Although he had to admit, even if only to himself, retro-cognitions did appear to answer some of his questions about having memories of what he considered a past event in which he could not possibly have been a part of. So for lack of anything else to do that he could manage, he sat in front of the laptop and continued to explore the possibilities and the improbabilities of things he didn't understand.

******

Julie had started early, having slept another night in the guest bedroom. There was no way she could bring herself to sleep in the master bedroom, having surmised what had taken place in that bed during her absence. And as she drove away from Nashville, she changed the radio channel from country and western to something more viscerally pleasing. The thought came quite as a shock when she first realized that had she arrived home announced, the secret affair would have continued on undetected. And for how long? How long would she have continued cooking and cleaning, pleading for his attention? How long?

It felt like a crushing blow and smacked hard against her emotions. For the second time in her life, she had been cheated. Her memory replayed the events of her first love and his betrayal to remind her she had been down this road before. *Men are freakin bastards. Uncaring, self-satisfying bastards.* It had been a hard lesson to learn, and she vowed there would be no need for a refresher course. But as the miles passed away behind her, Julie's mood lightened in the sense of newfound freedom, and she promised herself not to look back.

Her mind merged into happier times with Travis, mom, and dad. When she was the big sister and everything was somehow simpler, she wished mom and dad could see how well Travis had turned out. Although not wanting them dead, she was also grateful they had not lived to witness Steve's adulterous behavior. And, even though he had proved to be a bastard, she had to remind herself to give him credit for helping Travis as he struggled with their death. *So maybe*, she concluded, *he wasn't a complete bastard, but a bastard just the same.*

There was no way of knowing when thoughts about Deb popped into her mind. How could she have known Deb was a lesbian? Julie smiled, remembering she had offered to sleep in the same bed, and curiously wondered what that might have been like? Then quickly dismissed the thought. But now she knew the truth, and she had to admit, she liked Deb. Her outspoken personality and lack of inhibitions, although surprising, had allowed Julie to explore herself and her thoughts. And being wrong about Deb gave credence to the possibility that she may have been wrong about Mac? But she couldn't go there, not yet.

And Travis, he was still her hero. The tall, dark, handsome young man who thrived on adventure and captivated her spirit with his stories. Her little brother with two loves and no lover, it doesn't get any more gentlemanly than that. How wrong she'd been about so many things lent conviction to how little she had known. And so Julie continued her way forward as mile after mile swept away behind her.

******

"Morning Travis." The blinds snapped open and the bright sunlight filled the room instantly. He may have missed his sister, but he sure as heck hadn't missed her morning ritual.

"Come on, here's your coffee. Let me help you sit up. Breakfast will be ready in fifteen minutes." Her words held a tone of precision about them, he thought, denying him any room to maneuver or delay the inevitable.

"Morning Sis." There was no hint of enthusiasm in his voice as he half-consciously complied with her request.

******

Mac sat across from Deb at the small cabin table and amused himself with a deck of cards while Deb keyed her report into the laptop. He didn't need a report to confirm what he could see for himself every time they dived. The coral reefs were in decline and dying due to boats, careless divers, and contamination. And from a political standpoint, if Deb's report told the truth, which he was sure it would, the board of tourism and dive centers would not be happy.

Happy, he wasn't feeling happy. The woman who filled his thoughts with love was thousands of miles away, and if she wasn't already back with her husband, it was just a matter of time. But no matter the time, distance, or circumstance, he could not deny his truth. He loved her more than life itself, and the life that he had lived for so many years had to come to an end.

Chapter 18

With fingers available, Travis instructed Julie how to open up his underwater cameras and retrieve the SD cards. Afterward, he walked her through the necessary cleaning and preparation of the equipment before replacing them into their storage cases. During that same time, following the brief explanation she had presented him with the night before, Julie continued to confide the realization of the facts she had discovered about Steve and his adulterous affair.

"Sis, I don't know what to say. I'm so sorry. I can't believe Steve would do something like that. And that it had been going on for so long, I'm at a loss for words. It's unbelievable; I don't know what to do. Do or say really, it would seem unfixable unless you determine it can be fixed."

"Huh, no way, his betrayal is humiliating, his deception is unforgivable and I have no desire to kiss and make up under any circumstances. That door has not only closed. It's also been bolted."

******

It had not been an easy call to make and had it not been for the emotional turmoil; the explosion of deep feelings he felt towards Julie, the call would probably not have been made. Even now, knowing he may never hold Julie in his arms again, Mac understands he can no longer sustain the vagrant lifestyle he had surrendered himself into living. If nothing else, Julie had become a beacon of light showing the way, casting everything else in shadow and darkness. For Mac, there was only one choice.

******

Sam felt agitated and concerned in equal measure. Agitated by Travis's need for distance and space. Agitated by the deep feelings she felt and being denied any opportunity to express them and confused by Travis's non-committal text message. '*Sam, I received the painting. Thank you.*' No expression of emotional thought or feeling felt shocking and plagued her senses as if he somehow might not care. Then there was concern as to why his sister Julie, had also left on the same day she was asked to leave. Did Travis want to be isolated and alone? Why? Sam wished now that she had asked Julie in greater detail. Yes, Julie has a husband and probably felt the need to return to Nashville, but why had she left Travis to fend for himself under the circumstance of his injuries. To Sam's mind, she had witnessed the limitations Travis faced and felt her own desire to care for and assist. Nothing seemed to make a whole lot of sense. She knew and had firsthand experience of all the shared emotional fulfillment their connections have expressed and relayed from one to the other. Some of which stayed, even now, as Travis remained inside her being. '*The two shall be as one,*' that thought, and the reality of its experience left no room for doubt. But Sam felt forced to conclude there was something else, something she was unaware of taking place. Something she needed to find out about. No matter what, Sam determined, it would not come between them.

******

After Travis had transferred the images from the SD cards to his laptop, he set about separating the 'fun shots' of the last dive he, Mac, and Julie had taken from the 'business shots.' It took a couple of hours to determine he had enough to present to the magazine once he had correlated them and written a back story. During that time frame, Julie had been to the store and was now in the kitchen, filling up the refrigerator and restocking the pantry.

"Hey Sis, come and take a look at these." Julie came over to where Travis was sitting, stood behind him, and looked at the screen. In the underwater world she had just recently discovered, the images displayed in sharp resolution, without any distortion, were of her. Image after image portrayed her as if weightlessly drifting, flying almost, through a beautiful garden filled with a kaleidoscope of colors. She was surrounded by marine life, the likes of which she could only have partially imagined existing before her adventure. Even now, it was breathtaking or would have been if almost all of the shots didn't include Mac.

For Julie, it was haunting. Mac was always there, slightly behind and above her. Mixed feelings, memories, and the invasion of his presence. The just not knowing what to think or believe. Breathless and anxious simultaneously, a paradox of emotional turmoil with unanswered questions that were never asked and the probability that they never would be. Creating a veil of uncertainty as to the reality of what took place.

******

Deb's assignment was nearing conclusion, one more day of diving, one more night of finalizing her report, then the sail back to port. Wicket behaved more like himself, which pleased her and presented a dilemma. After finding out what she knew now, how Wicket felt about Julie, could she tell him about her and Travis? Especially now, they were planning to meet up in the UK immediately after she arrived home. There was no telling how Wicket would take the news. It was one thing for Travis to say; he'd take care of it, but Deb had this strong feeling it would be better sorted before she and Travis initiated the physical aspect of their relationship and bonked the hell out of each other. She couldn't wait for the event to finally take place. Even in knowing, due to circumstances beyond her control, it might still be at least a week away unless. *The mind boggles with ideas and creativity.* But Deb had this distinct feeling about Wicket, and it would be like hitting a man when he's down.

******

Julie had just finished getting Travis bathed and into bed when she heard her phone ring in the guest bedroom. Quickly saying goodnight to Travis, she closed his bedroom door and when to answer the call.

"Hello."

"Julie, it's Sam. I hope I'm not intruding."

"Hi, Sam. No, it's fine. What can I do for you?"

"I have a question. Considering Travis's injuries, I'm concerned; I wondered why you also left the same day I did? I mean, shouldn't someone be there to help him?"

"You're right. There was a slight misunderstanding. Funny really. But it's been taken care of. I'm back with him in Pensacola, so you can rest assured he's well taken care of."

It took Sam a second or two to make sense of that, but the reasoning was probably none of her business. "How is Travis?"

"He's doing well. In fact, he's planning to fly to England in a few days. Something to do with a painting of a building, and a friend, Deb, said she knows where the building is located."

Sam was shocked, uncertain how to pursue without appearing overly inquisitive and raising alarm. "Please give Travis my love. I miss him and wish him safe travels."

"I will. Goodnight."

Sam was bewildered. She was trying to digest and come to terms with the information she'd just received as question after question raced through her thoughts.

Chapter 19

Deb had several long flights ahead of her, from Borneo to Kuala Lumpur. Kuala Lumpur to Bangkok, Bangkok to the Arab Emirates, and London Heathrow. Twenty-three hours and forty-five minutes travel time, but it wouldn't end there. After arriving at Heathrow and meeting up with Travis, at least that was the plan. Next, they would get on the underground train and make their way to Euston Station. From there, catch a high-speed inter-city train to Nuneaton in Warwickshire, and finally, a taxicab would carry them to her home in Hinckley, Leicestershire. All-in-all, Deb was looking at somewhere between twenty-eight and thirty hours before arriving at the journey's end if everything ran smoothly and on time.

But that wasn't her focus at the moment. It was Wicket.

"Well, Deb, that's ya bag taken care of."

They were standing near the departure gate, and Deb had finished checking in for her first flight. Mac, as usual, had escorted her to the airport, and as was usually the case, this was the awkward moment for goodbyes. This time more so than before.

Deb searched Wicket's eyes; she felt the need to be sure. She watched his facial expressions and listened for any indication in his voice. Strangely, she was feeling more unsettled than he was behaving, and as far as she could tell, Wicket had listened to her the night before when she told him about her desire to be with Travis. He'd taken the news much better than she could have imagined. Wicket had said he was okay with it and happy for her. He also told her that after meeting Julie, he understood her hearts need to be with the one she loved. Deb had felt like she was seeing Wicket in a whole new light and was convinced about the sincerity of his affection towards Julie. In that, she felt sadness in understanding Wicket's predicament. He had fallen hard, Julie was a married woman, and in that frame the outcome didn't look good.

There were many things they could say to each other, and usually they did before parting ways. Right now, the moment hovered solemnly as if neither he nor she knew what to do next. Fear of the anticipated change in their relationship, whether imagined or real, lent uncertainty about what to do next. Finally, Deb couldn't stand the tension any longer. "Come here, you big lump." Grabbing the bull by the horns, she pulled Wicket into her arms, kissed his cheek, and held on tight. Mac, as usual, didn't know his own strength.

"Ouch, Wicket, I'll be bloody flat-chested in a minute."

Mac eased back to allow a little breathing room. "I love ya Deb, ya and Travis are my best mates. I'm gonna miss ya."

"Love you too Wicket. You're my guardian angel. Are you going to be alright?"

"Sure thing Deb. Now ya best be off, or ya will miss the flight."

Deb noticed the tear in the corner of Wicket's eye as they ended their embrace. She felt her own tears beginning to blur her vision as she smiled and turned towards the ramp leading her to the waiting plane. Wicket watched as she walked away. "Goodbye, mermaid." He whispered with heartfelt affection. Once out of sight, Mac drew in a slow deep breath, and just as slowly, he released it before turning towards the airport exit.

The cab ride back to the boat felt mournful, and with nothing to do but sit, he felt stuck in the emotion. The heaviness that he felt was not about Deb. It wasn't about Julie either. Both of them were good, decent women. He pined for one and was content and happy for the other. The heaviness was personal, about himself, knowing himself and finding no satisfaction in who he had become. That had to change. He demanded it of himself, and in a couple of days, after he had returned the boat to its owner and shipped his and Deb's diving gear off to their respective addresses, he would fly to Australia in search of redemption.

Chapter 20

The following morning, after her telephone conversation with Julie, Sam had devised a plan. She was enthusiastically informing her mother and father about the letter she had received from Dr. Samuels. Carefully, she prepped their encouragement during breakfast, producing the letter and enlightening them about the tremendous opportunity and prestige she would garner professionally by accepting his offer. Sam knew her parents well, and when she was sure of their support, she initiated the final phase. "There is a magnificent collection of Mayan artifacts currently on display at the British Museum in London. And I believe it would be beneficial for me to fly there and learn everything I can before going to Mexico. So, I'd like to spend about a week there with your permission." Academics and professionals themselves they were delighted to entertain their daughters' desire to further her career. So, Sam made the arrangements to fly to London the very next day. After which she determined, it would be a case of stealth and luck.

******

Travis had spent the day working diligently on his back story, knowing all too well it would be edited to the point of becoming unrecognizable as to something he had produced. Some young professional writer would undoubtedly turn it into something worth reading. But, *what-the*-heck, he concluded, *he had no aspirations in that arena*. Task complete, he placed the thumb drive containing the back-story and images into a Fed Ex overnight envelope and called to schedule a pick-up.

"Hey, Sis, how about I take you out for dinner tonight."
"Great, I'd love it. What time is your flight tomorrow?"

"Four-thirty in the afternoon to Atlanta and pick up the connecting flight from there. Should arrive in London just after seven the next morning."

"Are you sure you're going to be okay? I mean, taking care of yourself until you meet up with Deb?"

"I'll manage, and if I have to enlist the help of a pretty flight attendant, well, who's to say how interesting that might get."

Julie gave him a look of disapproval. "I think I might talk with Deb, make sure she understands what she's getting herself into."

"Just kidding Sis. I am a bit concerned, especially about buttoning my pants. But I came up with this."

Travis held up what was once recognizable as a large paperclip. Now reconfigured, he demonstrated how he could thread it through the buttonhole, grab the button and pull it back through the buttonhole. "Voila."

"Clever. Maybe you could market that and make a bunch of money. Anyway, where are you taking me to dinner so that I can dress accordingly?"

******

After a late lunch the following day, Julie drove Travis to the airport.

"Sis, it occurred to me late last night, or should I say, in the wee hours of this morning that I might be abandoning you in your hour of need. If that's the case and you'd rather I stay here with you, just say the word. I'm sure Deb would understand."

"My hour of need? Hum. Steve should have recognized that many times over the past three years. But, no, Travis, I'll be alright, I'm fine, and I'd sure hate to disappoint Deb. Besides, without you to look after twenty-four-seven, I can get out and explore all the stores in Pensacola."

"We have a pretty nice beach too, Sis."

"And young pilots, from what I read in the paper. The Blue Angels are stationed here. I might feel inclined to visit them. Who knows what mischief I might get up to while you're away?"

Travis wasn't sure how he felt about that statement. Maybe it wasn't such a good idea to leave her alone at this time having witnessed her newfound freedom while out on the boat. Julie just smiled.

******

Sam had already touched down at London Heathrow and the compelling argument she had concocted and convinced herself was such a good idea didn't seem so brilliant right now. She was alone, amid a multitude of people, in a strange city, on a different continent. 'The plan,' more or less, ended there unless she was fortunate enough to spot Travis. And the reality was, she had no idea when he was scheduled to arrive. So there was a plan 'B.' Not really, but if all else failed, she could go to the British Museum and see if they had any Mayan artifacts.

With a suitcase and carry-on bag to contend with, she thought about contacting Julie again and gleaning more insight into Travis's travel arrangements. However, Sam realized that it contained the risk of awkward inquiries about her interest. She pondered the dilemma by taking a seat in the arrivals area where she had wandered back toward after claiming her luggage. Remembering Julie said Travis would be leaving in a few days. If she took that figuratively, 'a few' usually referenced more than 'two.' Otherwise, people used the word 'couple' in conversation, as he will be leaving in a couple of days, meaning two. It wasn't an exact science, but, she thought, Julie appeared to articulate her words well. So, she concluded Travis would probably arrive tomorrow or the following day, but when?

To figure that out, Sam opened her notebook and connected to the available Wi-Fi with an unspoken question in mind, which airport would he fly out of? Pensacola seemed the logical choice but offered no direct flights to the United Kingdom. So, on a connecting flight, he would fly to a hub, an airport with direct flights to the UK. At first, the choices overwhelmed her. He could have gone in any direction except due south. Sam tried to narrow it down by focusing on three leading commercial airlines, but that still offered too many choices, which left her with, *'what would she do.'* If she were Travis, *'how would she choose to fly?'* *'No, how would a man choose to fly,'* appeared to be a better train of thought to follow.

A moment of light relief found its way through the seriousness of her quest when she thought, *'it depends which brain he's engaged. Top or bottom.'* The answer to her question amused her, and she smiled. But it didn't last long. She was hungry, tired, and perplexed. Then, as if a revelation had suddenly occurred, she determined to put her research on hold, place her notebook inside her carry-on, find the shuttle bus and go to the hotel.

******

Julie had prepared and cooked quiche. Having eaten a portion accompanied by a freshly made salad as her evening meal, she dutifully went about washing the dishes and tidying up the kitchen. Even so, a twinge of suddenly feeling alone passed through her mind occasionally. She hadn't expected or anticipated it, and it contained an element of surprise each time it struck. Once she was satisfied with the kitchen, Julie unthinkingly moved from room to room picking up odd items, straightening things, and unconsciously upon inspection decided that everything was in order. Unfortunately, television held little appeal, and she felt it was too soon to retire for the night, which somehow led her to sit at Travis's desk. The laptop lay there, right in front of her.

If asked why she had opened a file containing pictures of their recent adventure, she'd have no concise or intelligible answer. It was there, on the screen, and she had just double-clicked the mouse button. The first three images contained no human lifeforms and transported her back. There was no living vicariously through these pictures as she had so many times before, as Travis relayed an adventure he alone had participated in. Instead, she felt her re-emersion into each scene and remembered the movements and sounds. The multitude of physical and emotional experiences which had and still do, hold her in ore and inspire further investigation. Time passed. Dozens of images, some smiles, some tears, some plausible regret, but with an ever-growing sense of accomplishment without need for recourse towards the three people that made it all possible.

Realizing the time, almost midnight, Julie made a conscientious effort to evaluate the time difference in London and concluded Travis would be landing in about two hours. It didn't seem that long ago when she said goodbye to him at the airport. But soon, she surmised, he and Deb would hold each other tightly in their embrace. The happy thought meandered through her mind, which carried her to the feelings she felt while held firmly in Mac's arms. Having determined that it took two to tango, there was no remorse, and even though the dance was not finished, it had been a wonderful experience. A soft woeful sigh mixed with a tingling memory saw Julie close the laptop, rise from her seat and think about going to bed.

******

It took Travis about twenty-five minutes to clear customs and immigration before he walked into the arrivals area. He saw Deb immediately, she looked well-traveled and tired, but her face lit up with a big smile upon seeing him. They were enfolded in a lover's embrace in less than two shakes of a cat's tail. The kiss, so much more than a greeting, as the humdrum of the world around them seemed to fade away. It couldn't last, they both knew that but they gave it their best shot before accepting they were not alone.

"I've missed you," Travis whispered into Deb's ear before pulling back to look into her eyes.

"Don't go getting all soppy on me Sage. I'm so tired; you might end up carrying me. By the way, I missed you too."

They kissed and embraced once more as Deb melded her body into his. "I love you Travis."

"Now, who's getting soppy Deb?"

"I'm a girl. It's okay for girls to get soppy. Come on, let's collect your bags and get out of here before someone tells us to get a room."

"Don't have one to collect Deb. I figured it would be easier to ship it directly to your address."

"So, you're good to go?"

"You bet-ya."

"Then let's get this show on the road."

Their happiness radiated through their eyes and their smiles as Travis hooked his good arm through the shoulder strap of his backpack and then stooped to pick up Deb's canvas hold-all. Deb likewise hooked her arm through the strap of her backpack and pointed in the direction they needed to go. With anticipation for all that they longed for in front of them, neither would think to look back.

Chapter 21

Sam learned quickly; sleuthing wasn't for the faint of heart and nothing like they show on television, and having witnessed the affectionate exchange, she was angry. But there was no time to cry, no allowance granted to rationalize the situation, and definitely, it was not the time to scream. The chase began fast, and like a storm blown by high winds, people moved in every direction, halting mindlessly in groups blocking her path. Luggage in all forms carried, dragged, pushed, and pulled. An ever-changing obstacle course of mass confusion, although she had to imagine most of them must know where they were going, lay bare the fact that she didn't, and they hadn't even left the airport yet. There was no choice; she had to keep up, remain undiscovered, hide in plain sight, and move swiftly.

******

Half a world away down under, the plane landed in Sydney Australia in the southern hemisphere. Home: now there's a word he hadn't used in a long time. The meaning of which seemed alien in many respects until... Mac knew the answer, *until Julie*. Even now, as he exited the plane his heart yearned for a different circumstance. Although, he knew the current circumstance was unchangeable unless and until he did something to alter his wayward path. Intellectually, Mac surmised his chances were slim. Julie was married, and although the interlude of romance had shown itself apparent, there was no verbal admission or indication given that might constitute a future. It was just a feeling, and if he was honest with himself, it was his feeling. An emotional sense of discovery and an instinct that inspired his belief Julie is the woman he was born to love.

The familiarity of the accent spoken by strangers surrounding him and that of the almost melodic voice of the female announcer wafting out of the overhead speakers took him by surprise. It had been a long time and punctuated his unfamiliarity with the sound of his fellow countrymen in its abundance. The feeling of being an outsider in his native land washed over him as he contemplated the discomfort of that thought. His family name meant something in this part of the world. But, at this moment, unrecognized, he stood alone waiting for his bag, knowing its content bore stark contrast to the style he had been accustomed to in this, the land of his birth.

An uncanny thought of the need to be recognized, for himself, by himself on what felt like a threadbare canvas, struck out at him as hard as any man's fist had ever connected with his jaw. Mac sensed his lack of identity in the unfamiliarity of the vaguely familiar scene as his vagrant, vagabond-self contrived to pull him back to the carefree meaningless life he had just walked away from. Defiant and determined, Mac snatched up his bag, mentally pissed on the idea of not moving forward, and then headed in the direction of car rental.

******

There were some noticeable changes, but the roads remained the same. Mac made his way onto the Hume highway out of Sidney towards the Southern Highlands in the rented Land Rover, ideally suited to carry him over the different terrain he would encounter as he continued towards the Blue Mountains. Although not a direct route to his final destination, Mac felt the need to get reacquainted with the world he grew up in.

Mac was in no rush, and there was no urgency to reach his final destination just south of Brisbane near the gold coast. However, this indirect route would first take him through the outback of New South Wales to a place he was very familiar with, Lightning Ridge. At about four hundred and fifty miles north-northwest of Sidney,

Lightning Ridge was the family business center. A business started back in the early nineteen hundreds by his great grandfather that has provided prosperity for each generation of the Adam's family ever since. The mining of Black Opals the most valuable of all opals.

    Driving through the wine region of Hunter Valley, everything became more familiar, the names of towns recognizable, and he would remember favorite stops. Places to eat, purchase a few items or just fill up with petrol. It was all coming back to him, the feeling of belonging, the knowledge and memories, the events of his life. The reflection and connections were good. Association and anticipation of what would come next rebuilt the foundation of his existence and purpose. Mac was finding himself and the demons of the past seven years, and the reason his course had initially changed began to fade as he breathed in deeply and laid claim to his old life. The life he was born into, the life he once again knew so well. *'Look out, Australia, Mackenzie Adams is back.'* He smiled and relished the thought.

Chapter 22

Travis opened his eyes slowly; the unfamiliar surroundings gave evidence that he was not in his bed. Although, glancing to his left and taking in the beautiful sight of the woman who lay beside him calmed any notion that he was in the wrong place. How long had they slept? He had no idea. What time was it? He didn't have a clue, except for the daylight creeping in around the edges of the curtains gave an indication it wasn't night. But that did not explain why he felt so tired or why he was awake. *A-ha!* The answer to the latter was near the foot of the bed. Vaguely he remembered the cat, who was kneading a comfortable spot between his feet. Having discerned all was well, Travis closed his eyes and went back to sleep.

******

"Damn it!" Mac slammed his foot on the brake pedal. The hard-packed dirt road provided little friction or resistance as the Land Rover careened forward, skidding out of control. Apart from suddenly finding religion and saying a prayer, his only option was to keep the wheels straight. He knew if she went sideways, the vehicle would flip side over side until all forward momentum was used up.

The arse-end swung out to the left; Mac yanked the steering wheel in the same direction, then slowly eased it back as everything lined up again. And finally, with the forward velocity giving way to traction, the Land Rover halted in a billowing cloud of dirt.

At first, Mac didn't move. Figuring it might take a pry-bar to release his fingers from the steering wheel and sure that he'd left permanent indentations in the leather. And his leg, the one on the brake pedal, was rigid. Eyes wide and focused on nothing in particular beyond the windscreen, as a wall of turbulent dust danced frantically in front of it.

As if suddenly realizing he'd been holding his breath, he exhaled. Then inhaled immediately to counter the action. "Damn it." He scolded himself for having forgotten about them as he looked over at the time illuminated on the dash. *'Yep, it was way past four.'*

He released the steering wheel slowly, took the engine out of gear, turned off the ignition, and finally removed his foot from the brake pedal. And as the dust cloud settled, he opened the door and climbed out of the vehicle. He was in the middle of nowhere, deep into the outback and he had to take a leak.

Looking back from whence he came and then in front, the direction he was traveling, nothing moved. He was alone, as alone as any person could be in this part of the world. Although it wouldn't surprise him if a bunch of Aborigines suddenly appeared out of nowhere, they were good at that. They didn't sneak up exactly; they just had the habit of arriving, then, just as quickly, they'd disappear. Much like the big red kangaroos. Why hadn't he remembered them? He had no answer, but he sure as hell just had his memory jogged. *'Fucking big bastards.'*

Everyone in these parts knew the 'big reds' start appearing around four in the afternoon and accumulate on the roads, especially at night. So, it was never a question of you might hit one. Because if you were driving at night, it was more of a question about when you'd hit one. Mac considered himself lucky as he zipped up his fly. He'd seen the bastard just in time and swerved to miss it. That is, if he considered almost losing his own life, lucky.

As the dust settled, the Land Rover melded itself to the same color as the dirt road. Even so, he checked around the body just to be sure 'big red' had not left its imprint. And, if a river or billabong was close by, he might have felt inclined to throw some water over the vehicle. But out here, there were more things that would kill ya than as wouldn't. Freshwater crocs, snakes, and even spiders don't think twice about taking a man's life.

No, it was time to move on and if memory served him right, a town called Narrabri lay no more than twenty miles ahead. But, driving cautiously, that was still a good hour to an hour and a half away. And his chances of meeting another member of 'big red's family' were almost imminent.

******

Manicured and pedicured Julie had even toyed with the idea of changing her hairstyle, but that was a big decision and warranted further thought. So, she had been to the mall, discovered South Palafox Street, and driven out to the beach. And, aimlessly driving along the coast road had crossed the state line into Alabama, where she discovered Orange Beach and Gulf Shores. Then, turning north on Highway 59, she found the Tanger Outlets Mall in Foley and had made a friend in the J Crew store. Julie was impressed; she had covered so much ground and found so many places. It was a whole different world on the Gulf Coast and she liked it.

But even though she would hate to admit it, Travis had been right. Well, partially correct maybe, in his initial concern about her staying at his place while he would have been in Borneo. The days were easy to fill and presented no problem, but the nights differed. What does a married but separated woman do in a city she is unfamiliar with during the evenings? By her own account, absolutely nothing it would seem and if there was something to do, was she ready to do it? *'Hmm,'* something else that would require further thought.

During these contemplative moments, she found little solace in her predicament, sitting alone with her iPad in her lap. Julie had yet to disclose and confide in anyone about the breakup of her marriage and was thankful that it took place after moving to Nashville. The hurt and anger still simmered beneath the surface, and honestly, she didn't want to say anything she might regret later. But that didn't resolve the problem. She thought about emailing Travis and typing, *'It's 8.30 pm. Do you know where your sister is?'* Wondering what his response would be if he responded, and if he did, would she feel forced into the pity party of woe is me? I feel so alone. No, that was so not going to happen. Besides, Travis was probably too busy with Deb to worry about his big sister. So, who? Who would welcome her email?

'Dear Mac....' *No, scary, too affectionate.* 'Hi, Mac....' *Better.* Although hadn't she wanted his affection, craved his attention....? *That was before. But what happened after didn't really happen, did it? It's so confusing; it's a mess. How did it get like this, and why in God's name did he stop? Why didn't he take me completely? I wanted him to...to...? To make me feel like a woman.* Tears formed, she felt vulnerable, and that made her angry. Afraid. Afraid in the memory and desire she still felt, and, in her certainty, it was too late to do anything to change things. *It was over and done with, just like her marriage.* There would be no email to Mac.

Chapter 23

It usually took Deb a couple of days to acclimate to the time difference when she arrived home, and under normal circumstances she had her routines organized. Of which, grocery shopping was about the most industrious. Following that, checking received mail and paying bills. Anything else took a backseat to sleep and taking care of Annie. But normal circumstances seemed unavailable as she and Travis grappled with the effects of moving through time. She had traveled backward, Travis had moved forward, and although her journey had been longer, the intricacies of their adjustments had them both off kilter.

The nuance of having Travis there in her home, in her bed, felt awkward and unsettling, new and exciting, all in the same moments of thought. Making her feel edgy and considering the tired dullness of her brain, Deb found it hard to relax amid a mixture of unexpected emotions. The jumble of feelings, crisscrossing and colliding, taxing her limited resource called reason. But, laying quietly beside him, feeling the warmth of his body, she was thankful. And although perplexed, she looked forward urgently to unraveling the secrets of this new experience. Her body wanted him now; her disquieted mind said, wait. But the complexity of her thoughts had more to do with her past and the memories which still lingered. Reminders of Christine surrounded her and gave evidence of their shared love. A connection to the intangible intimacy of their affection and the sweet sensation of touch. And as one complex thought gave way to the next, Deb suddenly realized *she was living with a ghost.*

As the stark reality of that thought seized hold of her mind, any idea of comfort disintegrated. Her eyes showed fear as she leaped out of bed and looked around the room. Everywhere, the imprint of Christine blatantly mocking her as if she, Deb, was the intruder in Christine's world. A cold chill brushed against her cheek as she sensed movement. Annie stood rigid, arched her back, and hissed vehemently as if she sensed unseen danger. A picture fell off the wall; Annie hissed again, jumped off the bed, and ran from the bedroom. Bewildered in uncertainty, Deb moved towards the fallen picture, unaware Travis woken by the sound of breaking glass watched and tried to comprehend.

"What happened?" He asked still struggling with the orientation of his surroundings. "Are you okay?"

Deb stopped and turned to face him. "I'm not sure. I think we have a ghost." Travis scoffed humorously as he flipped the bedside light on. "Interesting way to wake up Deb. I don't think I've heard that line before. Where is he? Did he rattle his chains?"

Deb chose to ignore the sarcastic attempt at wit and refocused her attention on the picture carefully picking it up without spilling any more glass shards. The image of her and Christine, the last of them together before....... Before, there were no more. Christine was....... The accident. Death by misadventure, the coroner's verdict. *'What just happened?'* Deb's thoughts were all over the place. *'Was this some sort of message?'* That was a frightening proposition and had to be dismissed. *'Hum.'* She turned again towards Travis. "I have no explanation; the picture just fell. I'll have to get the glass replaced. Did you sleep well?" Deb did her best to hide behind a smile.

"Like a log." Travis placed his feet on the floor, stood, and moved toward Deb. "How about you?" he wrapped her in his arms. "Morning Deb. I'll get this cleaned up if you tell me where you keep the dustpan and broom."

She said nothing, extracting every ounce of soothing reassurance his warm embrace had to offer. Push aside the uneasiness of the strange disturbance and refocus her thoughts. Her love for this man soon filled her mind, and the strong desire to be bonked quickly followed. The anticipation yearned to be satisfied in a most agonizingly urgent request as her lips discovered his and she conveyed her message.

******

Narrabri hadn't changed; it looked much like he'd remembered as he departed along the main road leading out of town. The incident with 'big red' the evening before was behind him, although not forgotten, and he was thankful the surprise meeting had not proved more serious. The hotel, if he could call it that, was nothing to write home about. But the bed gave comfort and provided a restful night's sleep. It was a new day, and Mac felt energized as thoughts and memories swirled through his mind. His destination, Lightning Ridge, where he had spent his childhood, was a mining community that bore the Adams family name. The only place in the world to discover the famous black opals.

It lay about 160 miles to the northwest and was an easy drive through open terrain and rolling hills. The outback at its finest for a city dweller. A positively urban experience if you consider it had dirt roads and a train track. It was almost civilized, in a wild sort of way. Tourist appeal for the adventurous though less daring explorer, who maintained a dependency on certain creature comforts? Although, even out here, there were creatures that would kill ya.

Then slap-bang, in the middle of all this wildness, sat Lightning Ridge. Which, to the casual onlooker, was definitely nothing to write home about. But for Mac, this had been home for many years until the family moved into the civilized world of city life on the east coast.

Lightning Ridge, in the best of times could claim no more than about 2,000 inhabitants. Mainly mine workers, those who provided retail services and their families. It wasn't one of those towns where, if you blinked while driving through, you'd miss it. No, you either came to Lightning Ridge, or you left it. There was no driving through. An odd sort of ramshackle community, with a hodgepodge of buildings to indicate someone might live there.

And there over to the right, set back off the road, just before entering the town, the sign. Adams Mining Industries Company Limited. Larger than life, it stood sentry, proclaiming its proclamation to all who ventured this way. Mac smiled, remembering once he had thought about burning it to the ground. He couldn't quite remember his reasoning now, but the idea had stuck in his mind.

Driving slowly, he looked around at all the choices. Jock's grocery store where you could choose to shop or not and go hungry. The bank? That was something new. Phelps' oil and petrol station, a grub hut called Molly's and Gibson's general store. That was about it, except for old Doc Fobs' surgery, the essayer's office, a couple of lawyers, and the undertaker who usually racked up a pretty good business. Down at the far end of the street sat the parsonage next to the church and beyond that, Digger's watering hole, the only pub in town. Well, there was one more outback, behind the general store which catered to the needs of the unmarried men.... mostly.

Mac pulled up and parked outside Digger's. It had either been there or Molly's. And at Digger's, he stood more chance of getting both needs met in one place. A pint and something to eat. It was a modern place if this had been in the early nineteenth century. Full of rustic charm might have been overkill in describing it. But it was the quintessential example of a typical watering hole in many outback towns. Complete with a bartender who looked like he'd been in a fight with a crocodile and almost lost.

Met with the polite customary greeting, "G'day, what ya havin?"

Mac told the bartender what he wanted as he walked up and stood next to the bar.

"Not from around these here parts. Where are ya comin from?" The bartender eyed Mac inquisitively.

Of the five or six other men lined up along the bar, Mac could tell without looking the bartender's question had drawn curious looks from the locals—all waiting to hear his answer.

"Brisbane."

"Brisbane aye. Ya, quite a ways from home, what brings ya to these parts, fella?"

Mac understood the interrogatory process; it was harmless. Even so, he wasn't sure how much information he wanted to share.

"Been away awhile, just doin walk-about, seeing the sites."

The bartender gave him the eye. "Comin from the cooler?"

"Prison!" Mac laughed. "Na, been overseas."

"Mac...? Mac Adams?"

Mac turned toward the man doing the asking, while trying to find a name to put to the face.

"Pete?"

The man rushed towards him smiling in disbelief, as if he wasn't certain but, sure that he was, all tied up in the same expression.

"Mac? I can't believe it. Mac Adams?" Their right hands met in a tight grip. "Hey fella's, this here's Mac; we grew up together. Don't any of ya recognize him?"

A couple of the other men did, vaguely. Then began to remember more things about Mac as the drinks were drawn and placed on the bar.

******

News travels fast in a small town. And although Mac had not intended to linger, several hours floated by unnoticed as several more men joined what was becoming a celebratory crowd. Until...

"Mac?"

The sound of a woman's voice. An unusual sound in a pub. Most men stopped talking and in hushed stares, their eyes focused on the woman in disbelief that she would enter this, their hallowed place.

"Mac?"

At first, he too, disbelieved his eyes, but for a different reason.

"Maggie?"

Chapter 24

The complexity of her thoughts. During the journey back to the hotel, just south of London near Heathrow airport gave Sam reason to question the sanity and consequence of her actions. And if she was honest with herself, her foolish behavior seemed *'borderline,'* although the thought was a hard nut to swallow, *'criminal.'* The reflective nature of her thinking begged understanding which appeared elusive—the justification foolish. *'Yes,'* her emotions were strong and filled with desire. *'Yes,'* she reaffirmed, the depth of her instinct and the inexplicable knowledge of somehow having known him. *'When?' 'Where?' 'How?'* These were the questions. They defied logic and all reasonable explanation. An illusionary perception of.... *Of what?* And after witnessing the affectionate kiss exchanged with the woman at the airport, *'Why,'* was she in such hot pursuit?

******

If minds could be read, both Travis and Deb shared a similar thought. They were content to stay right where they were, together, in bed. Delightfully bonked and creatively inventive, they made love. A euphoric rhapsody of emotions held them trance-like, wrapped in each other's arms. "I love you, Travis." Soft-spoken words preceded their kiss and.......... Annie jumped up on the bed and meowed discontentedly, stating her complaint. She had been ignored long enough, and she was hungry.

******

Mac opened his eyes to a confusing scene with blurred edges. The face of a small girl stood, staring at him. The surprise startled him, which in turn seemed to frighten the little girl, and she ran away. Still uncertain, he sat up and immediately felt the pain. Eyes closed, praying for relief, and in a moment of clarity he remembered the drinking. Eyes open again he tried to make sense of everything. He was on a sofa. His shoes were on the floor and he had been covered with a blanket. Nothing in the room looked familiar and he had no idea how he ended up where he was.

"Mornin?"

A female voice behind him.

Mac looked around; no one was there.

"Do ya still like ya coffee black?"

Same voice, different direction, in another room maybe?

"Ya, thanks."

The little girl reappeared in the doorway and looked warily at him.

"Hi." Mac tried to smile convincingly. "What's ya name?"

The girl remained silent and brought her hand up close to her mouth.

The woman entered the room. "Here, take these."

Mac saw the pills in her hand and then looked up.

"Maggie?" Revelation. It came back to him. Last night at the pub, Maggie? The shock.

"You look bloody mortified Mac; I don't remember ever havin that effect on ya?"

"Maggie? What are ya doin here? I mean, what am I doin here? Where am I?"

"Relax, Mac. Baby steps. One thought at a time. Take these pills and get some coffee inside ya. There's plenty of time to talk.

Mac couldn't believe it. It didn't make sense. "Maggie. What the hell are ya doin' here in Lightning Ridge?"

"I grew up here, remember?"

She was just as pretty now as she was....... "Ya, I remember. But ya moved, ya left here so why did ya come back?"

Mac watched her as she looked at him. Then her eyes focused on the little girl for a moment before looking at him again. "Life's a bitch sometimes."

Mac got the message. Now was not the time to talk about it.

******

This newfound sense of sensibility or as Sam would prefer to believe, the re-establishment of her common sense was not without its symptomatic ailments. Her stomach was in knots; her head hurt, and her heart ached. Mourning a loss of something which in reality she had little understanding of and as she somberly wandered around the British Museum gathering information and leaflets to evidence the fact that she had been there, the nagging thoughts persisted. *'Why'* had she made that journal entry *'My name is Anne'* so many years ago? *'How'* could she perceive the emotional connection within a painting? And just as importantly, *'How'* could Travis perceive what appeared to be a similar emotional link? *'What'* happened, really happened when they touched each other. And the confusing exchange of prior knowledge, the knowing and sense of belonging they had transmitted one to the other through their eyes? Sam struggled with inner loneliness, a lost feeling she had never experienced before.

******

Mac had so many questions he didn't know where to start. The logical entry point, at least to him, considering his confused state was.... "How did I get here?"

"Mac, ya were in no condition to drive anywhere last night. So, what was I supposed to do, just walk away. Did ya have someplace to stay? Because ya didn't seem to understand that question when I asked ya last night."

"So, where am I?"

"Ya been in this house a thousand times Mac. This was my mum and dad's place. I guess ya didn't hear. My mum passed away two years ago. So, I live here with Becca, my daughter."

"Okay. But how did I get here?"

"Ya Land Rover is parked in the drive. How do ya think ya bloody got here? I drove ya here; ya was acting like a drunk, no wait a second, ya were a bloody drunk. What's happened to ya Mac? Where have ya been all these years? Where did ya go? Do ya mum and dad know ya here?" Her tone sounded harsh, annoyed. Angry almost?

"Maggie, please?" Too many questions; slow down, is there any more coffee?"

Mac got up off the sofa. The little girl watched, somehow reassured by the tone in her mother's voice that this strange man posed no threat. Mac touched the top of her head as he passed by and ruffled her hair with his hand on his way to the bathroom. Which somehow, he appeared to know where it was.

******

When he returned to the living room he was alone, Maggie and Becca were in the kitchen. Mac sat on the sofa and put his shoes on. "Maggie, I'm sorry for the inconvenience. Can I get cleaned up before I leave?"

"Do ya want breakfast?"

Mac hesitated. Uncertain. The edginess was still in her tone. "Don't go to any trouble on my account Maggie."

"It's no trouble, ya need to eat something."

"Okay. But let me get some clean clothes out of the Land Rover and get washed up."

"Go on with ya then."

Mac made his way out of the house unaware Becca was following him. Watching him; either curious or suspicious, she wasn't going to let him out of her sight. Outside he looked up and down the street; yes, the familiarity came back to him. He knew this place well, and as Maggie had said, he'd been here a thousand times. A smirk or smile indicated the memory and reminded him, he had lost his virginity in this house and so had Maggie.

Grabbing what he needed from the vehicle, he turned to go back inside the house. Becca stood, stationed right in front of him. "Becca!" Unsure what to say he took note of her facial features, she looked just like the younger version of her mother, so beautiful. He held out his hand and after a brief moment of thought, Becca placed her hand in his and they returned inside together, holding hands.

******

"Why did ya come here Mac?" Her tone had softened. Mac was seated at the small table in the kitchen eating breakfast. Becca sat across from him and silently they were exchanging silly facial expressions. Maggie was at the kitchen sink washing the frying pan.

"It's a long story Maggie; if I had known ya were here in Lightning Ridge I probably wouldn't have come, or if I had known, I'd have done my best to keep out of ya way. I'm sorry Maggie, I know that doesn't sound too nice, but the last thing I'd want to do is rake up the past and upset ya in the bargain."

Maggie thought about that. "Upset Mac? I'm not upset. Well, maybe I am a bit. Shocked is more like it. Ya can't begin to imagine how it felt to find out you were in town. But then, when I find ya, you're a drunken fool, incapable of giving me any kind of straight answers. So, what was I supposed to think? Seven years Mac, seven years. Not knowing if you're alive or dead. Never havin a chance to explain or tell ya how sorry I am for what happened."

"It's okay Maggie; water under the bridge, the last thing I'd want to do is upset ya."

"Mac, I'm not upset? I'm beside myself with relief, I need a chance to explain. Stay a few days at least, Give me a chance to say what I couldn't say before. Ya have no idea how much I regret hurting ya. I need this, just a few days Mac, please, I beg ya."

The pleading expression on Maggie's face. The tears in her eyes betrayed the emotional need to cry. She was struggling to stay composed and losing the battle fast. Mac felt unsure yet somehow sensed he might need this too. The moment was fraught with tension. What about his mum and dad? There were wounds to heal there as well. Becca looked uncertain in her conception of what was taking place and at this moment, any reassurance would rest on his next words. To tarry or not to tarry, and what would be the emotional cost? That's the question.

Chapter 25

Sam had to concede as things stood, she had no plan. No idea really what her next move should be. Thoughts about Travis still permeated her emotional desire but seemed out of reach. He chose to be with someone else and there was nothing she could do about it. Trying to fool herself that she didn't care appeared contrite and that he didn't matter was at best, an unconvincing argument which she knew she was not going to win. She did care, and he does matter. Her feelings, although to this point had proved obsessive and even fanatical were, when conditioned with temperance, good feelings. But under the circumstances it seemed her feelings didn't matter. At least to Travis they didn't and therein lay the rub.

Trying to make the most of her time or fill her time with distractions, Sam had been to Buckingham Palace and watched the changing of the guard. Westminster Abby, the Houses of Parliament and Big Ben. To the Tower of London to view the crown jewels and even taken a boat ride along the river Thames to Hampton Court Palace. She marveled at the grandeur or would have, if her thoughts were not centrally convened on self-recrimination for past actions. But she blew it and she knew it. It was not a happy thought.

******

Mac called his dad, told him where he was and that he would stick around for a few days before heading east. It was a good conversation; even so, Mac sensed a bit of disappointment in his dad's voice and understood the anticipation and now the delay. Maggie said she had to get ready for work and Becca, it appeared, was determined to become his shadow.

"Becca, are ya ready? Time to go. Mac, help yourself to anythin in the fridge, and thanks again for stickin around."

"Maggie, where do ya work?" That question popped out for two reasons; one, the outfit she was wearing and two, why was she taking a kid to work? It also just occurred to him there wasn't another vehicle in her drive besides his Land Rover.

"Molly's Grub Hut." She saw his surprised look and knew the reason for it. "Mac, there's not a lot of openings around here for a woman with a business degree. Especially a divorced woman with a kid."

Mac understood her answer. He didn't like it considering he knew how proficient she was in the business world and how successful she had been. But he understood. "And Becca, where does she go?"

"She's comin to work with me. Sometimes Mrs. Farley down the road watches her, but she had somewhere to go today."

"Do ya want me to give ya a ride?"

Maggie smiled. "That's the Mac I remember. Always the gentleman."

While driving Mac asked. "Maggie, it's not a good idea for me to stay at your house. Wagging tongues, you being a divorced woman, I should git a room? Does Widow Duncan still take in boarders?"

Maggie laughed. "Accordin to the wagging tongue's society, I've slept with half the men in this town. The truth of it is, I haven't had sex in so long, I can't remember what it feels like and no, Widow Duncan is dead. Her son sold the house and moved on. Honestly Mac, I don't have a problem with ya stayin at the house."

******

After several hours wandering along Pensacola beach, occasionally picking up shells and examining them. Julie felt positively old. For the most part, her one-piece bathing suit made her feel *'geriatric.'* Seemingly, the *'trend'* placed her in the dark ages of unliberated womanhood and made her very self-conscious and out of step. Sure, there were women in one-piece suits, and several appeared much younger than she, but their one-piece suits utilized half as much material and were so revealing they left little to the imagination. Overwhelmingly, the two-piece ruled this beach, shockingly in some extremes.

And the men, how did they get away with wearing so much? As much as ten times the material count of their respective female companions. Julie was forced to wonder how they could sunbathe when so much was covered up. Maybe, she surmised, they were afraid of catching a chill. It seemed an unlikely deduction, considering the temperature was within the '90s. Even so, she appeared to glean no attention from the male populous whatsoever, which concerned her.

She thought about Mac, a bittersweet memory now, and remembered his eyes upon her for the very first time. The visual undressing of her in his mind, and her sensed appreciation of what he appeared to have imagined. And the appreciation he continued to exude visually and orally during the days that followed. And then, there was that night? The mere thought of that night.... Julie found herself hot and bothered, in need of....... What? A shady palm tree wasn't going to cut it. Neither would a cold drink. For the first time in what seemed like a long time, Julie wanted.... Mac? Wanted to feel his kiss upon her lips. Yearned to feel his hands touching her body. The frustration of the imagined illusion and the recognition of the experience screamed out mercilessly to be acknowledged, conceded, and re-measured. Not incompletely, but sanctified completely, to the depth of all understanding and then some.

Julie felt like a bolt of lightning had just struck her. The intensity was so powerful she felt forced to sit or fall down. Whichever came first? The air had somehow been sucked from her lungs and the headiness of her mind gave clarity to just one thought.... Mac?

A sensation of being lost and needing to be found stumbled and tumbled through the darkness out into the light. With distinction, resolution, and no room for doubt, Julie spoke the words with conviction. "I love you Mac. I love you." Happily, she acknowledged her tears and willingly felt the acceptance of this truth.

******

Travis took in the sites of Hinckley's pedestrianized downtown shopping area as he and Deb walked hand in hand with the aura of togetherness surrounding them. The old redbrick edifices of the quaint storefronts, some painted over and some not, lent themselves to a time long passed and yet, still functional in this more modern era. It was different in a nice sort of way and even though he was acutely aware of the apparent busyness of the people out shopping, he and Deb were meandering along unrushed, engaged only in each other.

******

"Well, I'll be... Look at what the dust storm just blew in? Mackenzie Adams. I heard ya were back in town. Come here son, let me take a good look at ya."

Mac smiled. He had followed Maggie and Becca into Molly's grub hut. "Mrs. Aldridge."

"Look at ya all grown up and lookin handsome. Call me Molly, you ain't no kid anymore. I can still picture ya and Maggie over in that corner booth being all secretive and lovey, thinkin ya had us all fooled. After all this time I can't believe it, and then to walk in here with Maggie. Who would have thought? Come over here, sit down and tell me what ya been doin all this time. Hi, Maggie. Tell me Mac, what do ya think of Maggie? Ain't she just as pretty as ever? And Becca, ain't she the spittin image of her mother?"

Mac did his best to work his way through the answers. Molly just kept piling the questions on, usually without waiting for his response. Mac took it in stride; he was the latest gossip, the novelty. Finally, the prodigal son had returned home and everyone was curious.

After three cups of strong black coffee and a 'deluxe' sandwich, ordered up by Molly and made by Maggie, Mac took Becca's hand, and together they went walkabout around town.

Chapter 26

Mac kept his shadow with him for the remainder of the afternoon and evening and at seven-thirty, they drove back to Molly's to pick up Maggie.

"Hope ya don't mind, I've made dinner."

"Wow, that's a treat. Ya didn't have to do that Mac but thank ya."

After arriving home, Maggie took a quick shower while Mac put the finishing touches to the meal. During the afternoon Becca had opened up and was now talking to Mac quite freely. He took that as a good sign but really, it was his first meaningful interaction with someone so small. A child who, through no fault of her own, lacked an adult male figure in her life. He hoped under the circumstance it would be a good experience for both of them.

Once Becca was bathed and in bed and Mac had finished cleaning up the kitchen, Maggie joined him in the living room.

"Thanks again for dinner Mac. A girl could get used to that in a hurry."

"Hmm I hope not, I don't want to disappoint ya Maggie, let's talk."

Maggie, for all intent and purpose, was just taken aback. Mac's comment had a finality to it. Not that she was expecting something magical to happen, but a girl could have a little hope couldn't she? "I'm sorry Mac, I didn't mean to imply anything, it was just a nice thing for ya to do and I appreciate it. Where should I start?"

"Ya could start by telling me who's Becca's father?"

To Maggie that was like a knife to the jugular. "Alex, ya met him. I didn't know it at the time when we broke up."

"Broke up? Maggie, we didn't break up. Ya were sleeping with him and I found out about it."

She took a deep breath. Maggie was well aware of what she had done and just listening to Mac, she could tell her betrayal still hurt him. "Mac, I'm so sorry, I let ya down, I betrayed ya trust, ya love and I know ya were hurt. I'd give anythin to go back and do things differently and not make that mistake again, but I can't. I've cried so many times. It was a mistake that almost drove me crazy and ya just disappearing didn't make it any easier.

"Easier Maggie? Ya think I should've made it easier for ya?"

"No, Mac, that's not what I meant, I just wished I could have talked to ya. I was in the wrong, not ya, we both know that. Ya didn't deserve to get hurt. To this day, I don't know why I did what I did. I don't have any good reason; ya loved me, ya respected me, and ya trusted me. We had been together since we were kids, just like Molly said. Everyone knew I was with ya and ya were with me. It was easy when we lived here; I got myself mixed up in somethin in Brisbane that shouldn't have happened. I should've had more sense; I knew it was wrong from the beginning, I won't even try to deny that, but foolish me, ya can see where I am now?"

"That's just it Maggie. Where are ya? And...... I don't just mean right now, even back then, when we were planning our wedding. Where was ya Maggie? Did our future mean so little to ya? What was goin through ya mind that made it so easy for ya to destroy me? Take my love and my life and throw it away as if it meant nothin to ya. What did I do wrong Maggie?"

"Mac, stop for a minute. Hear me. If I was offered the opportunity to give my life in exchange to remove all the pain ya have felt in your heart, I'd gladly give my life even in knowing I'd make Becca an orphan.

******

Deb told Travis it was curry night which meant going to the Lime Kilns. That didn't make a lot of sense to Travis. He knew what curry was and had some idea what a kiln was used for—but putting lime in a kiln? And who would use a kiln to make curry? At the risk of sounding stupid. No, more information was forthcoming. "We'll walk along the canal path to the Lime Kilns so we had better take a torch." Fascinated; Travis could visualize a thick stick with tarred cloth wrapped around one end, it sounded positively medieval or Viking-like. And they were going to carry this torch along the edge of a canal in the dark, find some lime kilns and hopefully eat curry? *'Huh, this should be interesting. Just hope we don't fall into the canal?'*

******

It's a pity we don't speak the same language. It turns out a torch, translated means a flashlight. *Pity, Travis had kinda looked forward to making a torch.* But the walk along the canal path was no joke. It was still light when they set off beside the canal along a dirt track, and looking at the dark brown, murky canal water he kinda wished he had brought a stay-dry deep-dive suit and helmet with him, and worn it as a preventative measure, just in case?

They walked for more than a mile before reaching the Lime Kilns which turned out to be a pub. *'Huh, who knew?'* And even stranger? It had a perfectly good road running right beside it. *So why had they risked life and limb to travel on foot and taken the long way or should that be the wrong way to get there?*

But the curry was good and the local customers *who, by the way had all chosen to travel by automobiles,* were jovial.

"Hey, Deb. That picture of the arch, you said you thought it was near here, right?"

"Yes. I'm fairly certain it's in Warwickshire the next county over, in the town of Atherstone."

"How far away is that?"

"Only about eight maybe, ten miles."

"Will you take me there to see it?"

"Yes. We can go tomorrow if you like?"

"Assuming of course, we survive the walk home along the canal path?"

"Travis, the exercise is good for you."

"It's not the exercise I'm concerned about and besides, I can think of a much better way to exercise?"

Deb smiled knowingly. "Hum, I'd be interested in having you show me later?"

******

Sam was seriously considering it was time to fly home and having done that, get in touch with Dr. Samuels to accept his offer. How she had let everything get so far out of hand didn't bear thinking about anymore, and she was blatantly aware of all the mistakes she had made. She had been considered a precocious student in high school and college. And she would consider herself anything but intelligent in her handling of this relationship with Travis. Sam concluded that no matter what the unusual circumstances were. No matter what the strong attractions or significant unprovable facts suggest, the writing was on the wall. And like it states in the gambler song, you've got to know when to hold, know when to fold'em. Know when to walk away, know when to run. It was late; she wanted to take a shower and climb into bed.

Chapter 27

Shortly after breakfast, they set out—Deb behind the wheel and Travis riding shotgun. The morning sky was overcast as Deb entered the roundabout and took the exit heading west along the A5. Travis felt speculative and uncertain of what to expect? Remembering when Sam had presented him with her phone, he gazed first at the picture and then eerily into the scene and felt connected to it. The sense of it still defied logical explanation but the fact of it happening had drawn him to this moment.

The road to either side was open land. Farmland for the most part, with occasional clusters of trees. Woodlands, some covering more area than others and an isolated house or building scattered the scene as they moved towards Warwickshire.

It wasn't that far, no more than minutes. They left Leicestershire behind and drove by a small enclave of homes before the land opened up once more.

Passing the road signs indicating turn-offs for Witherley and Mancetter, which meant no more to Travis than did the name Atherstone as they entered the outskirts of the town. Only then did he begin to feel something? Odds things. The recognition of a building, a feeling of knowing and yet not quite remembering how to associate his thoughts. And a few minutes later, they were in the town looking for a place to park.

Turning left onto Coleshill Road, then right. Travis imagined a strong familiarity wash over him. Accompanied by an ominous foreboding as they parked and he stepped out of the car. The sense of recognition consumed his awareness of knowing exactly where he was?

"Hey, Deb. It might sound crazy, but please just go with it and let me see where we end up. I want to lead us to the arch without help from you?"

"Travis?"

"I know Deb, but just bear with me. I have a strong feeling I know which way to go?"

Deb, a little confused hunched her shoulders momentarily. Finally she gave Travis the suspicious eye and indicated her agreement to follow. "Okay Sage, lead on."

Travis turned towards the back of the stores that fronted the main road through town without further ado. A road called Long Street, formally known as Watling Street. It was part of a road network first built by Romans as a troop and supply route.

"This way Deb." Travis was fast approaching the back of the stores. To the unknowing eye this would have been a dead end. The store backs presented a barrier against access to Long Street. But almost hidden from view, between two old buildings was a small, covered alley which provided a narrow walkway, a tunnel almost, leading out onto the main road. Deb continued to follow him curiously.

Standing on the curb directly across the street from them another road lay perpendicular to Long Street and Travis could see a church at the end of it. The church, which he somehow imagined was hidden from view in the painting. He took a moment to absorb the scene. "Hey Deb, it's up that street isn't it, over to the right of the Church?"

"Travis, how…….?"

"Come on Deb."

He took Deb's hand in his and crossed the street, moving towards the church.

"How can you know this; how do you know?"

"It's a long story Deb. I'm having a hard time coming to terms with this myself."

Halfway along what he now knew was Church Street he stopped suddenly. Deb walked right into him.

"Oops, sorry Deb." He saw the Arch cattycorner from where they were. "Somethings wrong Deb?"

"What do you mean?"

"There should be a building here, between where we are and the arch. It was a tall redbrick building; I was sure of it?"

"You're starting to worry me. I don't understand?"

"I'm sorry Deb, I should have told you before?"

"Before what Travis? What are you saying?"

"I'll make you a deal. Let's just look at the arch then find somewhere to sit down and I'll tell you all about it?"

Deb was reluctant, Travis seemed to have all his faculties but he was sure acting weird. Finally, not certain if she even had a choice she nodded her agreement, they stepped across the street and proceeded to cover the remaining distance to the arch.

A sign mounted on the wall on this side of the arch, over to the left read Friar's Gate, which seems relevant to Travis somehow, but it was a mystery yet to reveal itself. He surveyed the structure and the attached buildings on either side. Nothing appeared remarkable or offered any insight. By now Deb was a little leery and stood watching Travis, who, for all intent and purpose appeared to be watching the building while working something out in his mind? Without a word Travis stepped beneath the arch, and instantly felt an ice-cold chill envelope his body. He staggered and reached out his hand to steady himself against the wall.

"Travis?"

Deb moved quickly to his side and took hold of his arm. He was trembling. "Travis?" But he appeared unaware of her presence. The color had drained from his face, it was ashen, and for all Deb could surmise, he was not standing there with her in that exact moment.

Chapter 28

Instinct kicked in as Deb sensed the gravity of the situation and was terrified of losing him. Even though she had no rational understanding of how that was possible, it was a moment of choice. She could stand there in hope. Not an option as she remembered what Christine had been forced to do. It had been swift, it hurt, and it was necessary. With no further hesitation, Deb clenched her fist drew back her arm, and slugged Travis hard in the face.

His reaction wasn't much, but it was enough to put a chink in the spell. Deb grabbed his body and literally pushed him out from under the arch. He went down to the pavement and Deb tumbled down on top of him.

******

Sam was just about to pick up her phone to call the airline and make the necessary changes to her flight schedule and fly home tomorrow. When without warning, her hand felt like ice. The agony of it stunned her; and as if she were a mannequin she could not move. She felt trapped in a motionless stare at her hand and incapable of producing any intelligible thought.

And then just as suddenly she was released. "What the f....?" A typical human reaction. Followed quickly by "Travis?" Because she knew, without a shadow of a doubt that she had just experienced the force of death. "No! Oh God no." There was no way of measuring the time she had been held captive; a minute, an hour and no time to waste even thinking about it. As she frantically threw the last items of clothing in her suitcase, picked up her bag and her phone, looked around one more time and hurriedly left her hotel room. She would not be coming back.

******

It took Travis a few seconds and then a few seconds more and still, he didn't understand why he was on his back on the pavement and more importantly, why Deb was on top of him.

"Travis, are you…?"

"Deb, we can't bonk in the street."

She felt like slugging him again and people were starting to gather. Deb struggled awkwardly to get off him and stand up. "Sorry?" That comment was not addressed to Travis. "This wanker slipped over and I fell on top of him." The concerned looks on their faces began to relax. "Are you okay Travis?" That comment was addressed to him, but it wasn't sincere. She thought Travis should count himself lucky she didn't kick him in the balls for the comment he'd just made. And she was glad when the people began to disperse.

Travis had finally got enough sense to get to his feet and stand up. "Thanks everyone?" Although no one seemed to pay him any attention, and Deb didn't look any too happy with him either. "Sorry Deb."

"You just scared the living crap out of me. I think you had better tell me what the fuck is going on?"

Travis knew he had some explaining to do.

Not waiting to be asked, Deb led the way across the open square and walked straight into the pub. "Brandy, please."

"And you sir, what can I get for you."

Deb was surprised that the bartender would even assume they were together. She was so upset with Travis.

"Beer please."

"Deb picked up the glass of Brandy and knocked it back in one swallow. "I'll take another one."

Travis got the impression that the bartender was as shocked as he was.

Deb marched over to an empty table and sat down. Travis followed her with the drinks and took up residence in the seat across from her.

"I owe you an apology Deb. I'm sorry."

"That's not nearly enough. You owe me a lot more than that Travis Sage, a whole lot more and you know it?"

This was serious, and yes he knew it. Their first lover's spat. It had to happen sooner or later, but if he had been given a choice. Well, he had and he knew that too. "Deb, what I'm about to tell you will sound...?" He had to think about it, it was crazy, unbelievable, but somehow he had to convince her he was telling the truth.

"I'm waiting?"

"Deb, before making the trip to Borneo I visited my sister Julie and her husband Steve, who had recently moved to Nashville Tennessee. On the second night I was there, Steve's company held a social event. Steve and Julie invited me to go with them, and I did. I wasn't doing anything when suddenly I noticed this girl, a young woman and she noticed me. Honestly, I don't know what happened. She looked into my eyes and I looked into hers, and we were stuck. Neither of us could, nor wanted to break eye contact. It was as if we were in a trance, and I swear to you Deb, I felt like I knew her. I mean, I knew her in the biblical sense. Yet the reality is, I'd never seen her before in my life."

"Are you talking about Sam, Samantha?"

"Yes, how did you know?"

"Julie mentioned her. I asked her if you had a girl back in the states."

"Oh?"

"Carry on Travis. Don't let me distract you."

"Why would you ask if I had a girl back in the states?"

"Travis!"

He smiled, a knowing smile.

Unwilling to entertain him, Deb simply picked up her glass and took a sip.

"Hum, okay. Where was I? Anyway, the feelings we exchanged were intense; for some unknown reason I called her Anne, and she fainted. Right there in front of me, her eyes rolled back and she collapsed. So I caught her in my arms, then her dad came over, picked her up and carried her away and that was it.

"What do you mean, that was it? What about the birthday dinner?

"How much of this do you already know. Did Sis tell you my life story? I feel like I've been....... Undressed? Put on display. Do I have any secrets left?"

"I'm sure you do. Anyway, Julie said you and Sam went outside for a while. What was it she said? Ah yes, you and Sam were as thick as thieves."

"Damn! I think I need to keep you and Julie separated."

Deb smiled for the first time. "Tell me, what was Sam like? Would you like to know her in the biblical sense, or do you already know that?"

"No Deb, and that's crossing a line. Things in the past should stay in the past, agreed?"

"Okay. So, you didn't want to know her in the biblical sense?"

"I didn't say that Deb, but....... Can I get back to my story?"

"Be my guest. Go for it."

"Damn my jaw hurts. Like somebody hit me with a sledgehammer."

Deb laughed, quickly putting her hand in front of her mouth.

"It's not funny. I must have done it to myself when I hit the ground, I just don't remember. Hum? The thing is, Julie couldn't tell you what happened when Sam and I held hands. I don't know how to explain it myself. So, I'm just going to say it was intense. Same with the eyes, looking into each other's eyes. It was like exchanging bodies; honestly Deb, I was inside her and knew everything about her. Intense doesn't begin to explain it. How do you begin to describe knowing someone that intimately when the reality is you don't know them at all?"

"I think I do, in a way. Isn't that what love is? To be completely attuned with your lover. To imagine the intensity of them through touch. To look in their eyes and see the love reflected towards you. To just know by instinct, you're connected?"

"Yes, I can accept that, but the odd thing about Sam is that I also feel weary. On guard and feel the need to protect myself, I can't explain that either. It's like she's two different women. I feel I know one and the other I don't know anything about. She broke into my house while I was in Borneo."

"What? No? She didn't?"

"She did, but anyway. I haven't told you about the painting yet, or the journal. If you think that other stuff is strange, wait till you hear this." That painting, the picture you saw on my laptop of the archway across the street."

"That's what this is all about? You're saying this is all connected?"

"Yes, more so than you can imagine. Stay with me Deb don't start thinking I'm crazy, we've come too far to turn back now. Something very frightening happened today; I'm sure you're unaware of it, but something terrible happened when I was under the arch."

Deb considered her thoughts. Important pieces were still missing. "Tell me about the painting."

Travis had to quickly reshuffle his thoughts. "It was when we were at the birthday dinner. I was seated next to Sam; she had a picture on her phone, and she showed it to me—the arch. At first I saw the picture, just the picture but then something appeared within the picture. It felt like Sam's eyes were looking at me, only it wasn't Sam it was Anne and I felt this incredible attraction drawing me towards her. Sam told me that when she looked at the painting, which she owns by the way. It was hanging on her bedroom wall. She saw my eyes in the picture looking out at her, drawing her into the actual painting. Explain that; I can't? And the journal, that's weird too. When Sam was at my house, she left her backpack in my bedroom. Well, she said the reason she broke into my house and was living there when Julie and I arrived home was that she wanted to know me better through my things? You know, be around my stuff. Live amongst it. Yes I know, I didn't quite get that either. Anyway as I said, she left the backpack in my bedroom. So, tit for tat, I thought I'd see what she had in her backpack. Not a lot really, girlie stuff and two journals. One in current use and an old one. Pre-teen years and I read through it. You can't begin to imagine my surprise when I came across an entry she had written back when she was eleven. In her own handwriting she had written Anne, my name is Anne!"

"That's fucked up Travis. Are you sure? Did it look authentic? I mean, did you compare the handwriting with other entries?"

"Yep. Matched perfectly."

"It's impossible."

"I would agree with you if I hadn't seen it myself. Take that and add the weird effect of the old painting. Mix them together with the visual and physical and there's no logical explanation. That's why I researched the Déjà vu theory, precognitions—just trying to find answers. Come up with a reason which might make sense of everything.

"And did you find an answer?"

"No Deb. It's part of why I took the opportunity to fly over here. You said you thought you knew where the arch was located and I need answers."

"So, what happened inside the arch?"

"Death happened."

The instant change in Deb's expression, from curious to.... To what? Travis struggled to define description. Terror maybe? No, fear, foreboding, a memory?

"I'm sorry Deb." Even in his moment of realization of the words he'd spoken, 'death happened.' His conscious thought wrestled with his sudden awareness of what he had experienced. Travis felt conflicted and somewhat unable to define this thought, its conclusion or how it had manifested itself. It was more a sense of something, instinctual perhaps, which he seemed to know but lacked the linkage to put it all together.

Deb still looked shaken and confused; hurt, in an agonizing moment of recognizing her interpretation and understanding of the words and her familiarity with such an event.

"Come on Deb. Let's get out of here." Travis got out of his seat and gently took hold of her arm. "I've seen enough." Even as he said it he knew it wasn't true, but his concern for her overrode his need for a better understanding of his confusion. "Why don't we find something else to do."

It took Deb a while to come around and relinquish her thought toward the recollected memory of what 'death happened' had given a vivid reflection to and then refocus. Still somewhat unsettled by the event in her bedroom when the picture fell off the wall, and now this stark reference had been unnerving. But willing it aside, by the time they reached her car Deb had decided for her at least, the past must remain where it belonged and with conscious effort, determined this day would produce a good memory.

"Okay Sage, get in I'm taking you to a medieval castle. Possibly the best in all of England."

For Deb the conversation was nowhere near over, merely paused. Suspect to further investigation and inquiry. The look she had witnessed on his face, the strange feeling she had surmised, and the forceful need to rescue him from imminent danger lingered. Yes, she had questions, but her concern lay more in the possible answers and potential outcome of this inexplicable circumstance. It was a bridge that at this time she felt neither she nor Travis was equipped to cross over and instinctually, she sensed fear and the need to put distance between this place and themselves.

Chapter 29

To have openly acknowledged her deepest feelings, if only to herself didn't erase the seemingly insurmountable reality of the facts. The conclusion of which besieged Julie's emotions with justifiable doubts. She had no idea where he was, how he felt or what he might be thinking. And although she ventured to guess that Travis might have some idea where Mac was, there was no reason to believe he would share his thoughts and feelings with her brother. Her thoughts were in a quandary, and she was afforded little comfort and no contentment in her desire to seek reassurance that her love would not go unrequented. (unrequited*)

But being alone in a house gave no justification for losing it and having an emotional outburst. What would be the point? With no one to witness the event it would be an exercise in futility. At least for now, Julie concluded. But she was keeping her options open.

The logical approach would appear to be to contact him. The illogical aspect seemed to be the simplicity of words. What would she say and how much worse would she feel if he didn't respond? The anxiety of her dilemma had placed her on the verge of tears and yet angry for being so indecisive with momentary relief found only in the photographs on Travis's laptop, and her passionate memories of a night beneath an Asian moon.

******

Having paid the taxi driver Sam stood and looked at the house where several days ago Travis had entered behind the woman who met him at the airport. It was late afternoon; the temperature was cooling rapidly and Sam now stranded could only hope for two things. One, to discover Travis was okay and two, he would not get too angry at her arrival. The fact of which, with regards to the latter, he had every right to be and probably would be once he inquired as to how she knew where to find him but, as she quickly learned no one was home. The pending surprise, inquiry, trial, and verdict were suspended leaving her with no place to go and no means of getting there.

******

It was an impassioned kiss full of affection shared between two people who had known each other intimately. The years of separation and pain vanished within the unspoken message of forgiveness and being forgiven. For Mac, it was a moment he could never have imagined and yet so badly needed to heal. For Maggie, the heavy weight of guilt released her from its grip. "I love ya Mac, I always have."

"I know Maggie." Looking deeply into her eyes he had always known always felt a strong connection. Stepping back a little more he gathered his thoughts he was so thankful for this moment. "I have to leave?"

"I know ya do Mac."

"Maggie I'm grateful for having these couple of days with ya."

"Mac you're welcome here anytime don't forget that." Whatever Mac was about, he was still the most amazing man she had always known him to be. Her heart ached as he climbed into his vehicle; somehow wishing he would change his mind and stay even if only for just one night. One night to feel his passion and experience him once more. Unbearably holding back tears she stood and watched as the Land Rover backed out of her driveway and moments later he was gone.

He'd sensed the danger felt the urge and knew what he had to do. There was love in his heart, a passion he knew well but it was a yesterday feeling. One which used to fill all his tomorrows and every day in between. It had been difficult to drive away although he knew it was the better thing to do. If he could wish for something and make it come true, he'd wish that no more hardship befall Maggie and one day perhaps Becca would have a daddy and Maggie would feel loved too. He sighed at the thought of where he was, in his vehicle and where he could have remained. The contrast was black and white with no gray area in between and had the situation been different......? No, he didn't need to go there. If the situation had been different and he had never met Julie, he would have had no reason to be back in Australia. Meeting Julie had been the key and no matter what else the future held in store, his love for her had influenced his reunion with Maggie. It was a good feeling—a sense of putting things to rights, changing the outcome, and moving forward. But there will be no more moving forward tonight. 'Big Red' and many of his relatives would be out on the roads and having no desire to make their acquaintance Mac pulled up and parked outside Digger's and went inside.

******

After spending the better part of the afternoon at Warwick Castle, Travis and Deb decided to have dinner while they were out and about. It turned out to be a wonderful day, especially for Travis as he excitedly explored the castle. Deb found her joy in just watching him have fun. It was a one-hundred-and-eighty-degree turnaround in comparison to the experience in Atherstone. He seemed delighted with the reality of something which, up until this time had been an imaginary concept. Knights doing battle, protecting the castle from all invaders. Deb smiled as Travis led the way, they climbed the stone stairways, walked the ramparts, and looked at the weaponry and suits of armor. He had behaved like a young boy who discovered Disney World for the first time.

******

Out of frustration and with few choices available to her, Julie determined to compose a platonic message to Mac. It was a difficult task the weight of which held everything in the balance. In its simplest form the question was simple, he loves me, he loves me not and he will either respond or he will not. The 'not' posed unrest and complicated her choice of words; the right words, words that might convey connection and yet provide her with a protective shield.

******

"Sam?"

It hadn't taken many seconds to figure that out. Even so for Travis, it seemed an illogical conclusion. It was impossible and yet, unless his eyes were playing tricks on him the only other rational conclusion was that it was her. "What the fuck? Sam?"

Deb looked on as Travis moved towards the person sitting on her doorstep illuminated only by the light issued from the streetlamp. She looked like a vagrant or would have, had it not been for the expensive look of her luggage and hearing Travis call out her name, Deb immediately became concerned as she too moved closer.

Sam was cold, tired, and hungry, and having sat curled up on a doorstep for so long trying to keep warm, she found it difficult to stand up. Affording her a moment to sense her relief that Travis was okay but that moment passed quickly, and in hoping to make eye contact she was foiled. His eyes were in deep shadow, and as if by instinct he diverted his gaze. It was an unnecessary act of which he was unaware. Yet to reveal itself a truth lay deep within him, denied and silent.

Chapter 30

"I've got to be honest with you Sam, I don't trust you." He was sitting across the room from her wearing his mirror-finish Ray-ban sunglasses. Deb looked on, trying to make sense of Sam's story. Julie had been correct; Sam was beautiful and Deb guessed she must be about ten years younger than she was. It was hard for her to imagine this young woman had stalked them all the way from the airport to her house, never mind the fact of having flown all the way from the states in pursuit of Travis.

"I don't blame you Travis if you consider everything I've done. I'm sorry and honestly I was about to call the airline to change my flight and go home this morning."

"So why didn't you?"

"My hand, something happened to my hand. This morning, almost like it had been frozen I couldn't move. I'm not sure for how long, a minute, an hour, but when it passed, I felt something terrible had happened to you."

Travis and Deb looked at each other, but Deb spoke next.

"What time this morning?"

Her question was directed toward Sam. It was the first time she had interrupted their conversation and it had taken Sam by surprise. She had to pause for a moment and think.

"I guess it was after ten, ten-twenty maybe?"

The shock was evident in Deb's expression. That was around the same time Travis was under the arch.

******

Mac stirred and with the way his head felt, he wished to God he hadn't. Peering through mere slits because his eyelids refused to open wider he took stock of where he was. How he ended up in the cargo area of his Land Rover, still parked outside Digger's lacked necessary explanation because the why he'd ended up there was painfully obvious, but the urgent call of nature took precedence. He was in desperate need to take a leak.

Thirty minutes later he ambled into Molly's or was that stumbled into Molly's.

"Mackenzie Adams, what the hell as happened to ya?"

The startled expression on Molly's face clearly indicated he didn't look his best. Mac sure as hell didn't feel his best either and the volume of her voice seemed to resonate violently between his ears. Meekly Mac slid into a booth as Molly approached with a mug of hot coffee in hand.

"Morning Molly."

"If ya feel as bad as ya look son, I'd say death would be a blessing. What the hell have ya done to yourself?"

That in itself, seemed to be a very good question but the necessary brain function appeared unable to tackle it, at least in the current state of his condition and feeling fragile he could only hope Molly would lose interest and leave him alone.

"Mac?" Her sympathetic expression matched the softening of her tone as she slid onto the bench seat across from him.

"Ya didn't get into a fight with Maggie, did ya?"

He offered a somewhat halted half-smile and lazily shook his head to indicate he hadn't, but the thought of, if he had stayed with her last night the wrestling action in bed would have seen him with a broad smile on his face this morning. A comparison that offered humiliation for the choice he'd made.

"No Molly, just the opposite. We still love each other but it's not what I came here for."

Molly placed her hand over Mac's. Her concern searched his face for clues; more insight and a better understanding but somehow, she sensed she already knew there was no happy ever after to this story.

******

Deb shivered, feeling the sense of a cold presence in the room and it spooked her.

"Christine?"

Jumping out of her seat in horror, Deb glared at Sam in disbelief, unable to comprehend why Sam said that, or how she could possibly even know. Travis was only a split second behind her in realizing what just happened, and in knowing what that name meant to her.

"Sam!" Travis said forcefully, while pulling Deb into his arms to shield and protect her from.......... God knows what? "Sam...... What......Why......Where? How do you know...... Why did you say that name?"

Sam sat in utter confusion trying to understand what had just happened. What changed?

"Honestly Travis, I don't know." She felt frightened by the look of fear on Deb's face and almost terrified by the 'ready to defend until death' posture Travis had quickly established.

"What just happened?" Sam cried out incredulously in need of explanation.

Travis drew Deb's eyes toward his by gently placing his hand on her chin. "Deb, it's okay." It wasn't okay and he knew it. For starters his Ray-ban sunglasses were in the way and after that, how could he even begin to think anything was okay. He removed his glasses but remained focused on Deb.

"Sam.... Just stay where you are. I need to make sure Deb is alright."

Travis led Deb into her bedroom with a protective arm around her shoulders but almost immediately after crossing the threshold, Deb spun around. "No Travis, I need to know." Then with determination she returned to the living room and squared off in front of Sam.

"Why did you say Christine's name? What do you know about her? How do you know about her?"

Sam sat bewildered, threatened by Deb's close proximity and the demanding tone in her voice.

She tried to think quickly but nothing came to mind. "I don't know. The name just came into my thoughts. I can't think why I said it. It holds no relevance to me. I'm sorry, really I am."

Even with the intense emotional overload pulsating at high speed through her mind Deb knew she was telling the truth. Unfortunately it didn't explain anything or ease the pain she was experiencing in her chest, or her compulsion in that next moment to break down and cry. Instinctively Sam stood, wrapped Deb in her arms and held her close.

******

The clear blue sky and the warm touch of sunlight on her face greeted Julie as she stepped out into a new morning. The fragrance of magnolia mingled with the gulf breeze intoxicatingly invigorated her sense of smell and mesmerized her thoughts as to how paradise should be imagined. It was a beautiful morning; she was in love, and she planned to go shopping. Travis would arrive home in a few days, and just as importantly he would bring Deb with him. She missed her brother almost as much as she looked forward to spending more time with Deb. It was hard to put into words, but she sensed Deb had so much more to teach her about the woman she had always been but had somehow failed to understand for reasons unknown to her. And although her wetsuit hung quietly in the guest bedroom closet she intended to get it wet again soon. It was a beautiful day and fifty miles away, the Tanger Outlet Mall in Foley Alabama stood waiting for her arrival.

The Gulf Beach Highway via Warrington carried her through Navy Point, Perdido Key, across the state line, and on through

Orange Beach. Mile after mile of pure white sun-kissed sandy beach lay to her left, caressed by the aqua-blue waters from the Gulf of Mexico. Julie felt contrite now to think she had chastised her brother for preferring to live so close to the coast. Nashville is a memory fading fast as her thoughts about the future are pleasantly inspired by the natural serenity of this seascape. With Jimmy Buffett songs on the radio, a cheeseburger in paradise seemed to be quite within her reach. Yes she thought, it's a beautiful day.

Her response from Mac had arrived fast and greeted her before breakfast. He loves me, he loves me not. He loves me, yes. *'Julie, I love you. Mac.'* It's a beautiful morning. *He's in Australia, he sure gets around.* Half a world away and yet Julie can feel his presence. It's a beautiful day.

******

Eventually things appeared to calm down, even so Travis remained suspicious of Sam. Not once had he felt the need to chase after her, track her down or stalk her. Break into her home, live among her possessions, or get on a plane and follow her to another continent. There was something wrong with all that and now this, uttering Christine's name out of nowhere? It didn't make sense, and the more he thought about it the more on edge it made him. Then just to complicate her seemingly obsessive behavior, how he thought, could he explain the entry in her journal—the perceived vision in the painting, and his experience beneath the arch. And if that wasn't enough, he was still struggling to understand this touch of the hand, the eye-to-eye transmission of thoughts and the terrifying premonition. For a man who thought he had a fairly tight grip on his life, in these things he was floundering. Adrift and alone with no knowledge of what would happen one minute to the next, and it all revolved around Sam, Anne, or both of them. And now Deb and

Sam were sitting together in conversation and he, as if excluded, sat in the armchair watching them with no role to play.

Chapter 31

Deb woke early and looked at Travis who still lay sleeping beside her. The evening had not ended well. Travis wanted Sam to leave and offered to help her find somewhere to stay for the night. Deb had insisted that Sam stay and noted the troubled expression on Travis's face when he finally succumbed to her wish, and she had felt the tension of his dissatisfaction as they prepared to get into bed. She found this whole situation troubling, overwhelming in fact and despite her reluctance to admit it, she too was now involved. The very mention of Christine's name had unleashed unresolved memories, heartache, and questions that had undulated silently beneath the surface of her thoughts and added to the sensation of feeling Christine's presence. It challenged Deb's ability to reason with any sort of certainty as to exactly what was happening.

Easing her way out of bed and trying not to disturb Travis, Deb felt inclined to wake Sam up and talk to her although the impulse stirring her motivation was unclear. The desire to wake Sam almost seems imperative and necessary and having quietly closed her bedroom door behind her, she hesitated to listen before opening the guest bedroom door.

Gently rousing Sam from sleep, Deb smiled to offer reassurance before holding her finger in front of her lips to indicate their need to be quiet. Sam smiled and immediately drew her arms from beneath the bedcovers invitingly toward Deb for a hug. Without thought, Deb accepted the invitation and only while held in each other's embrace did she stop to think, but it didn't feel strange. But strange or not, she could not allow it to continue and she could not contemplate the validity of her involuntary action because Travis was asleep in the next room. The quelling of emotions that stirred in an instant required expedient division without alarm. Deb brought the hug to a conclusion and gently drew back. Sam blushed and softly said, "I don't know why I did that, I just felt so happy to see you as if, I'm not sure, like I hadn't seen you in a long time and...."

"It's okay," Deb whispered, still trying to dispel her own emotional reaction. "I want to talk with you and get your thoughts on what it is you and Travis have experienced. I just don't understand and I need answers."

Following Deb's lead, Sam got out of bed and tailed her into the kitchen where Deb made coffee before they moved into the living room and sat on the couch.

Searching Sam's eyes Deb pondered where to begin.

"Sam, you and Travis met for the first time at a party and something happened. But before that, did you ever experience any strange feelings like the ones you've had since meeting him?"

"No, Deb. Never. I was just a normal person living a normal life. I recently graduated college and was looking forward to getting on with the rest of my life and wham, Travis came out of nowhere and nothing has been the same ever since. It's been crazy, I've done some stupid things, and it wasn't until yesterday that I decided to stop everything and go home. I don't want this to keep going on. Travis obviously doesn't love me, which hurts, but I want my life back. Then this thing happened again yesterday morning and threw me right back into it. I had to find out if he was okay. I couldn't just get on a plane and fly home not knowing but how many times will this keep happening, and what am I supposed to do when it does?"

"You mean when you felt something in your hand. It's happened before?"

"Yes, but last time it was my shoulder, my arm, and then my head. When he got hurt in the water."

"I don't understand?"

"I felt the pain when Travis was in trouble. Really, it was excruciating. I was at his house in Pensacola. He was somewhere in Asia, diving. He was in the water. I couldn't breathe."

Deb was stunned and almost certain that Sam was unaware she had been with Travis when the accident happened. "How is that even possible, Sam?"

"How is any of this possible, Deb? I don't know. I just thought our love for each other was so strong that somehow we shared a telepathic connection. I've heard of that happening, like when identical twins know when something happens to one of them, but this is different."

"What do you mean, different?"

"I've felt Travis inside me, and I feel like I've been inside him. We've talked about it. It was the most powerful thing I've ever experienced. I know him as well as I know myself, or I thought I did but he rejects me, and I can't understand why. It feels like love, but it's filled with hurt, or at least I keep getting hurt."

Deb saw the expressions on Sam's face and felt sympathy, knowing Sam was desperately holding back tears. Trying to be strong. It was a feeling she recognized and had felt at times when she and Christine were in contention with each other. It does hurt, but why does Travis seem immune to its impact? Her only conclusion was that he was not in love with Sam. But that didn't answer why they seem to share a vulnerability towards each other. Although, it did explain why Travis didn't want to be around Sam. Even so, that was only one facet, one possible conclusion, and Deb was still confused. "Sam, tell me about the painting."

It was only at that moment Sam realized Deb and Travis had talked about her. The sensation of having been stripped naked and laid bare, her thoughts and feelings gave cause for concern and constituted her imperative need to cover and protect herself. The thought passed quickly and was replaced with the feeling of wanting Deb to see her and, strangely, so much more. It was an unusual feeling and yet enticing and warmly welcomed. Her breath caught at the very thought of it, and she didn't know what to do.

Travis appeared in the doorway, holding a cup of coffee in his hand.

Chapter 32

Julie's trip had been successful and having found the beach attire she deemed appealing, she decided to sample a cheeseburger in paradise along with fries and a drink. It had been, in her mind, a wonderful day, and it continued to be until she saw Steve's vehicle parked in Travis's driveway. The sight of it felt threatening and it defiled her mood. Then, watching Steve open the driver-side door and step out of his vehicle as she pulled in added to her displeasure.

"Steve, what are you doing here?" Even as she said the words immediately after getting out of her car, she felt their redundancy. She knew there was only one reason he would drive all the way from Nashville and her resolve was unmoved. He had violated and humiliated her for far too long, even though the violation and humiliation lacked physical touch; it had insulted her emotional self-worth.

"Julie, I came to say I'm sorry. I know that may not sound like much, and I don't expect you to forgive me. I was wrong to do what I did and hurt you in the process. You didn't deserve that, but as a consequence, this is where we find ourselves, and we need to talk about it."

It felt like a slap across her face. His remorse was limited. He had not come to beg her forgiveness but merely to tie up all the loose ends. Angered by this continued humiliation Julie reached out and slapped his face hard. She wanted him to feel what she felt, even in the ineffectual satisfaction of her scorn.

"Steve, I feel sorry for you, you son-of-a-bitch. You are not the man I married, he was worthy of my love, and I respected him. Whoever you are now, you're not that man."

Steve was shocked by the force of her hand, and his visible expression acknowledged it, as did the strong impact of her words.

He could not have anticipated this strength; he was not accustomed to it and stepped back.

Julie stepped forward unafraid with the desire to slap him again but restrained herself, concluding he was not worth it and the fact that her hand still stung from the first encounter with his face.

"I suggest you get an attorney and if you try to cheat me again, I'll see you in court."

Her determination was to see him leave and never come back. She was afraid of the image she portrayed, never before having experienced it. It was powerful, invigorating, and resolute. Julie was uncompromising and steadfast in her belief of who she had become.

Steve backed away several paces before turning. Then, he silently got into his vehicle, closed the door, and drove out of the driveway.

Julie stood motionless; no clear, concise thought came to the front of her mind. In her victory, she had lost everything, but none of it was worth having, and in that, she was free.

******

Travis absorbed the scene with interest. Deb and Sam were sitting on the couch. Apparently, he had intruded in on their conversation and judging by the embarrassed look on Sam's face; the conversation was probably about him. And although Deb's smile looked warm he remained skeptical as to the value of it. The mere presence of Sam posed a threat. He couldn't explain it; it was just something he felt and at that moment, he was reluctant to invest any more time trying to sort everything out. Not only did he feel at odds with Deb and the decision she'd made last night, he felt at odds with himself. Something had changed and he wasn't quite sure what it was.

"Travis, you're not wearing sunglasses?"

Sam heard herself say the words with instant regret. He glanced at her to acknowledge her voice, then quickly looked away. '*Why,*'

Sam thought, had she forewarned him when her deepest desire was to look into his eyes and experience their connection.

"Travis, please look at me," Sam asked pleadingly, but he would not.

"Sam, this isn't what you think it is. Trust me, get on a plane, go home, and forget we ever met."

Even Deb felt the cold detachment of his statement and was surprised by the uncaring sound of it.

"Travis, that was harsh. Sam loves you, and no matter your feelings for her, you could be a little bit kinder."

"Deb, I'm not trying to be unkind and I do care, I'm trying to protect her. She needs to go home, it's safer there."

"What do you mean Travis? What exactly do you think you will be protecting me from?" Sam asked out of frustration. "The only person who is hurting me is you. Do I need protection from you?"

Travis chose not to answer.

Deb got off the couch walked over to Travis and kissed him. Unfortunately, he was not quite as responsive as she'd hoped.

"Travis, something is wrong, come and sit down, let's talk this out."

He allowed Deb to take him by the hand and reluctantly he followed her to the couch where he sat in the middle with Sam on one side and Deb on the other. It was the safest place for him to be, he had thought about this, thought about what happened beneath the arch. Thought about all the amazing emotions he'd exchanged with Sam. Thought about the deep feelings of love he held toward Deb, and the premonition he was in sole possession of. Affectionately he took hold of Sam's hand.

"Sam," he said in a quiet voice, "Yesterday when you sensed something was wrong. What did you feel?"

"My hand was cold, like ice."

"No, Sam, what did you feel in your mind?"

Sam knew what he was asking, but at that moment she was trying to discover why nothing happened when he took hold of her hand. Why didn't she feel the connection?

"Travis, I can't feel you; what's happened? What's wrong?"

"Please, just answer my question Sam; what did you feel in your mind?"

Hesitantly, Sam answered. "I don't know exactly how to describe it, cold, lifeless, empty. I remember thinking it was the force of death but I've never experienced that, so I'm guessing."

Keeping hold of Sam's hand in his left hand, he took hold of Deb's hand in his right.

"Deb, what happened beneath the arch?"

Deb replayed the sequence of events in her mind unwillingly, but she sensed her answer was important.

"I felt a sense of losing you, you were there, but you weren't. You were somewhere else, and in your emotionless expression, I thought you were dead or close to it."

"And, so you slugged me, right?"

"It was all I could think to do to save you. Wait, how did you know?"

"Do you mean apart from my jaw being sore? I remember you telling me what Christine had to do to make you realize what needed to be done."

Deb's eyes filled with tears. Travis leaned in and kissed her.

"I love you Deb and thank you. You probably did save me, and I'm trying to save Sam."

Turning his head to face Sam, he said, "Sam look into my eyes."

She did, and nothing happened. "I don't understand.'" She too, had tears in her eyes now. Something lost, something of great value to her was missing. She turned away to hide her face.

"Sam, look at me." She did as he asked. "It's still there Sam. I'm blocking it because I don't want you to see what I've seen or feel its pain but trust me, it's still there. Although you need to realize as I have, it's not what we thought it might have been."

Chapter 33

Mac and Julie pledged their love toward each other in a flurry of almost cryptic emails blazing across the internet. It was an exhausting pace to keep up with and then her phone rang.

"Julie?"

"Mac?"

They began their conversation filled with emotional relief, overwhelming joy, and a sense of togetherness. The depth of which had them breathless at times for something they had discovered within the confines of their hearts. They took turns explaining where they each were and more importantly, why they were there. And when the question arose, Mac explained why he had withdrawn from making love to her on the boat, and she loved him even more for his integrity in demonstrating his honor toward her.

"Julie, how would ya feel about flying down to Australia?"

It was a question that only had one answer and in giving it, she felt her excitement rise to a level she had never experienced before.

******

"I want you to fly home, Sam. Deb and I will take you to the train station. Call the airline and reschedule your flights."

Sam wanted to put up a fight, but there wasn't much fight left in her and the sincerity in Travis's opinion seemed to make sense even in the face of so many unanswered questions.

"One thing Travis, that's all I ask." She still could not believe being able to look into his eyes and not feeling the connection she once had, it was heartbreaking. "Will you take me to see the arch?"

"No, I'm sorry Sam. That's the last place on earth I want you to visit."

Deb had watched and listened quietly. The circumstance of so many things remained unresolved; she knew Travis, and if this dilemma held such grave possibility she would follow his lead, he was not a reckless man.

"Okay," Deb announced while rising to her feet. "I'm going to get showered. Travis: you come in in about ten minutes and we'll get you taken care of. Sam, you call the airline to see what you can arrange, then while you shower, I'll prepare breakfast."

"I'll make a fresh pot of coffee while I'm waiting," Travis stated as he rose from the couch and made his way into the kitchen.

Sam quietly walked to the guest bedroom to retrieve her phone and flight information. On her return, she stopped in the kitchen and touched Travis's arm lightly.

"Will I ever see you again?"

The lost look in her eyes and the sad tone in her voice moved him to take her in his arms and hold her close.

"I'm not sure Sam. Besides, if you're going off into the Mexican jungle to dig up old relics and artifacts, I don't think there'd be much need for an oceanographer to come calling, do you?"

She knew he was joking, but it had a serious side to it as well. Sam kissed his cheek and went towards the living room. Travis finished up what he was doing and then went into the bedroom.

Travis had reached a point where he could bathe himself. All Deb had to do, was help him secure a plastic covering over his cast. That done, she set about drying her hair. The thoughts mulling around inside her head presented many different avenues to explore in search of answers and combined, were just a muddled mess. The one that appeared to need her immediate attention was Sam. Why she had spoken Christine's name was just the tip of the iceberg, and considering she would be leaving soon was probably a question that would remain unanswered. But the affectionate hug this morning if Deb was honest with herself she had relished it. And the look in

Sam's eyes, moments before Travis entered the room, moved Deb to believe they were about to kiss. That bothered her in so far as she somehow craved the experience, and now it would never happen. What was it about Sam that she found herself drawn toward? How, having acknowledged her strong feelings toward Travis could she begin to entertain the idea of feeling affection for someone else. It wasn't right and thankfully the kiss had not taken place, but if Travis had been a few moments later? That was a scary thought. She turned the hairdryer off.

"Hey Deb, I'm sorry about last night, I'm sure you thought I was being a dick. Fact is, I probably was a dick and I apologize."

Deb smiled, then pulled the shower curtain back. "Speaking of dicks?" She removed the towel from around her body allowing it to fall to the floor and climbed into the shower with Travis.

******

"Honestly Sam, it might take me a while not to expect to find you wherever I go, but through it all you've meant no harm. You're a beautiful young woman. A bit crazy sometimes, maybe, but crazy in a good way and you'll be hard to forget. I could say you've made a lasting impression, so come here and give me a hug."

Sam and Deb had said their goodbyes. The train was waiting at the platform and it was time for Sam to get on board. With the hug came a parting kiss. "I love you Travis, don't forget that, please and don't forget me." She turned away and boarded the train. With her flight schedule changed she would be flying home tonight.

"Well Deb, you can't say we lead a boring life and just think in two more days we'll be heading to the airport ourselves. Do we have any time to sleep planned into our schedule?"

"Not getting knackered on me are you Sage?"

"I have no idea what that means. Do I want to know?"

Deb smiled. "How about I take you to Coventry?"

"Does it have a castle?"

Chapter 34

Taking the elevator to the top floor of the Adams Tower building, Mac, dressed in a tailored three-piece suit made his way to the executive suite moving past four secretarial stations and several offices as he went.

"Mr. Adams?" The inquiry came from a female secretary.

Mac turned in her direction. She looked familiar but he lacked her name, so he smiled.

"Mackenzie Adams?"

Mac smiled again and nodded.

"I can't believe my eyes. Sir, is it really you?"

Mac felt stupid as he nodded in the affirmative once more.

"I'm sorry Sir, I'm Lindsey Summers. I was you're temporary secretary for about four months. That must have been what, seven years ago, at least."

"Lindsey, it's good to see ya. How have ya been?"

"Well, Sir: and if I might say, ya looking pretty good ya self. Welcome back." She smiled from ear to ear before turning away.

Mac's eyes followed her for a few moments. He was amazed. Judging by how she looks now, she couldn't have been more than a kid seven years ago. There are child labor laws against that sort of thing, so it caused him to wonder.

Entering the executive suite, he greeted his father. "Hey, dad."

"Mackenzie son, you've cleaned up real nice. I thought ya weren't going to start back until next week?"

"Just thought I'd do a look-around dad. Ya don't mind, do ya?"

"Mind, Mac, no, of course not; I'm glad to see ya son, have a seat. Take a load off."

Seven years ago this was Mac's office and starting next week it will become his office once more. His dad had never been the type of man who was content to sit behind a desk, but with Mac taking himself out of the picture, his father had felt obligated to spend at least three days a week in the building and, as he put it, it was killing him. And, as Mac had yet to mention, he had no intention of spending the rest of his life behind a desk either. But that was a discussion he could hold over for a later date. Right now, he had to re-establish himself as the head of the Adams Corporation and oversee all its subsidiary companies and holdings.

It had been one hell-of-a homecoming. Mac's parents must have invited everybody who's anybody in Brisbane and when there's free booze, it looked like nobody had passed up the invitation. It had been a humdinger of a do, with many bloodshot eyes the next day to prove it, and necessitated Mac beating a retreat down to the family beach house along the Gold Coast for a few days. But things were settling down now and for Mac, that meant the business came first and it surprised him how easily he readapted himself to his old style.

"Here Mac." His dad slid a set of keys across the desk toward him; Mac picked them up and looked at them, then at his father. "Don't recognize them, son? They're the keys to your place. I kept the staff on payroll, so it should be just the way ya left it."

Mac didn't know what to say except, "thanks dad." But his feelings ran much deeper in thinking his dad had hung onto the only connections he had with his son, his possessions.

"I had to let ya Land Rover go through; it wasn't doing it any good just sitting there idle."

"Dad, I'm sorry; I should've come and talked with ya. I love ya dad."

"It was a bad time son, neither of ya was thinking straight. How's Maggie doing?"

"She's doing dad, that's about it. It's a damn shame though; we both know how good she was in the business. Ran circles around most of them, now she's waiting tables over at Molly's grub hut and she as her kid Becca to look after."

"Any chance ya can patch things up? I know that might be asking a lot son, but ya mother and me, we always loved Maggie, ya know that."

"Yes, dad, I know. If you'd told me eight years ago, I'd be sitting here now without her, I'd a laughed at ya. But to answer ya question, we've patched things up as much as we're going to, I still have feelings for her and she loves me, but I have someone else in my life."

"And when do ya plan on telling ya mother and me about this woman, son?"

"I don't, dad. I'm making arrangements for her to come and visit with ya and she can tell ya all about herself. But in the meantime, I guess I better go get me a new Land Rover; I can't have my lady walking everywhere can I."

******

"Travis, I'm curious about something; hell that's not the truth, I'm curious about a lot of things, but considering what you and Sam have told me, I don't understand how you blocked Sam from seeing in through your eyes. I mean, wasn't it an involuntary thing that neither of you had any control over?"

"Yes, Deb, you're right; at least that's the way we each perceived it. But I read a lot of books on precognition and similar subject matter, and I guess at the time of reading, I failed to understand some things. For example, somewhere in one of the books it suggested there are ways of blocking insight into yourself. I have no idea why I suddenly thought about that or how I remembered it. So, I had to prevent Sam from gaining access to my mind."

"So, how is it done? How did you do it?"

"It was hard Deb; I had no idea going in if it would even work, that's why I took hold of Sam's hand first. Hands are classed as secondary portals, whereas the eyes are primary and apparently, it makes a difference unless someone uses a pure telepathic transmission. But it has to do with brain rhythm. Our brain rhythm is too fast to be receptive in our normal everyday lives. But if you slow the brain rhythm down, it becomes a channel through which you can send and or receive information. And relaxation and meditation do slow the brain rhythm down, which makes sense to me. So, I guess when Sam and I met at the party, we were both in a relaxed state and able to communicate without conversation. But you asked, how was I able to block her access to my thoughts and feelings, right?"

"Yes."

"I had to stress myself out."

"No, that sounds too easy?"

"Deb, have you ever tried to stress yourself out intentionally? I didn't find it easy at all. I know it's easy to get stressed out over things that seem out of our control. But really, Deb, try stressing yourself out when you're in control. It's not as easy as you might think."

"So, what did you do to stress yourself out?"

"I started by getting into a disagreement with you over Sam staying the night."

"What?"

"Yes. Then I carried it into the bedroom by keeping myself agitated."

"You wanker."

"Then, when I woke up this morning, you weren't in bed and I imagined you and Sam hugging and kissing each other. So I was primed when I got to the living room, stressed out to the max."

Deb was quiet for several minutes, and then.... "I'm going to tell you something Sage, and you'd better listen. I have never loved a man as much as I love you, and yes I loved my dad, and I love Wicket. But you are the only man I have loved who I've given myself to completely, but you knew that. And I will forgive you for what you did last night because I understand the reason for it, but don't push your luck again. Now one other thing you need to know, is that kissing and hugging almost happened, but I question now if it was something Sam or I instigated or maybe, it was telepathically channeled by you. We did hug once and I had reason to suspect we were about to kiss, right before you appeared in the living room. So Sage, fair warning, be careful what you wish for.

Chapter 35

How could he tell someone he loved; that someone they loved, had tried to kill them when that someone was now dead? Travis wrestled with the complications of a ghost who, in life loved, and in near-death, wished them harm. The restless spirit is troubled, in limbo and unwilling to crossover. The premonition of which is infinite, without remorse and unyielding, and he is now Deb's only defense. The circumstance had revealed itself and relayed the images and truth through a powerful emersion of insight as he stood, caught, and transfixed beneath the arch.

Christine did not want to die alone. He felt the emotional agony of her final moments as the images and her thoughts played through his mind and he realized the hard punch she had delivered to Deb's jaw was not meant to save her but seal their fate. The perception of which is now clear, she is a possessive and jealous spirit; as she was in life, she is in death and yet in Deb's mind she has been immortalized as a saint.

Travis had picked up the picture that fell off the wall to examine the photograph depicting them as a couple. He saw the affection in Deb's expression and as if a new piece of the puzzle had just fallen into place, he met Anne for the very first time. The lips can smile and deceive, but the eyes tell the truth. In looking at the image of Christine he had found Anne. How Sam played into all this he still wasn't sure, and he was going with the idea she was just a messenger. A susceptible mind utilized by Christine to get him to do something, but what? That part wasn't clear yet.

And in a conversation with Deb, he had learned that when Christine was young, her family had taken to calling her Chris. But during her preteen years she had objected because it sounded like a boy's name, and insisted they call her Anne. But it wasn't until Travis looked closely at the framed college diploma hanging on the guest bedroom wall that he made his subsequent discovery; her full name was Christine Anne O'Connell.

******

"Hey Deb, just curious, when did you meet Christine?"

They were driving through Coventry about to make their departure toward home.

"Hm, let me think, about five years ago, maybe five and a half. We met at a dance."

"Locally?"

"Oh, yes. In Atherstone as a matter of fact, that's where she was from. Her family has lived in that area for generations."

"And their family name is O'Connell."

"Yes. How did you know that?"

"I saw it on a diploma in the guest bedroom. Are her parents still alive?"

"Her mum is. Her dad passed away before I met her. Why, is it important?"

"I'm not sure Deb; it could be. Remember the old painting of the arch? The artist's name was O'Connell."

Deb thought about that for a moment. "Would you like to meet Mary? I'm sure she would welcome a visit. Besides, I think she'd be upset with me if I go off to the US without dropping by to see her first?"

"I'd love to, if you think it will be okay?"

"Mary will eat you up. What with your American accent and handsome features, I might have to fight with her to get you back."

"Well, okay then. I'm game."

Deb took note of Travis's big grin and smiled. "It's about fourteen miles from here. I'll give her a quick call to let her know we're on our way."

******

Mary was an elegant woman whom Travis instantly liked, and he got the distinct impression she was quite taken by him. Perhaps Deb had been right, he thought. She might have to fight to get him back. English tea to drink and the best scones he'd ever tasted, he felt deliciously spoiled, and he loved it as the conversation moved along at a leisurely pace.

"Mary, are there any artists in the O'Connell family?"

"Yes, Christine's great grandmother was a painter. Why do you ask?"

"Recently, I was given a painting. The signature is O'Connell, and I was just wondering if you could help me identify it."

"I'll try. Do you have it with you?"

"Unfortunately, I don't, but I can describe the scene if that will help."

"Let's give it a shot then. I love the way you talk; I could listen to you all day. Deb, where did you find him?"

Travis blushed. Mary's expression and close proximity felt almost intimate in a most agreeable sort of way. Deb just smiled.

"Mary, the scene is set at the Friar's Gate in town. Looking through the arch towards where the church stands. But you can't see the church in the painting and the painting appears old."

"That's odd! I remember that particular painting very well. Where did you get it from?"

"It was given to me by a friend."

"Here, in England, you mean?"

"No, actually Mary, in the States."

"That really is odd. I can't even begin to imagine how it would have made the journey to America. Interesting. But, yes, I can tell you, it was painted by Christine's great grandmother Anne O'Connell. Christine was named after her. Christine Anne

O'Connell. In fact, this may seem strange. Christine had that painting hanging in her bedroom when she was a child. I don't remember now when or why we let it go. Maybe we gave it to a charity shop. I'm not sure, but I do remember Christine loved that picture. As a girl, when she was ten or eleven years old, she would go and stand under that arch and look out in the direction where her great grandmother must have sat to paint. And strangely, Christine would always be smiling. I asked her once why she was smiling, and she told me that the lady was smiling at her. There was no one there. So I just concluded it was a childhood fantasy and never thought about it again. Travis, would you be interested in selling that painting to me?"

"I would certainly consider it Mary, but I'd prefer to check with the person who gave it to me first. But yes, if they have no objection, I'll make sure you get it. The price will be one dozen of these fantastic scones. Do we have a deal?"

Apparently, deals are not struck with a customary handshake in England; or at least in this instance it wasn't. Instead, a really close hug and a kiss on each cheek sealed the deal. Maybe it's a European thing, he thought.

"One more question Mary; I like the way you seal deals, maybe we can forge another one. Is there some way of acquiring a copy of the history of Friar's Gate and if so, would you be willing to obtain it and send it on to me?"

"I'm sure there is Travis, let me work on that for you and I'll let you know what my price is."

If the sparkle in Mary's eye was anything to go by, Travis could imagine he was going to enjoy their arrangement. He was taken with her; she was a lovely woman, Deb better put on her boxing gloves he surmised with a smile.

"Oops, one more question Mary, then I'll sit back and let you two get caught up. In front of the church there's a town square. I think that's what you'd call it. Was there a tall redbrick building there at some point in time?"

"Yes, when I was a small girl, I remember it. I think it was a parish meeting room of some sort. I believe they used to have all sorts of events and activities there. I'm so used to seeing the open square now; I'd almost forgotten that building had been there."

That answer raised a question in his mind. When he first saw into the painting, he had sensed the church and the redbrick building beyond the picture of the arch. And the demolition of that redbrick building pre-dates the birth of Christine Anne O'Connell. So, with who's eyes and memory had he been allowed to see that far back in time?

Chapter 36

Sam had lied but to her way of thinking, she had good reason not to tell the truth. And even though Travis had every right to refuse to take her to the arch, he had no right in preventing her from seeing it for herself. He would have known nothing about it if she hadn't shown him the painting, and his reasoning for not taking her to see it lacked plausible explanation. She had come too far to leave without discovering for herself what it was about the painting that so mysteriously had brought her on this journey. And what was it that had entwined her heart to beat so precisely in time with his and yet, caused the painful rejection that she was forced to endure? Her name wasn't Anne. It had been a silly childhood illusion created in the sheer fantasy of a child's imagination to add dimension to an otherwise orderly existence. Much like the names given to her childhood dolls and the realistic roles they played in her games. Sam, she thought emphatically, is Sam. Samantha, the only identity she equated with, it's who she is, and somewhat adamantly, she determined that Sam has the ability to make decisions for herself.

Her flight schedule remained unchanged. And having disembarked from the train in a place called Crewe, she had made her way to Atherstone and the room she had reserved at the Red Lion Hotel.

The urgency of Sam's thoughts seemed more convoluted than ever now, and her arrival in Atherstone promised only a partial answer to her growing list of questions. How Travis had blocked her advance to connect with him gave rise to the feeling she had been manipulated, and in some way used. It was a horrible feeling, and in many ways she felt violated as a consequence. Why he would do such a thing was just another question on her list. And Deb? She had filled Sam's dreams with passion throughout that night and then to wake and find Deb beside her bed, smiling and eager to accept her invitation to embrace. She had never felt like that before, never desired to experience love in a woman's arms, but at that moment her craving wanted to know Deb wholly and intimately. Even now with few reservations, the urge to explore that possibility resonates playfully amid her emotional need for that first kiss. The tempting thought of a sweet gentle kiss filled her mind with wonder when without warning, she sensed the powerful masculine kiss only Travis could deliver, and she was filled with jealousy at the thought that she had been denied both.

******

Driving his brand-new Land Rover, Mac pulled up to the guard station of the gated community where his house was located. It had been seven years. He didn't recognize either of the security officers on duty and needed a resident sticker for his vehicle. However, it was not a problem; his father had called ahead and the officers were very accommodating. After which, one of the officers waved his vehicle through the opened barrier, and Mac continued along the familiar road.

Reaching his private driveway, he tapped his personal code on the keypad buttons and he was somewhat surprised it still worked, and the wrought iron gates swung open. The large colonial-style house looked stately amid the tall shade trees, flowering shrubbery, and majestically manicured grounds. Mac was home and to his mind, there was only one person missing, Julie.

******

In utter confusion and tormented by her thoughts, Sam struggled to comprehend and make sense of something that made no sense at all. Then, finally, she could remember the arch, stepping forward, and in her next moment of awareness, her hand was pressed against a door.

The chaotic turmoil of her mind sensed a small vortex angrily darting about beyond the door and somehow she controlled it. Or did it control her? In a panic she gasped, pulled her hand away and stepped back from the door suddenly realizing where she was.

Her thoughts still grappled to make sense of it, struggled to find some clarity. It was beyond reason. "How?" Her spoken word appeared to linger in the air surrounding her and mingled with the unspoken thought of why. They seemed important, yet the necessary infrastructure to construct qualifying answers remained elusive, shrouded in a mysterious veil of emptiness. Sam could not comprehend what had happened, but she recognized Deb's house and had the strangest feeling that she had left something there.

More than eight hours had passed, Sam was in her hotel room and she had no idea how she got there or exactly where else she had been. Finally, consumed by fragmented thoughts and overcome with exhaustion, she collapsed on the bed and cried herself to sleep, unable to fear what she had yet to understand.

******

A sense that something was wrong struck Deb as soon as she and Travis entered her home. The visible signs were very apparent as they moved further into the dwelling. Deb's first thought was Annie had run amuck or as she quickly explained to Travis, Annie had been on a naughty adventure. Which he thought, was possible having no prior understanding of the cat's nature, but the extent of the disarray alarmed him. Two dozen cats maybe he thought, but one cat, he wasn't convinced. His sensibility of the scene they were surrounded by as they moved from room to room could not qualify Deb's initial assessment, and he felt an ominous stillness and quiet about the place which he hadn't noticed before.

"So, where is this rambunctious cat?" Travis asked while picking up a few items off the floor.

"Annie?" Deb called out as she left Travis in her bedroom and searched for her cat. He heard her call Annie several times as she moved from room to room while he continued to put things back where they belonged. Finally, Deb returned with a quizzical expression on her face, "I can't find her?" Her concern was audible in her tone so he joined her in the search, and after having looked under beds and other large furniture items, opening and closing closet doors and checking behind things, they were both at a loss as to where Annie could be.

Panicked, Deb when outside and walked around the house calling her name, which to Travis didn't make sense. If she had been left outside she couldn't have made the mess inside, but he was not about to voice that thought, and when Deb came back inside she looked visibly worried.

Holding her in his arms and trying not to amplify his thoughts of concern, he suggested that perhaps they should start cleaning up the mess and wait to see if Annie just showed up of her own volition.

The ominous feeling of stillness keenly remained in his thoughts as they went about the task of putting the house back in order. With a heightened sense of awareness, he was experiencing the feeling of being observed, watched and sized up, as if an adversary were examining him for weakness, points at which they could make their attack and successfully defeat their opponent. His sensed awareness also revealed the many items in this house that appeared to be reflective or related to Christine. And the idea that he was standing in the middle of a shrine flashed through his mind. It was an odious thought which sent a chill racing through his body. One more night he thought, we only have to get through one more night. Then added 'and find the cat.' One more night and they would be heading over to the states, which would seem to offer sanctuary to his current way of thinking.

******

As if like magic Annie suddenly appeared and announced her presence with a snarl, first at Travis, and when Deb went to pick her up she snarled again and violently clawed at Deb which took her completely by surprise. Shocked Deb drew back, unable to comprehend Annie's attack and then she looked at the lacerations on her hands and forearms as the blood began to flow.

"Oh, my God, Travis!"

Quickly Travis led Deb to the kitchen sink, turned on the faucet and guided her arms under the flow of cold water. Deb was visibly shaken.

"I can't believe that just happened," Deb stated, "she has never behaved like that before?"

Travis remained focused. His priority was to clean the wounds. "Do you have a first aid kit?"

"Yes, it's on the top shelf in the linen cupboard down the hall."

He went to retrieve it and returned to the kitchen. "Keep your arms and hands under the flow for a minute or so. Then I'll inspect the wounds." He was concerned; they looked deep. That cat meant business, but to lessen the chance of infection, he had to let the blood flow.

"I can't think what's gotten into her?" Deb said, almost as if she just needed to share her thoughts.

Travis thought it best not to share his thoughts but concerning the cat, they were not very kind.

Fifteen minutes later, with band-aids on the backs of her hands and both forearms bandaged, Deb held out her arms and laughed. "Well, this could prove quite interesting when we get in the shower."

Travis smiled, but he was still annoyed with the cat who had not shown her face again yet.

******

After eating dinner they set about packing their bags.

"Deb, do you have a pair of thick leather work gloves?"

"No, why?"

"I'm thinking ahead. Tomorrow we might need some protection to get Annie into her travel crate."

"She doesn't have a travel crate. Usually, I just sit her in a shopping bag."

"Good luck with that idea. If today's tantrum is anything to go by I'm not sure how safe we'd be, trapped inside a car with a wild cat on the loose."

"Travis, honestly, Annie has never behaved like that before. I can't think what got into her and besides, if necessary I will give her a sedative mixed in with her food first thing in the morning. Have you seen her? I haven't since she scratched me?"

"No, she's hiding somewhere, but I'll sleep a lot easier tonight if I know where she is. Preferably if she's behind a closed door, like the guest bathroom just to be safe and you're right, I can't imagine what got into her either but she attacked you, and it was vicious."

"I'm worried Travis. What if something is wrong with her? Tomorrow, I'm taking her to Jackie and Tony's house and they have two small children. I don't know what to do."

"Well, my best suggestion would be, let's see how she behaves when we find her again.

As far as Travis was concerned, the cat was only part of the issue, he still sensed unrest of some kind and realized how much of Deb's home was dominated by memorabilia depicting Christine and the life she and Deb had shared. It almost appeared to lack any personal imprint of Deb's since that time except Annie. Still, Annie might have been Christine's cat and he wasn't sure if he should ask.

Turning his thoughts completely, he thought about his sister. He was looking forward to seeing her again, hoping she was enjoying her time in Pensacola. But then he remembered her comment about the Blue Angels and hoped she hadn't had that good of a time while he'd been away. She was his sister, after all but even so, he hoped she was okay. Then he thought about Sam. She would be back home in Nashville by now. He liked her but it was better this way, and besides, she would go off to Mexico and forget all about him, which was okay too.

******

With their bags packed it was time to find Annie. Travis grabbed a bath towel just in case as the hunt prepared to begin. Deb grabbed a bag of cat treats and smiled before calling Annie and shaking the bag. Within seconds a docile bunch of fur came into the room.

"Damn, that was easy," Travis exclaimed with a sigh of relief.

Deb allowed Annie time to eat a few treats, stroked her back and then picked her up. Travis stood back and watched, unconvinced that this was the same cat.

Chapter 37

Jarred from sleep at *God only knows* what time, both Travis and Deb sat up in bed bolt straight. In unison their immediate awareness of the loud noise that had suddenly erupted violently vibrated in their ears. Without looking at each other, they threw back the bedcovers and dashed towards the epicenter in the living room. The combined noise bellowing from the television and stereo system at high volume seemed indescribably obnoxious and damaging. Deb sprang for the television remote while Travis searched for the stereo's power button. And then, silence. Its presence felt deafening immediately after the noise abated and it took several moments for their ears to adjust.

"What the hell just happened?"

Deb may have posed that as a question, but he got the distinct impression she wasn't asking him to come up with the answer. Because he concluded, how the hell would he know? But there had to be an answer somewhere, Travis felt certain of it. But were they going to find that answer now, this early in the morning when they should be asleep? He had doubts, but he checked to ensure the guest bathroom door was secure before returning to bed.

******

It was barely light outside when the construction crew or was that demolition crew started tearing into Deb's kitchen. At least that's what it sounded like with the clattering of metal and the breaking of glass violently pulling them from sleep.

"What the fuck is going on?" Deb said as she threw back the covers again.

Travis wasn't as quick this time, but he caught up with her at the entrance to the kitchen as they both stood and looked at the disarray.

Cabinet doors and drawers were open, contents strewn across the floor, it was a mess and if for no other reason than to discount it, he looked back along the hallway. And, as if they were the actors in a movie called, The Cat from Hell, Travis said his line.

"Deb, the bathroom door. It's open!"

Standing there naked Travis suddenly felt defenseless and exposed. Troubled, as he imagined where a female cat might strike first. Trapped as they were in a narrow passage with broken glass on the floor in the kitchen behind them. He could almost imagine the theme music from the movie Jaws playing in the background as the cat stalked them and cunningly brought them to this spot.

"Travis, you can't honestly tell me you think Annie has learned to turn a doorknob?"

He could still hear the theme music playing in his head as he cautiously made his way back toward the bedroom to get dressed.

Deb couldn't believe her eyes. The kitchen was a disaster. The whole night had been a disaster. No, she mentally retracted her last statement. The first part had been.... Amazing, but after that, definitely a disaster. She smiled as Travis turned back towards her bedroom, thinking 'cute bum.' And she guessed sleep time was over for both of them. Augh, she felt so tired and suddenly....... So horny!

"Travis, I hope you're not dressed yet?"

******

Getting a late start, Travis cleaned up the kitchen while Deb took Annie over to her friend's house and returned with breakfast in a bag.

Keeping his thoughts to himself, he found the events of last night inexplicable. He had no history to determine the cause but if he had to guess, considering his sensitivity and awareness of some unexplained presence it might start to make sense. Maybe, he thought, Annie was just as much a victim as he and Deb were. It would make sense if he could...... But the taxi had arrived to take them to the train station. He wished he'd thought of it before.

******

The confusion of her dreams seemed almost detached. As if they didn't belong to her, although in many ways they did appear familiar and upon waking this morning Sam felt drawn towards the arch once again. But the antipathy of her thoughts could not overpower the pressing desire she felt bound to obey and as she stood before the arch, as she had the day before, Sam was afraid of the beckoning force that compelled her to enter.

Beyond the arch she saw the easel, the back of the canvas and behind that a woman, whose radiant smile offered affection and warmth, Sam smiled. With her eyes transfixed in their connection the passage of time seemed superfluous and held no meaning as Sam slowly moved forward. Without any sense of movement in her body she was drawn closer and as she exited the far side of the arch; the sunlight obstructed her vision. She blinked several times, tried to refocus and looked around but the woman was gone. Yet, chilled in her recognition, terrified to accept what her eyes told her was true, she saw the familiar figure of a young girl beneath the arch and realized she was looking at herself. And as if further evidence was needed to convince, the young girl said, "Anne, my name is Anne!"

******

Travis had closed his eyes almost from the first moment they took their seats, but he wasn't asleep. He had felt Deb rest her head against his arm, heard her soft sweet sighs and felt his love toward her. His momentary imagination carried him back to the many times she had cuddled up beside him on board the various boats where they had come together on an assignment. The many times he had felt the strong desire of love wash over him and the restraint he had felt forced to bear. But it had been a journey that had led to this, their journey together.

Thoughts changed from one moment to the next as he contemplated the unusual feelings he'd experienced inside her home and tried to navigate his way through them. The presence, the unrest, and the shrine-like atmosphere challenged his need to do something, but what? He didn't appear to have the answers or know what questions to ask. And the crazy episodes from earlier this morning........? He was tired...... Everything would have to wait.

******

The vast amount of information transmitted back and forth between Julie and Mac could; she thought, probably fill a book as they did their best to translate feelings and thoughts into words. Words to describe past and current events. Hopes and fears about the future and imagine how Travis might react to the news of their relationship. It felt like a coin toss really, an uneasy coin toss because the possibilities could easily go either way, and a deep friendship was at stake not to mention a brother, sister relationship. Mac had suggested that he should be the one to broach the subject directly. Julie understood the predicament but reasoned he had a responsibility to his parents and the business dealings he had so recently shouldered. As the days passed and the time drew closer for Travis to arrive home, the indecision intensified. Julie felt conflicted and unsure about whether she could hide her feelings. Half a world apart and yet, Julie feels Mac's presence so intimately close it takes her breath away and makes her heart flutter from both memory and anticipation.

******

Mac is doing his best but he would be the first to admit, *'it ain't easy.'* The business side of things is not the issue. Like a duck taking to water he knows what he has to do and having done it before, it's more a question of getting up to speed on the latest developments and changes. No, it's more a question of this aching in his gut, this yearning in his heart and the responsibility of knowing he just can't say *'fuck it'* and follow his desire. It's a traumatic situation waging war on the inside which has to remain unreflective on the outside and in many ways, especially at night *'it's killin him.'* But, like a trial by fire, Mac instinctively knows what he has to do for himself, Julie, redemption, and love. Mending fences, building bridges, melding two lives into one, reconstructing himself back into the person he once was, and in many ways, placing value on that which he devalued for many years.

There was so much to do, so much he wanted to share with Julie, and right now, the most significant obstacles are time and distance. Time in the urgency to share emotions and distance in the desire to touch. Touch and be touched, kiss and caress, gaze into her dark brown eyes and lose himself to her pleasure. Time, distance, the heart cries out, the mind must stay strong as the soul weeps.

Chapter 38

Time flies when you're having fun, but when disaster strikes, for a few moments at least, it's as if everything runs in slow motion, then WHAM, the impact. Travis took another swallow of Coors Lite, set the bottle down, picked up the tongs and turned the ribeye steak over on the grill. Was he angry? From his perspective, he felt he had every right to be. *Women! You can't live with them, and you can't live without them.* It was an old cliché, but it seemed to fit his mood. He blamed Julie. Why, the day after he and Deb arrived did she announced her intentions to hook up with Mac, and even now it still seems ludicrous.

The idea of thinking she and Mac could have a relationship was too farfetched. Mac is a loner, a womanizer and moves around from place to place, no strings attached. Travis scoffed. It was beyond belief that Julie would act so irrational and the fact that she left and drove back to Nashville proved it. But he concluded, going back to Nashville was probably a better choice than chasing after Mac. The trouble with that was he was alone. Deb had taken Julie's side in the argument, cut her vacation short and flew back to England. It had been a nightmare, both of them with bags packed. Julie drove Deb to the airport, dropped her off and started her journey to Nashville and since then, going on two weeks now neither of them would return his calls or respond to his emails. He had even thought about contacting Mac. Run through the issue, maybe laugh, and get some positive reinforcement that he was right, but he knew how much Mac cared for Deb so he hadn't quite gotten around to making that call yet. In any case, the cast was off, the stitches had been removed and his arm felt okay. Within a few weeks he would be ready for his next assignment and he'd be in touch with Mac anyway.

Standing near the grill, he took another pull on his Coors Lite. The evening air still warm as the light began to fade, he contemplated that he too, like Mac appeared to be a loner. Travis had not thought about it, his lifestyle in quite that way before. He thought more about being busy going somewhere on assignment, busy on completion and getting ready for the next task. Always busy, this downtime was getting to him; he had far too much time on his hands. Too much time to think and it was only today when the large envelope arrived from England that his thinking took a turn and he thought about Sam.

The envelope contained the historical data on Friar's Gate, which Mary O'Connell had obtained for him. Considering everything it seemed redundant, but she also inquired about his willingness to part with the painting. Travis determined the need to contact Sam and seek her approval so he sent her an email. Reflected momentarily and hoped she was happy digging in the dirt. The information went back in the envelope and haphazardly placed on his desk without much interest in reading through it. That's what brought about his mood. He could have had Sam. He could have been with Deb. He and his sister Julie might not have been at odds with each other...... If? If he had behaved differently. That didn't make much sense, but in some ways it was true. He knew it, but there was no way he would stand by and watch his sister make a fool of herself. As for Deb, she had made it pretty clear what she thought about him. *'A domineering, chauvinistic arsehole.'* And that was one of the kinder thoughts she had verbally expressed. The salad was pre-made, the baked potato ready and the steak was done.

But then again? His thoughts had been compounding during these past two weeks of solitude. What if...... What if Julie was the innocent party? What if Mac had taken advantage of her situation? What happened on the boat when they were alone together? Deb's words reverberated through his mind. *'What are you, some sort of judge who gets to decide who should be with whom? You need to butt out and mind your own business. If they want to have a romantic fling, that's their choice. They're adults.'* Had Mac betrayed him? Was there some sort of plot conceived between Mac and Deb? And yet wasn't it he himself who set the ball in motion by asking Mac for a favor? To take Julie out for a couple more dives. Travis quantified his idea in that he naturally assumed Deb would have been right there on the boat with them, not in his hotel room. Which in turn led his thoughts into that night when.... Deb.... He reluctantly accepted his loss. After two weeks of silence, what else could he do? Was his relationship with Mac also in question? Would Julie eventually come around? Maybe he thought he should make the next move. Travis toyed with the idea of driving to Nashville. Perhaps if he considered Julie's whole situation and was a little more understanding, it was something to think about rather than sitting around feeling sorry for himself and inventing conspiracies. The steak sat half-eaten; he had lost his appetite along with feeling the loss of so many other things.

******

Travis woke the following day feeling much the same as he had felt the preceding morning and the ones before that, confused. Too many thoughts and things were out of whack and off-balance. Something had to change and he needed to do something for that to happen. The change had to start somewhere and with time on his hands, which was unusual, he felt it was time to act. Before long he had eaten breakfast, cleaned up the kitchen, taken a shower, dressed and packed a bag. His conclusion was to sort this mess out one step at a time and Julie was the first person on his list.

******

The undertow of Mac's thoughts carried concern and anger in knowing that it would not end well if he and Travis were put in the same room. Some of the things Travis had said about him to Julie, although true, belonged in the past to the person he was and the sting in the recrimination of past actions hurt him deeply. There was guilt and he had to bear it, not only in silence but also in confession, as he laid out his wayward lifestyle to the woman he loved. From the start Mac had confessed that he *'ain't no Saint,'* he'd made mistakes and for reasons he could only be thankful for, Julie had not turned away. He was a fortunate man and he knew it, which made it harder to accept the current situation between her and Travis. Fumbling for ideas, he had suggested that Julie should fly to him, he should fly to her, he should confront Travis and in all, Julie had conceded to none. *'Travis should be given time to stew in his own juice.'* She had determined, and Mac had the good sense not to cross her.

Mac's life down under was back on track. His dad still came to the office once or twice weekly, albeit more of a social visit. Mac knew his dad had felt the pain of disconnect once and sensed he wasn't so willing to let that happen again. Neither was Mac, which made his next decision a crucial move and carried a risk he hoped he would not live to regret.

******

Divorce carries all the cliched comments and remarks purported to damn someone or support them, had played through Julie's mind. Different thoughts at different times, but she never once lost sight of the fact that Steve, for all his good points, had been dealing her sucker punches for the past three years. She felt no hypocrisy for having offered herself to Mac, even at a time when the truth had not been revealed. The notion that the marriage was falling apart was instinctually felt long before she realized its reality. Julie felt fortunate that the newly purchased home held no equity and no emotional ties. The furnishings, some new, some old, had no sentimental attachment, which alleviated the pull on the heartstrings or the necessity for removal or storage. On more than one occasion,

Julie was surprised by her simple detachment from what was and what is still yet to be. The simplistic sense of walking towards a door, opening it, stepping through and drawing it closed behind her. It made perfect sense and better still, it felt logical.

Days and nights, because of the time difference seemed to blend into a continuance of one email to the next or one phone call followed by another in an ever-growing fusion of learning, understanding, grasping images and concepts to the deepest feelings of love in their verbal and written expressions, through to the sadness and longing of being so far apart. And, of course, Travis and what a pain in the ass he has turned out to be. But, as Julie has told Mac several times, *'he is my brother; let me deal with him first. Then, after that you can have him.'*

Earlier that afternoon, the meeting with Steve and their attorneys had been amicable. Steve would take possession of the house and pay off all credit card debt. She would receive fifty percent of his stock portfolio and monthly alimony payments for a set period, keep her vehicle and sign off on his. Julie considered it a fresh start and a fair agreement and the attorneys inferred their willingness to deal with it quickly. And when she arrived home Travis's vehicle was parked in her driveway.

Chapter 39

Both got out of their respective vehicles and stood on the driveway facing each other.

"Travis." Julie's eye contact was guarded unwilling to show emotion.

"Sis."

"Why are you here?" The memory of a similar circumstance with Steve not so long ago crossed her mind.

Why he should have hoped for a better reception could hardly come as a surprise, but it did. It was new, cold, and disarming.

"I think I owe you an apology. Maybe I could have handled the situation differently."

"How, differently?" Julie's eyes narrowed. Suspicion was written across her brow. Almost threatening Travis to say the wrong thing, give the wrong answer and blow his chance.

He wanted to say; *I've known Mac for a long time. I love him like a brother and I've known you my entire life, but.........?* No, he suddenly realized that wouldn't work. Scratch that thought. "Maybe I should have listened more."

"Go on!"

Funny, in the non-humorous sense of the word; it hadn't happened since they were kids, at least he was a kid. She had always been the big sister and as he remembers it now, she wasn't always nice. He had forgotten about this side of her.

"Look Sis, do we have to do this on the driveway. Invite me in, ask me to stay awhile; I'm not going to bite your head off in fact, allow me to invite you out to dinner tonight. Call it a peace offering, you choose the restaurant. We can talk and try to patch things up or save the talk for later and just enjoy an evening out together. What do you say?"

Julie seemed to allow a meager smile. He almost missed the inflection of it before she turned towards the house. He assumed he was supposed to follow on behind her, so he did.

"I'm sleeping in the guestroom. You can use the master bedroom; fresh towels are in the linen closet but you know that already. Help yourself."

Her tone was dismissive which made him wonder if he were to go back out to his vehicle to get his bag, would she bolt the door and refuse to allow him to re-enter her house? *Tough choice: better to get it later maybe the situation will improve. He was walking on eggshells and felt it.*

"So, Sis, got any good news to get the conversation rolling?"

"I met with the attorneys this afternoon; Steve agreed to the terms of our divorce."

******

"I hope I'm not being premature in saying this Travis, considering you drove up here but I got to thinking while I was getting dressed that no matter how hurt I was, how demeaning your words were, you are making an effort to correct your mistake and I appreciate it. Thank you and thanks for bringing me out to dinner. Honestly, I'm tired of being cooped up in the house and I'll be happy when this divorce has been finalized so that I can put it behind me."

There certainly were a couple of opportunities presented to open up the conversation. Why then did Travis perceive them as traps? Demeaning? His mistake?

"I am sorry that things got so heated and out of hand, and I can't say with any real sense of certainty that I know how to fix everything or if some things are even fixable although I feel obligated to try. Tell me, how I could have handled things differently and achieved a better result?"

"You mean without squashing a person's feelings, crushing their heart, ridiculing their thoughts and making them feel like they don't have a brain or an ounce of common sense? Honestly, Travis, the better result would have been produced by keeping your opinions to yourself. To have been too afraid to let anyone know that you had those thoughts in the first place and maybe, just maybe, you should have just listened to what was being said. Think about it, did anyone ask for your opinion?"

"When you put it in those terms I can see your point. You didn't ask for my opinion and neither did Deb. Wow, when did I become such an asshole?"

"You didn't. After giving it a whole lot of thought I realized that even though twisted and overbearing, you were trying to protect me. I should have forgiven you sooner, but you were just as hard on Deb when she tried to defend Mac. Honestly, you were not forgivable then, you verbally lashed out uncontrollably at the slightest provocation. Not your most inspiring moment I'd say, and so if I forgive you it will be conditional. Conditional on you quietly sitting there and listening to me tell you about the Mac I know. Your opinion is not asked for or required, can you do that?"

******

"Maggie, it's Mac. Do ya have time to talk?"

"Mac, what's up? Is something wrong?"

"Not really Maggie, I've got this idea and I want to run it by ya."

"Where are ya? Are ya back in town?"

"No I'm in Brisbane. Look Maggie, I want to make ya an offer. How would ya feel about coming to work for me. We could get ya moved here; find ya a nice place to live and pay ya a good salary."

"Woe, hold up a second Mac, let me sit down. Are ya serious?" It took her a few seconds to gather her thoughts midway through getting ready for work, but everything stopped. The things she'd been thinking evaporated, a moment of empty headedness followed quickly by a concerted effort the concentrate and focus on what Mac was suggesting.

******

It was out of desperation his wife suggested calling Julie and Steve. There had been no contact with Sam their daughter for over three weeks. The police department in Nashville had interviewed both parents as a couple and then two days later individually, which left Helen and Richard with the distinct feeling they were suspected of a crime. The absurdity of that and the fact that no one in the police department seemed very concerned or willing to mount a concerted investigation demolished any faith Richard held towards law enforcement. Yes they had confirmed Sam took a flight to the UK. However, the airline had also confirmed that she had not shown up for her return flight to the US. One detective stupidly, in Richard's opinion, suggested his daughter Sam might simply have become involved in a romantic relationship and in the heat of youthful passion, responsibility becomes irrelevant for a time. Richard's interpretation of that statement was that the detective was unwilling to get off his fat lazy ass unless and until a dead body was found blocking his parking space and interrupted his daily routine.

******

As requested, Travis kept his mouth shut and listened; it wasn't easy considering the amount of information Julie shared about Mac, which at times made him wonder if she was talking about the same person. Mac, his dive partner; the man he loved like a brother, trusted with his life on many occasions. The man he had worked with during the past three years; side by side in sometimes dangerous situations, was cast in a totally different light. The unfamiliarity of it made Travis question his own belief. But if true, how could he not have known, and just when he thought it might be safe to ask questions, Julie's phone rang.

"Hello."

"Good evening, my name is Doctor Richard Sanders, am I speaking with Julie?"

"Yes, this is Julie."

"Ha, good. Julie, I'm not sure if you will remember me. My wife Helen and I ate dinner with you and your husband Steve a few months ago to celebrate my daughter's birthday and if I remember correctly, it was also your brother's birthday."

"Sure, I remember you Richard, and Helen, your wife. Travis and Sam share the same birth date. How are you both and how is Sam?"

"Helen and I are well, thank you for asking, but the reason for my call is to inquire if you or your brother Travis kept in touch with Sam, and have either of you heard from her recently?"

"Hmm, the last time I saw Sam was several weeks ago at the mall. We had coffee together and if I remember correctly, we spoke briefly by phone about a week later. Why, is something wrong?"

Not intentionally eavesdropping, Travis began to pay more attention to Julie's side of the conversation at the mention of Sam's name.

"Well, Helen and I are concerned. We haven't been able to contact Sam in more than three weeks which is unlike her. She flew to London to visit the British Museum and missed her scheduled flight home. That was over two weeks ago and as I mentioned already, we've had no communication with her. So I'm grasping at straws, hoping I can find someone she has kept in touch with just to have peace of mind. I'm sure you understand?"

"I certainly do understand Richard, you and Helen have every right to be worried and I wish I could be more help, but as I said the last time Sam and I spoke was about a month ago and she never mentioned taking a trip to London. So, I'm sorry please let me know when you hear from her."

Travis was frantically waving his hands, indicating he wanted Julie to hand over her phone.

"Hold on a moment Richard; I believe Travis would like to speak with you."

"Hello Richard, first allow me to apologize for interrupting your conversation with my sister, but please, tell me what is going on with Sam?"

It didn't take long for Travis to assess the gravity of the situation, put two-and-two together and surmise what Sam had done or was attempting to do. It was not a good feeling; he knew the danger and how headstrong she could be.

"Richard, I don't wish to impose on your time, but I think we need to sit down and talk. Please text your address; this is urgent and I don't believe we can successfully navigate it over the telephone.

Chapter 40

Sitting there with Richard and Helen, listening to Travis relay details about Sam's misguided reason for visiting the United Kingdom seemed incredulous and intelligible. And for some unfathomable reason Julie felt gobsmacked. That word had never been part of her vocabulary until she met Deb, and even then the understanding of its meaning had to be explained to her. Shocked and speechless, yes she confirmed her thought. She was gobsmacked. The how and why questions mounted in number in her mind with every statement and disclosed fact Travis shared. Only overwritten by an even more pressing question, how come she was unaware of any of this? Why had Travis, or even Deb not thought to mention Sam had shown up in England?

For Travis, imparting the sequence of actual events as he knew them to be was relatively easy. In a step-by-step process, walk through the park timeline from when he and Deb discovered Sam on Deb's doorstep to where they said goodbye as she boarded the train bound for London. But even while speaking he knew his summary would open the floodgate to a thousand inquiries, most of which would begin with why? That would be the complicated part to navigate. Their first meeting at the party; the birthday dinner, Sam breaking into his house plus everything in between, during, and after. Tangible facts, but the whys were surrounded by intangible sequences lacking substantial understanding and acceptance. Heck, he thought, I'm an involuntary participant struggling to understand it even now. As to his thoughts about Sam, if he could take hold of her right now, he would feel very strongly about turning her over his knee for a sound spanking. Not so much out of anger for her bad choices or crazy decisions, but more towards his need to vent his relief in knowing she had come to no harm. Well, except for the hardness of his hand across her butt.

The why questions came, and in their complexity Travis thought it would be easier to go right back to the beginning under the circumstances. No one was going to get any sleep tonight anyway; Sam might have placed herself in grave danger and he was the only available link as to her possible whereabouts and the reason. It was a judgment call and he knew it might sound crazy but his gut feeling was to preclude abandoning her in their collective experience.

After validating some of the events she had witnessed, Julie remained quiet and listened. She was stunned by the intrinsic details of anomalies she could not grasp. The depth of the transmitted emotions and thoughts became almost acceptable compared to the unacceptability of a painting that somehow came to life. Richard appeared to draw a line in the sand regarding the artwork and voiced his objection. On the other hand, Helen remained quietly attentive as if intricately weaving threads into fabric as the night dwindled towards the dawn until finally, the how and why questions appeared to be exhausted.

"Travis, this lady friend of yours, Deb. Do you have means of contacting her?"

"Yes, Helen what do you have in mind?"

"Please call her and ask if she has had any further contact with Samantha. And the arch, what was the name of the town?"

"Atherstone, it's located in the county of Warwickshire."

"Richard, get on the computer, bring up Atherstone. See if you can find a site for the local police department and send them a picture of Samantha. Tell them she is missing and that we would appreciate any help they can provide, also, do the same with any hotels listed in that area."

Helen looked at her watch. "I have a work associate who might be very interested in listening to what you have shared with us, would you be willing to speak with him, Travis?"

He was listening to the ring tone on Deb's phone but acknowledged Helen with a nod. Deb didn't answer her phone so Travis typed out a quick text to explain the urgency to make contact and sent the message.

Julie went into the kitchen to make another pot of coffee and discover what food items were available to put together some kind of breakfast. After all these hours, it was evident that this meeting was not nearing a conclusion. So much for being treated to dinner out on the town she thought. They had not even served the first course when Travis announced they were leaving. The sound her phone made distracted her, a message from Mac. A broad smile lit up her face as she read his greeting into this another new day knowing he was considering the time difference between them, and timing his message perfectly for her to begin her day was so romantic and usually caught her as she woke each morning. Julie paused to consider this last night, this morning, where she was and the reason that brought her here. Her smile disappeared and was replaced with a serious frown. There was no way she would or could include Mac in this mess, let alone try to explain what was going on. It was all just too much and far too complicated.

"Travis, it would appear that there is a link between you and Samantha. An understatement as far as you're concerned, I'm sure." Helen projected. "Metaphorically speaking, a lock and a key, but I'm unable to determine which of you is the lock and which is the key. However, what you have told us bears evidence you are both, which is unusual. Also, and I will admit I'm having a difficult time excepting the possibility that Samantha has exhibited characteristics of being both lock and key as well. Which, going by everything I have studied would be deemed impossible. In theory at least."

Maybe the blank stare on Travis's face prompted Helen's following statement.

"Oh, forgive me Travis, I am a psychiatrist. I thought you were aware of my occupation, exploring the mind and its many facets."

Travis was surprised and still confused. "Lock and key?"

"Yes. From what you have described in your experiences, you have exhibited actions that would indicate you are both the initiator and the beneficiary, which I find fascinating. Of course, that is just an assumption on my part, but for the moment please allow me to assume I am correct. What is unimaginable is if Samantha is also an initiator and a beneficiary. That, under different circumstances would be, how can I put it, a eureka moment for science. A phenomenon not yet understood. But then again I'm using layman's terms and with the limited knowledge available, who is to say what is and is not possible. Everything is speculative until proven one way or the other."

Travis felt the need to think about that. The strange thought of him and Sam locked away in a laboratory somewhere with lots of wires attached to their heads came to mind and he was thankful he had shared so little and apprehensive about divulging any more details. Kind of like what happens in Vegas, stays in Vegas type of deal.

"Breakfast is ready" Julie announced, poking her head into the room. "Come and get it while it's hot."

Richard had indeed found a website for the Atherstone Police Station and sent a request for their assistance. Accommodation-wise there wasn't an abundant choice available, but he had contacted all that offered a website. It was only now while tasting the fresh coffee, Travis remembered and checked his phone messages. "Hmm?" But before jumping to an assumption he mentally figured the time difference only to conclude perhaps Deb was ignoring him.

"Hey Sis, would you mind calling Deb's cell phone, she might still be upset with me?"

"Travis, I'm fascinated not only by the painting of the arch, but the actual attraction the arch itself seems to have in drawing you and now Samantha towards it, and I have a strong feeling it might be the epicenter to everything that has happened. You said Samantha sent the original painting to you, correct?"

"Damn it, Helen, stop going off on tangents, this is Sam, our daughter. She could be in trouble; focus on that that is the priority, not a stupid painting and some cockamamie notion about supernatural hocus-pocus. Now let Julie and Travis enjoy breakfast." Turning his focus towards them, he continued. "You have been very helpful. Helen and I thank you, but we have kept you here far too long and I'm sure you understand we need to do everything we can to find our daughter and bring her home." Pushing his chair back from the table, he stood and left the room. The tension in Richard's face was evident and his patience was wearing thin.

******

Really it was a no-brainer. Maggie accepted Mac's offer with little hesitation. One or two more questions, satisfactory answers and Mac ended the call with, I'll be there in a few days to pick ya up and in that short space of time Maggie's world changed completely. There was no need to ponder what she would wear; Maggie knew nothing in her wardrobe was up to date and suitable for a Brisbane business professional. She'd be lucky to find something suitable for the journey. But the real magic, her reason for excitement was that Mac was coming back to get her and carry her into the world they had become accustomed to living in together. No, she knew he hadn't said that out loud, but he was thinking about her and this could be the first step in the right direction and bring them so much closer.

******

There he was thinking all this time that Sam was digging in the dirt in Mexico, he should have known better his entire experience of her had proven she was flighty, undisciplined, and rebellious. Why he believed even for just one minute, when they put her on that train she would actually stay on it, then go to the airport and fly back to the states. Again, he should have known better. Now look where they are and the situation she has created. Yes, Travis was worried, and knowing what he knew he had reason to be. "Sam, you damn fool." He said that, but his strong emotional connection could not be denied. There was no way he could just turn his back on her not knowing and come to think on it, he still had to make peace with Deb and he wasn't sure if the equilibrium had been reestablished with his sister. The evening had definitely not gone the way he intended but as weary as he was and as tired as he imagined Julie must be, he was ready to hoist a white flag and surrender to whatever came next.

Chapter 41

Mac had a plan. No, he thought, he had ideas like jigsaw puzzle pieces in a pile, waiting to be sorted and slotted into place. Pieces like Maggie and Becca, his mum and dad, Julie sweet Julie, and Travis. Especially after he received an email from Deb; Travis was now on his shit-list twice although Mac realized Travis was just trying to protect Julie from the only Mac he had known and he could deal with that. But what Travis had done to Deb; now that was a different kettle of fish and it stank. Breaking Deb's heart had got Mac steaming and if it weren't for his agreement with Julie to wait, he would move mountains to get in her brother's face.

******

Travis looked at his phone. Nothing, nada, not a single reply from either Deb or Sam.

"Hey Sis, did you get in touch with Deb?"

"I tried calling her this morning, but she didn't pick up so I left a message."

Julie was fixing dinner; the day had been a write-off. After she and Travis had arrived home this morning most of the day had been spent sleeping. Travis was dressed after taking a shower and had just entered the dining area.

"Sis, I'm concerned; Sam never left England, Deb flew back to England and now this, no contact. They are both in real danger and don't realize it."

"What do you mean, real danger? That's a bit dramatic for you Travis what's going on? What do you know?"

Just then, Julie's phone rang.

"Hi, Helen, any news, have you heard from Sam?"

"I was going to ask you that very same question, or if Travis had heard from his lady friend in England?"

"No, I'm sorry Helen, Travis and I were just saying it's strange not to hear back from either of them."

"Well, we have some news but I'm not sure if it will be useful. We received an email response from a hotel called the Red Lion in Atherstone. The manager confirmed Sam had stayed there over the weekend, four weeks ago then checked out. From a previous conversation, he assumed she would catch a train to Heathrow airport."

Julie switched to speakerphone mode quickly once the conversation began.

"Helen. It's Travis. Do you have the manager's name and the phone number for the hotel?"

******

No sooner than Mac pulled up, parked and got out of his Land Rover on Maggie's drive, than Becca came running excitedly out of the house. He bent at the knees and opened his arms in what he could only imagine was a knee-jerk reaction. He certainly had never done that before and at that exact moment, when Becca wrapped her arms around his neck Mac realized with a feeling of guilt that when he left last time he had not said goodbye. She held on tight and kissed his cheek as he stood straight holding her gently in his arms. He didn't want to squeeze her, Becca weighed almost nothing to his way of thinking and he was afraid she would break. A sensation of lightheadedness played with his emotions as he tried to determine how he felt, but no answer had been reached when Maggie appeared beside him, "Hey Mac." She too reached up and kissed him.

For Mac, it was emotional, as memory upon memory played back through his mind about how, a long time ago he had envisioned his life would work out. Maggie, his wife, and the children, their children, as they had imagined within the blissful union of their love. To be standing there now with Maggie beside him and Becca in his arms, fulfilled the fantasy but quickly mocked his inexperienced idealisms of youth. It was a wretched circumstance to carefully lower Becca to the ground as he gathered his thoughts together and pushed back the resentment which had surfaced toward Maggie. Something stolen, something lost, the affection still lingered but love's trust had been violated.

It had been Becca's squeal of delight as she ran out of the house that alerted Maggie to Mac's arrival and reaching the open door she saw the smile on Mac's face as Becca leaped into his arms. A smile she recognized; had seen a thousand times and felt the radiance of his love toward her. Her heart shattered and mourned the loss; her breath caught and she wanted to cry as she waited and watched their embrace. The desperation in Maggie's heart longed to be held in Mac's arms again, to feel his kiss upon her lips and be told she had been forgiven.

******

Travis had no way of explaining how or what had happened. It may have had something to do with Helen saying he was the key, Julie saying he was being dramatic, or the knowledge that Sam had been to Atherstone and probably discovered the arch. All he knew with any certainty was that the time for wondering and talking had to stop. It was time for action, and hope he was not too late. But unfortunately, he didn't have the answers and the clarity of his thoughts terrified him in knowing what he would have to confront for Deb, Sam, and himself.

Julie couldn't quite grasp the change. One minute they had been talking while she finished preparing their meal, the next, after a short telephone conversation with Helen, Travis announced he was leaving.

"What's happening Travis? What's going on?" Julie entered the master bedroom and watched him hurriedly stuffing his clothes into a bag.

"Sorry Sis, it just occurred to me that I'm the only one who understands the danger both Sam and Deb are in so it's up to me to do something."

"I still don't understand. What danger?" Julie could see the determination on his face and even without knowing why, she felt her concern. Where was he going? What was he going to do, and what perils would he have to face? "Travis, at least eat something before you go and take a few minutes to explain where you're going and what you plan to do."

Pausing briefly to seemingly assess her request and balance it against his quest he conceded. "Sure Sis, there's not much I can do tonight except drive back to Pensacola."

******

Molly wanted to believe in the fairytale ending for Maggie and Mac, she had watched them grow up and considered them family. Maggie's announcement had been bittersweet; she was losing her best employee but more than that, Molly was losing her friend. She was happy that everything was working out for Maggie, and that Becca would have a good man to help raise her but still, she knew she would miss them which was the sad part. She had often caught herself in a stare during the past week looking at Maggie, and sometimes Becca as if fixing images in her mind. She was building one last set of memories, wondering if she would ever see them again. Molly considered herself a strong woman, a fine piece of leather that was well put together. As a woman, you had to be tough to survive here in the outback, few men would cut you slack and weakness would win you no favors.

Lightning Ridge was a place for roughnecks, where most men were so ugly they'd make a dirt road do a U-turn, and most women would make an onion cry. No, she thought, although she loved Maggie she didn't belong here. It was time for her to go, and because you couldn't keep anything quiet in this town the Grub Hut was packed. The business was brisk, and Maggie was the main attraction. It seemed like every man wanted to get one last look, one last smile before the mirage disappeared and their fantasies evaporated. But Mac had arrived, this was Maggie's last shift and everyone sensed a change was coming.

******

Julie stood in her driveway and waved as Travis backed his vehicle out onto the road, and seconds later was gone from view. She didn't know what to think, and as she stepped back inside the house an ominous thought flashed through her mind, would she ever see her brother again? She was afraid.

******

Travis had so many things to be considered and his ability to prioritize was clouded in guilt. Why he thought had he not confided in Deb. Told her about what he had concluded from the experience under the arch. His strong feelings about an unnatural presence in her home and the atmosphere of an almost shrine-like memorial to lost love and the death of a saint. Why had he failed to understand her affection and loyalty toward Mac when he himself shared that same loyalty and devotion. Yes, he had felt sideswiped by Julie's announcement and had spoken his mind. Looking back now, he knew he had been blunt. Especially after Julie and Deb closed ranks and united their forces to combat everything he thought was true. Even so the outcome was, he concluded, an overreaction by all of them. Tempers had flared, hurtful comments had been exchanged and no one was willing to back down or compromise. The consequence of which saw Deb head straight back towards the complicated web of unsolved mysteries and his guilt hung heavy in the knowledge he had allowed almost four weeks to pass knowing she was the target. As for Sam, she was a quandary in her own right, a contradiction to sensibility. Why hadn't she simply stayed on the train to London, caught the flight home and gone digging in the dirt in Mexico? It defied his logical thought process but then again, what, he asked himself was rational about anything to do with everything that had happened? But even more unsettling was not knowing what he had yet to confront.

Chapter 42

Molly came over to Maggie's house early the following morning to say a final goodbye, wish them well and take possession of the house keys. She had been left in charge of selling the property. Maggie had determined to close this chapter of her life and never look back. Opportunity had opened a door and she was eager to embrace it, although cautious not to overstep any as of yet unidentified boundaries. Last night she had prepared and waited with anticipation, hoped Mac would enter her bedroom and although disappointed this morning that he hadn't, it was forgivable. They faced a long arduous drive today and there would be many more nights in front of them. Maggie knew she had to content herself and let Mac take the lead on this, at least to a point. She would need to be attentive and look for openings, be desirable without appearing too forward or pushy, despite her urgent desire to be taken and delightfully devoured by him every time he got within arm's length. And today there was little chance he would be out of arm's length except during toilet stops and petrol fill-ups. Although in moments of rational thought she knew Mac was unlikely to get amorous with Becca in the backseat. But she hoped it would happen soon and remove the anxiety of not knowing what he had in mind. So with minimal clothing for her and Becca, a couple of boxes of knickknacks and memorabilia, they got into the Land Rover, waved to Molly, and headed out of town.

******

As the dawn light began to make its presence felt Travis pulled his vehicle into his garage. Priority one was to get the coffeemaker primed and producing the stimulant his body craved. Priority number two, fire up the laptop and arrange his flights, quickly followed by locating the painting Sam had sent, and the envelope containing the history of the arch from Mary O'Conner. Drink coffee, eat breakfast, shower, and get some much-needed sleep. Packing a bag for the trip could wait until later. Time was the enemy and utilizing it to his full advantage would take precision.

******

Discreetly, knowing Richard would disapprove, Helen had called her colleague John and arranged to meet with him. To her, everything Travis had disclosed offered clues to something, a phenomenon outside the realms of everyday thinking which could if interpreted correctly, lead them to her daughter. Richard was wrong in her opinion, to dismiss offhandedly the possibility of life forces outside his comprehension interfering and interacting in both positive and negative ways. She loved Richard; even so, he could be an ass at times. Together they loved their daughter Sam and in Helen's opinion no stone should be left unturned in their combined effort to be reunited with Samantha and bring her home safely.

"What you have described Helen goes far beyond anything currently understood, are you sure? No, perhaps I need to rephrase that, how confident are you about the character of this man, Travis? How well do you know him?"

"John, do you think I would bring this to you if I didn't have a high level of trust that Travis was speaking the truth as he believes it to be, and we are talking about Sam? You've known her since she was born. Of course I'm sure and I also believe Travis is withholding information about some things for fear of ridicule. I want you to meet him and talk to him because as you have alluded to, these phenomena go off the charts compared to what we currently understand, or even surmise as a possibility."

"But Helen, you have said you believe the arch is the epicenter. Samantha was last seen in the town where the arch is located; so much began to unfold here in Nashville, and this man Travis is in Florida. So, I ask you, where do we begin? How do you propose I, or we, approach this and how do we formulate a plan considering the urgency to locate your daughter? The investigation's feasibility is enticing, but it has to be weighed against the viability of reaching a verifiable conclusion. Again, we are talking about events on two continents."

"John, I've never known you to discount a challenge or dabble in the impracticability of furthering the advancement of knowledge and understanding. Travis is here in Nashville; at least agree to meet with him and judge for yourself. Right now, I can call his sister Julie, and set up a meeting."

Sigh. "Very well Helen, make the call."

"Hello Julie, It's Helen, could I speak with Travis?"

"Hi Helen, I'm sorry Travis left last night. He drove back to Pensacola with every intention of booking a flight to England."

"Why? Has he heard from Sam? Is she alright?"

"No, but I'm scared; he said Sam and Deb are in danger and he is the only one who knows what is happening."

Helen knew her assumption was correct; Travis knew more than he had divulged.

"Julie, did Travis say where in England he was going?"

"Well, he knows where Deb lives and that is within easy driving distance of Atherstone. That is where the arch is and the last known place Sam was seen. So it would be my guess that's the area he will head for unless he gets a different lead. But Helen honestly, the way he left here, his determination to resolve whatever it is that has been going on, I'm afraid and have wondered if I will ever see him again."

Helen's admiration for Travis instantly leapt to the level of 'a knight in shining armor.' That or a complete fool who had no idea what they were getting themselves involved in. Either way, the mere chivalry of his act found Helen decidedly in favor of having him as her son-in-law. "Julie, your brother is a remarkable young man and I intend to do everything in my power to make sure he returns to the US safely. I will keep you informed of my plans so don't worry, it's a sad situation that he is the first person to realize the need for action. I will call you again with updates. Bye for now."

"Well John, the field of play has just narrowed. Travis is on his way to the epicenter. The last known location Sam was seen and so, it would appear to me, if we join him there you will have a contained theater of operation."

******

Mac, to his way of thinking, was doing a good thing; not only for Maggie and Becca, but he would also benefit and indirectly so would his parents. It appeared to be a win-win situation where Maggie would have the opportunity to have a great job, which he already knew she would thrive in and be able to provide well for herself and Becca, he in turn, would become unshackled from a desk job and the everyday monotony of paperwork. Furthermore, as his administrative assistant, he knew Maggie had the skills and the mindset to oversee the day-to-day operations, keep him informed and navigate a smooth course.

A smooth course was the part he was having difficulty with as the familiarity of past affection and intimate interaction seemed to flirt with his senses. Was it him or was it the way Maggie smiled, sighed, spoke, and walked, or was it the look in her eyes? It was something, and whatever it was it penetrated his sense of propriety. The familiarity felt good, but he also knew he would feel relieved to have this journey behind him. Having contemplated the possibility of misconstrued intentions, the hotel suite he had reserved for

Maggie and Becca was a much better option than to have invited them into his home.

******

Only when Travis was seated on the plane did it cross his mind that perhaps he should have removed the painting from its package and looked at it. The question of whether it would have provided insight was now obsolete. Still, he considered it an oversight and considering everything that lay in front of him, oversights and mistakes were things he felt the need to minimize. Everything could turn into a life and death struggle with little or no warning, and he knew from experience there might be no second chances. The fact that Deb was ignoring him didn't help. Yes, he knew he had behaved badly, but to his way of thinking so did she and Sis. A simple case of everybody was right, and everybody was wrong, but four weeks of silence. He still loves her and would find it unbelievable if she were to announce that she no longer loved him. Everyone has disagreements from time to time then they kiss, make up and move forward. He hoped that he and Deb would, but four weeks is a long time to be mad at someone you professed love toward. Which led to the thought of whether it would be wise to show up on her doorstep unannounced? Remembering the last time they had arrived together at her door; they were both exhausted and he would be in a similar condition this time. Would he be better off spending the first night in a hotel? Would Deb then construe that circumstance as standoffish and find fault in his reasoning? How was he supposed to know? And Sam, that was the big quandary, like think of the logic, throw it out of the window and do precisely the opposite. So, assuming she had been to the arch, what might have happened? Not much apparently, because she had returned to the hotel to collect her bags. But what happened after that, that was the question. The best-case scenario he could think of was that she had returned to Deb's house. That was illogical; Deb was in the US but it hadn't stop Sam from breaking into his house in Pensacola while he was away. It was something to contemplate but didn't explain why she had not contacted anyone. And the worst-case scenario would be if Sam had somehow convinced Deb to revisit the arch together. The messenger and the prey, one leading the other right into harm's way. Travis paused instinctively knowing he should have taken the painting out of its box.

After dinner, he pulled out the large manilla envelope that contained the history of the arch from his carry-on and first looked at the return address. He was thankful for that; he would have had no way of getting in touch with Mary without it. Hopefully, there would be no urgent need to make use of it, things would be resolved, and only then would he feel obliged to make a courtesy visit. Even so, he still held fond memories of Mary and her out-of-this-world scones.

So, he read that the arch had been built in 1795, which only added to the complicated question of whose eyes were allowing him to see the things that no longer existed, the tall redbrick building? First, he would need to discover when that building was constructed. Then, as he continued to read, to confuse the issue more, he learned the first monastic site in Atherstone was an Augustinian Friary founded in the center of the town in 1374. So, it would seem like a logical deduction on his part to conclude Friar's Gate (the arch) would have some connection to the Friary. The information Mary had gathered and sent to him proved to be a fantastic history lesson but lacked the dedicated insight he was looking for about the arch. So, as to when the arch was actually built? Who built it, and why the building traversed the road beneath it remained clouded? But he certainly had learned a lot more about the town and its history and knew, in a sense, to walk its streets would be, for him at least, like walking on hallowed ground. Romans, Saxons, Normans, and

Vikings had walked those same streets along with Lords, Ladies, Knights, Kings, Queens, and many famous historical figures.

******

Maggie was surprised when Mac pulled up in front of the hotel downtown but it had been a long journey and she didn't question his decision.

"They have a reservation in ya name, and a rental car should already be in the parking garage. Here's a credit card, so ya can get whatever ya need for yaself and Becca. I'll come by tomorrow so we can talk about finding a house and gettin ya sorted. If ya need anythin call me." The porter arrived beside Mac's vehicle to collect the luggage. Mac got out of the Land Rover, walked around to open the door for Maggie then opened Becca's door and helped her out. Maggie wanted to object but caught herself. "Good night Mac, thanks for everythin." A simple embrace: Mac returned to the driver's seat and pulled away from the curb.

Maggie felt stunned and paused for a few moments before taking Becca's hand and following the porter inside the building. Her heart was aching and she felt lost, bewildered that Mac would behave so cold. But she thought she understood when she caught sight of herself in one of the many mirrors in the lobby. The reflected image portrayed a woman who belonged in the outback, wearing a drab dress that had seen better days, hair that had not seen a professional stylist in years and a deep suntanned face without makeup. Mac would have felt ashamed to have been caught with her in such an elegant setting, she concluded.

******

After touching down at Heathrow, Travis navigated the London Underground like a pro. At Euston railway station he purchased a highspeed intercity train ticket to Nuneaton and had time to grab lunch before his departure. He was tired but not overly so, anxious, and full of anticipation to finally sort things out with Deb, hold her in his arms and confirm she was safe. The why question was simple. Why had he not arrived here two or three weeks ago? The answer was sheer stupidity. In fact, the why he had carried their disagreement to the point where she left Pensacola in the first place and returned to the United Kingdom, was in itself an act of pigheadedness. The why in hindsight we can recognize these traits only after the fact begs the question, are we really an intelligent lifeform or a form of life who only by accident gets some things right, some of the time?

About an hour by high-speed train found him in Nuneaton getting into a taxi to cover the last five or six miles to Hinckley in Leicestershire. Travis hoped the first few moments of looking into Deb's eyes would resolve the quandary as to whether their love was stronger than the disagreement. There was a knot in the pit of his stomach. The tension in his chest felt like it was determined to restrict his breathing, and the back of his neck felt stiff. These final few minutes were proving worrisome, and he wanted desperately to get them behind him.

The taxi pulled to the curb and stopped. Instinctively Travis held the English currency in his hand, to determine the correct denominations to pay the fare when he glanced toward the house excitedly. Every motion stopped, and he stared. Finally in disbelief, he asked the driver if he was sure this was the correct address and was assured it was. Opening the passenger door, his eyes still fixed on the house, he stepped out of the vehicle, and moments later he seemed to hear the taxi driver's door close and could only assume the man had also gotten out of the taxi and came around to join him. "I seem to remember reading about this in the newspaper several weeks ago, tragic."

"What... What happened?" Even as he verbalized his thought, Travis knew what must have happened; it was evident from the yellow caution tape surrounding the burned-out shell of the house, what had happened. Not to mention the scorched brickwork of the houses on either side of what was left of Deb's house.

"I'm not sure what caused it," the taxi driver replied. "It was front-page news, and there was an investigation as far as I can remember. They found the remains of a woman." Travis stumbled forward feeling weaker with each step and dropped to his knees on the pavement directly in front of the pathway leading to where a front door had been.

"Hey pal, are you feeling alright?" The driver approached Travis and saw the tears and the forlorn expression. "Look, pal; it's obvious you won't be staying here. Is there somewhere else I can take you?"

Chapter 43

After checking in at the Red Lion Hotel in Atherstone, Travis solemnly made his way to his room. The agony of heartache filled every part of his body and mind, and it took a concerted effort to construct a cryptic email to Julie telling her about his discovery. Afterward, he lay back on the bed exhausted and at some point, fell asleep.

******

Julie woke to a brand-new day full of anticipation and eagerly reached for her phone and the inspiring daily email she had become accustomed to receiving from Mac. Seeing she had also received an email from Travis did not alarm her. He was probably just letting her know he had arrived safely and all was well. Julie chose to open Mac's email first, but after only glancing through it, she was reminded of her ominous feeling and the dangers her brother had gone off to face. She closed Mac's email and opened the one from Travis. Within seconds her heart felt like it had been wrenched from her chest, and she was crying inconsolably.

******

Having woken early, Maggie was on a mission and bathed Becca and herself. Then, she had room service deliver breakfast to their room and located the rental car in the parking garage. She was determined to obliterate any recognition tying their appearance to the outback as quickly as possible; consequently Mac's credit card was hot from continued use throughout the morning hours. It wasn't everything she needed but it was a good start and after a fast lunch, with Becca positioned in the seat next to her, she instructed the hairstylists to perform their magic and the manicurist to create a miracle. Mac had not given her the exact time he planned to arrive, and she prayed the transformation would meet with his approval in more ways than one.

Mac felt the need to rearrange some aspects of his plan in light of the previous day's journey, or it could have something to do with what Molly had inferred when she had spoken to him privately for a few minutes the evening before that, while Maggie was working her last shift. Molly seemed to have the impression that he and Maggie were getting back together. She hadn't come out and said it like that, but the implication definitely indicated she had that understanding. Molly was a straight shooter and called it as she saw it, and Mac could only think of one person who might have given her that impression. So this morning he called his mum and dad and invited them to join him for lunch at the hotel with the intention of surprising them.

Lunchtime had come and gone and Maggie and Becca were nowhere to be found. So the best alternative for Mac was to talk to them more about Julie and his intentions toward her, and end the conversation with, "by the way, I've brought Maggie and her daughter Becca to Brisbane. I've asked Maggie to be my executive assistant and she as accepted my offer." Of course, that started a completely new conversation and the promise he felt coerced into making, to bring Maggie and Becca by their house tonight for dinner, along with one other guest currently staying with him. At two-thirty in the afternoon, with still no sign of Maggie and Becca, he left a note at the reception desk and exited the hotel.

******

The instant Travis woke and gathered his senses, tears filled his eyes; he knew he could have prevented this if he had not been so adamant in his opinions. Not saying some of the things he had spoken to defend his posturing, and begged Deb not to leave, or if he had come looking for her sooner. He had been given plenty of opportunities to change this outcome, and had missed every one, and for what? What was so much more important? Julie was a grown woman and old enough to accept the consequences of her own decisions, just as he must now face the consequences of his choices. Deb was dead, and he was responsible for that. He had loved her for so long and when acknowledged, had let her down. He was damned and felt the need to seek absolution in his damnation.

Dressed and suitably attired for the ever-changing English climate, he made inquiries at the front desk and was surprised by how close he was to Mary's address. He had been assured about a fifteen-minute walk and so, off he set unaware of the type of reception he would receive. A slap across his face and a door slammed, barring him from entry felt appropriate. And yet, another surprise. Mary greeted him with a warm smile and a friendly hug before inviting him inside. Her surprise to see him lay in the disclosure that there was still no date set for the funeral because the authorities had not yet released the body. Although Mary did not understand why Deb was at home, when she was under the impression Deb was going with Travis to the US? A precarious state of affairs in which once he revealed the truth, he still could receive that well-deserved slap across his face and quickly be invited to leave.

He accepted her offer of tea and scones, and slowly they exchanged their personal insights about the events that brought each of them to where they are now: Deb's death. Mary was a gracious woman and generous with her understanding. Travis would have almost preferred the cold hard slap across the face; Mary's forgiveness was far too kind. Then their conversation turned to Sam and his desire to find her and make sure she got home safely, which opened the door to all the events that had brought him to Atherstone to see Friar's Gate. Mary appeared intrigued and dumbfounded as each new piece of information was divulged and then suddenly astonished, as if a recollection of something long past was unpleasantly remembered. Finally, she grew reticent, and Travis got the distinct impression he had overstayed his welcome.

******

Mac couldn't believe his eyes when he read and then re-read the email he had just received from Julie. His first thought defied logical interpretation; his second thought was, "What the hell as Travis been drinking?" But he knew something was wrong and couldn't stand back and do nothing. So quickly, he shot an email back to Julie.

******

Julie was waiting for Mac's reply when it arrived. She read, was shocked. Re-read to be sure and determined she would not be sidelined. It just didn't make any sense.

******

Mac knew this would be as inconvenient as hell for his dad; but he felt he had no other choice, so he made the call.

******

When Travis walked into the hotel dining room for dinner that evening he did a double take with his eyes. "Helen?"

"Hi Travis, we have been waiting for you. First, allow me to introduce my good friend and colleague, Professor Tanner. John, I would like you to meet Travis."

Rising from his chair, John extended his hand. "Travis, I'm very pleased to make your acquaintance, finally."

The word, 'finally' made the hair stand up on Travis's neck. He took John's hand in his in greeting and smiled; his curiosity and apprehension intermingled with his assessment of the man and the reasoning behind this 'chance' meeting. And not one to beat about the bush, as soon as they were all seated Travis asked, "Okay Helen, I can understand your reason for being here, but where is Richard and what interest does John have in finding your daughter?"

Helen had not anticipated the directness of Travis's question. "Travis, I can assure you we are all here for the same purpose, to find Sam and bring her home safely. Richard is at home in case something new develops at that end. John has known Samantha since birth and offered to assist me in whatever way he could. Right now, he is acting as my travel companion. Have you discovered anything since your arrival?"

"Nothing related to Sam, but Deb is dead. She was burned to death in a house fire."

"Travis!" Helen reached over and covered his hand with hers. "I'm so sorry. How? When did that happen?"

"I don't have all the details yet; I spent the day with a close friend of Deb's, and tomorrow I had thought about contacting the authorities to try to piece everything together."

"Travis. Forgive me for asking." John hesitated, then continued, "Were you close?"

Travis wanted to smack the man, but this was not the place or the time. "I was in love with her, I had been for quite some time."

It was not an easy conversation, guarded inquiries and hesitant questions throughout dinner. Some were relevant; some were not. Travis sensed John was trying to break the ice and find common grounds of interest. Helen attempted to develop inroads into the paranormal events related to Sam, her involvement and precisely what Travis's relationship was with Sam. Travis knew he had an obligation to find Sam, but tonight was not the night to turn his focus in that direction. He had someone else on his mind, and out of love, out of respect, and out of his deep sense of guilt, he would not deny her, her rightful place in his thoughts.

******

Maggie was completely surprised when Mac's dad greeted her in the lobby that evening. Mac's note said he would pick her up and take her and Becca out for dinner, and Maggie was dressed to seduce.

"Maggie, it's lovely to see ya girl, and who might this young lady be?"

"Walt, it's great to see ya, this here's Becca. Where's Mac, is somethin wrong?"

"No, not really, I don't suppose. Maggie, ya look amazing. I can't wait for mum to get an eyeful of ya. She's excited; been fussing in the kitchen all afternoon, ever since Mac told us ya was here. Anyway, if ya ready, my cars out front.

Maggie took Becca's hand and moved toward the glass doors. Walt still thought of Maggie as part of the family and was taken back by how Becca was the spitting image of Maggie when she was a young girl. Although, it kinda took his breath away to see them both, he felt smitten with joy and looked forward to seeing mum's reaction.

******

Travis didn't know what to expect or what he was hoping for later that evening in his room, when he unsealed the box containing the painting. He felt resentment toward Christine in that she may have won. How he could imagine that, was a question he didn't have the answer for. He positioned the painting on top of the desk stepped back, sat on the bed, and looked at it. He waited, watched, and looked for a clue. Silently he challenged it, her, to show herself but nothing happened. The temptress would not reveal herself, and the painting looked dull and boring. But suddenly, he felt cold, damp, and hungry. He was lost in a dark and lonely place. It didn't make sense and was hard to shake. He finally tired of looking at the painting; getting up from the bed he turned it face down on the desk and went into the bathroom cursing under his breath.

******

If Maggie ever wanted a new mum and dad, Mac's mum and dad would be her first choice. She knew they loved her and she loved them, and how they fussed over Becca was wonderful. And if she was honest, she did want them as her mum and dad and as grandparents for Becca. But there was an order to it, and that order included Mac as her husband, and Mac, as she now understands, has a love interest called Julie, who mum and dad are impatiently waiting to meet. An American no less, who to the best of their knowledge, has never stepped foot in Australia?

The evening had gone well, a chance to reminisce through countless memories most of which were good times. Talk about her parents, her marriage, the struggles of life in Lightning Ridge and raising Becca as a single parent. Yes she thought, Mac's mum and dad are great but Walt hinted that he would be overseeing her introduction into the business, because Mac was going to be out of the office for a while. She didn't understand that; she had spent the better part of three days with Mac, and he hadn't mentioned it or anything about Julie either.

But Maggie determined she had come too far to turn back. Life is a series of steppingstones; as long as she was careful, remained steadfast and balanced each move, she would get to where she wanted to be. Becca was asleep. Maggie took a long look at herself in the mirror and liked what she saw. Hardly a trace of the outback woman was visible. The new and improved Brisbane professional was ready to make her mark.

Chapter 44

Standing on the curb in front of the burned-out shell of what had been Deb's house, Travis would not have been able to explain why he had felt the need to revisit the site; it was personal. The taxicab driver was keeping his meter running. Mary had told him yesterday that he would need to contact the police station in Hinckley, and so he had called and made an appointment. But that didn't matter for the moment; Travis had something to say to Deb. Something he wanted to share with her, feelings that could not be put into words. Thoughts about the past, everything that had transpired between them, and the hopes that he knew now would never be fulfilled moments of joy, remorse for his inactions, and the affection that lingered in his heart. And strangely, he wondered what had happened to Annie, her cat? That thought seemed to detach any perceived connection and brought his attention back to the waiting cab.

At the police station, Travis was escorted into an office to meet with the detective assigned to the case and asked if he would like a cup of tea by a pretty policewoman. The courtesy was unexpected; he smiled politely at the hospitality but declined the offer.

Although as he quickly learned when talking with the detective, information was a one-way street. The detective wanted to know everything Travis knew but appeared unwilling to share anything but minor facts, quoting several times that the investigation was ongoing. Naturally, therefore, he could not disclose the details.

"Did you find a cat?" Travis had no idea why he asked that question. Maybe it was just to get a definite yes, or no answer. But unfortunately, it didn't work and he was left to assume that the detective didn't know one way or the other. And so, at the conclusion of the interview, Travis knew just as much as he had when he arrived. It was a futile attempt to bring resolution and lay Deb to rest.

Meanwhile, back in Atherstone, Helen had fliers printed with a picture and information about Sam and a contact number to call and had spent several hours distributing them around the town. Professor Tanner had been to Friar's Gate, spoken with the Vicar of St. Mary's church, and made inquiries about local paranormal anomalies. That last part did not appear to go over too well with the Vicar or the senior residents he confronted on the street. By late afternoon when he and Helen regrouped, they concluded they needed help from Travis.

Finding a taxi outside the police station proved exasperating, and when he asked, he was directed toward a bus stop. Travis could only guess at his next thought; it just came out of nowhere. Deb's car? He hadn't seen it parked on the street. But then he remembered; she had said it was always a hassle to find a parking space on her street. Travis estimated that he was two, maybe three miles away from Deb's house and although he didn't know the exact route, he had a general idea of the direction so he started walking. He knew the car must be there somewhere; Deb had been home. That wasn't the point. There was no point he concluded, but the vehicle had belonged to Deb and he was going to find it.

His acceptance of Deb's death was starting to sink in. Words used in the past tense seemed to summarize the circumstance but did not lessen the heartache and sorrow. He just needed to continue putting one foot in front of the other and moving forward. And then, again, the transference of his thoughts moved toward Sam, and he did not resist. Where was she, and how was she, held some priority and he wished he knew where to find her. He thought back to that night and their first meeting—the intensity of their connection and the spiritual aspects of shared knowledge. The intimate understanding of something beyond the physical ignited and rekindled a metaphysical plane, seducing them both in that exact moment, of which fragments remain.

Following one of the main roads; walking along the sidewalk passing homes and occasionally mom and pop type stores, he continued moving in the direction he hoped would lead him to Deb's house. If his memory was correct, he should be getting close to the pedestrianized shopping center, which he considered the downtown area, and he had a pretty good idea of which way to go from there. But something he wasn't sure what, caused him to pause. It was hard to determine, a feeling, a thought, an instinct of recognition maybe. Looking around there appeared to be nothing familiar in sight; he was standing in front of a boarded-up house. The homes on either side looked occupied; turning, he looked across the street before shaking his head, took one more look at the vacant house, dismissed his thought and started moving again.

******

Helen and John sat at the hotel bar enjoying a drink, waiting for dinner to start or Travis to return. Both events really, but in no particular order, but as John had pointed out it would be nice to know where Travis had been all day and what he had been doing. They casually talked about how to gain Travis's trust to extract the key elements for their investigation to move forward. John especially was aware of his botched attempts to build a rapport, and there had been several times during dinner last night, where he wished he could have stopped Helen and her relentless questioning. Unfortunately, it had not gone well and John had recognized Travis had taken a deflective stance.

******

Returning to the Red Lion Hotel; Travis paid the cab driver and got out, intending to go straight to his room, get cleaned up real fast and go out again to find somewhere to eat. He did not want a repeat performance of last night. But as he stepped toward the entrance a second cab pulled up to the curb. The cab door nearest to him shot open.

"TRAVIS!" He turned quickly and saw his sister moving toward him fast.

"Sis! What are you doing here?" His reaction was dictated by her arms taking hold of him in a hug and if that wasn't surprising enough, he saw Mac get out of the front passenger door over her shoulder. "Mac! What the hell's going on?"

Mac stepped forward as Travis relinquished his hold on Julie, and he and Mac met in their customary Titan hug fashion. Julie was surprised the ground didn't quake as they made contact; the force made her blink as she stepped back to a safe distance.

"What's going on? Why are you here?" It sounded lame, even to Travis as he said it but he was confused.

"Okay Wicket. You've had your turn. Get out the bloody way."

For Travis, his world stopped in that instant. The familiarity of Deb's voice sounded so real. So alive? Mac looked into Travis's eyes, saw the facial features contort, and wasn't sure if he should let go of him. Travis appeared to collect himself and take a deep breath as Mac released his grip and stepped to the side.

In total disbelief Travis felt his legs go weak. Wavering, he reached for Mac's shoulder for support. Eyes fixed, afraid to blink in case her image disappeared. His lips moved but there was no sound as tears slowly ran down his cheeks.

"Pull it together Sage. I've got enough on my plate with my house burning down without having to take care of you, you silly sod." Deb stepped forward, reaching her hands around Travis's neck she pulled his head down a little and kissed him passionately. Julie smiled and kissed Mac.

Travis heard Mac say, "This calls for a drink." But he was so stunned that he was still trying to decide if he'd kissed back. He had felt the warmth of Deb's lips on his, her embrace, and the reality of her in his arms. She was real, and a thousand 'how' questions raced through his brain but he had yet to organize his thoughts enough to get vocal. Deb had stepped back slightly and was gazing into his eyes. Her radiant smile mesmerized the remnants of any remaining senses he had left. He heard Julie say, "Let's get checked in; I'm hungry." And still, he had difficulty associating any necessity for action until Deb said, "Travis, I love you, and I'm sorry for the way I behaved." He took her in his arms and held her lovingly. Understanding now the full measure of her value in his life. He heard himself say, "I was searching for your car?" Then immediately realized how stupid that sounded. Deb took him by the arm and led him inside the hotel.

Mind still in a daze, Travis looked at Mac, speaking to the young lady behind the counter. Next, Julie, who was aimlessly looking around, and then Deb, standing beside him still attached to his arm and it was only when the young lady referred to the bar and the dining room that his avoidance thoughts kicked in.

"Hey Mac, let's go find a local pub. Deb, remember that one we were in before? They serve food."

"Lead the way mate," Mac instructed, then turning to the young lady he asked that their bags be taken to their room. Mac took Julie's arm and followed Deb and Travis out the front door.

******

'It had been one helluva humdinger,' according to Mac. 'Like it always was, the first night before an adventure and Mac appeared to be the only one not feeling the aftereffects. Amid food, drinks and more drinks the revelations and complexities of events and lifestyles were all discussed. Mac had given Travis a good account of his life and the reasons for his actions. Deb explained that once the decision was made to leave Pensacola, she had emailed Mac. Out of concern

Mac had responded, suggesting she not immediately return to the UK.

Instead, he booked flights for her from Atlanta in the US to Brisbane in Australia. Deb had contacted her friend who was looking after Annie, and that was okay, so in Atlanta she secured the tickets. Although shortly before her first flight took off she visited the restroom and accidentally dropped her smartphone into the toilet bowl. It was insured, but in Australia they would not honor her contract, so Mac had purchased a phone for her to use. And as Deb had said, she didn't have access to anyone's phone numbers. Mac had given her the numbers for Travis and Julie. But she was upset with Travis, and Julie had her issues to deal with, so she just enjoyed her time with Mac and getting out and about in Australia.

The serious stuff was brushed over, like Deb's smartphone, her house and contents were insured, and nothing could be done about the memorabilia, it was gone. But there was one question that wasn't asked? Although Travis felt sure it was on Deb's mind and Julie's too. If not Deb, then whose body was discovered in the ashes?

Chapter 45

Julie was smiling through the lingering effects of alcohol and the exhaustion of jetlag. Once she had arrived at Heathrow she sat anxiously for more than three-and-a-half hours waiting for Mac and Deb to arrive. Another new experience flying alone to a different part of the world and seeing people she had never seen before. Watching them go about their business and wondering what their lives were like. The thrill of Mac taking her in his arms and their first kiss after an eternity of wanting to know and needing to feel. And her unabashed embrace of Deb replaced every second that she thought she had lost her. The compassionate hug shared with her brother. It was emotional; she remembered how she felt when their mom and dad died and what Travis must have gone through when he arrived at Deb's house. But a whirlwind of emotional twists and turns, alcohol infusion, and sleep deprivation could not hold a candle to Mac's amorous advances earlier that morning. Yes, Julie wore a smile and her heartbeat was still racing.

******

The telephone in their room rang irritatingly at seven in the morning, and after replacing the receiver on its stand, Deb tried to remember why she had asked for an early morning call. There was no up-and-at'em left in her, so after tussling Travis aggressively she crawled out of bed and Travis followed suit, grabbing a tee shirt, and putting on shorts before heading downstairs to the exercise room. They had got to get this poison out of their systems.

******

Instinctually there was a sense that Mac would not let Julie out of his sight. Travis would not lose sight of Deb, and Julie wanted all three where she could keep an eye on them. But when Helen and John entered the dining room the spell was broken, at least for Travis. He had a hunch and it was not good. Julie recognized Helen immediately and introduced Mac and Deb. Travis waited for the penny to drop. It didn't, Helen introduced John and they were invited to join them for breakfast. Travis continued to wait anxiously and was surprised when the expression on John's face changed and he looked inquisitively at Deb. Travis knew what was about to happen next, so he intercepted John's inquiry before he could ask it. "Helen, can I speak with you privately for a moment?" Then as an afterthought he included, "John, would you please come with Helen and me?" Somewhat startled, Helen stood. Travis moved closer and took her arm. John also stood and followed as Travis led Helen toward the door. Fifteen minutes later Travis returned alone.

There had been no ill-intent, Helen was an intelligent woman and once she became aware of who Deb was, and that she had not died in the fire, Helen would surmise the possibility of who else it might have been. Who was missing? And as Travis thought, that realization was better reached in private.

******

Priorities for the day, Deb wanted to see her house and lay claim to her car. Travis had found it yesterday afternoon parked on the next road over from the house, exactly where Deb had left it. Then she wanted to drive to the city of Leicester; the closest Apple store location and get her phone replaced, make important calls and if she had time, she felt obligated to inform the Hinckley police about her resurrection from the dead and so, that was the plan. All four of them were going on a guided tour of Leicestershire.

******

Travis felt torn; his obligation was toward Deb, the woman he loved. But his heart was conflicted, Sam had meant no harm and he sensed a responsibility. She was a kid really who had fallen in love. A young woman misguided by her emotions, perhaps? But, as such she had played her part well, and he could not bear the thought that her life might have ended so tragically. He had a role in this, and he knew he would have to see it through if he was ever going to find peace.

To have delivered the news to Helen, and then watch as she reached her own conclusion. To have witnessed a mother's love, as she broke down in tears. Listened to the mournful cry and tried to reassure her of the improbability of it, while knowing it was a possibility felt heartless. He knew then that he had a duty to perform and it would not be easy.

******

It was late in the afternoon when they arrived at the Hinckley Police Station. The policeman at the information window looked nervous as Travis and Mac entered through the doors. Two muscular, tall, suntanned giants of men wearing sunglasses were not something he was accustomed to seeing stepping up to his counter. He took two steps back before offering a cordial greeting and inquiring why they were there. Mac felt the only reason the police officer did not sound the alarm was that they had Julie and Deb standing beside them.

"I want to report a resurrection," Deb answered boldly.

"May we speak with Detective Myers?" Travis added, trying not to laugh.

Again, the pretty policewoman offered tea, Deb accepted for everyone and the informal interview began once all the formalities were dealt with, milk and sugar, one lump or two, except for the part where Detective Myers wanted to interview Deb in a room on her own. Travis objected, and a compromise had to be reached. Travis would accompany her, sit beside Deb and be quiet. He would not be separated from her that easily. Mac and Julie were offered more tea and left to sit holding hands, looking into each other's eyes talking softly.

The detective asked a question, listened to the answer, and took notes before asking the next question. It all seemed a little tedious to Travis, but he remained quiet until an hour or so into the interview when the detective said something strange, which inferred he already knew the victim was not Deb?

"Whoa? Hold up a minute, detective. Did you just say what I think you said? You already know that the person who is dead was not Deb? And you saw no reason to share that information with me yesterday? What the fuck is wrong with you? I came here brokenhearted because the woman I love was dead, and you saw no reason to tell me otherwise?" Travis was hot; he wanted to grab the man and shove his foot up the guy's ass. But only after he banged the guy's head against the wall a few times to try to knock some sense into him. The meeting came to an abrupt stop.

The detective knew he had made a mistake and was sidelined as a consequence by his boss. Travis was asked to calm down and if he complied, the senior detective would share specific facts with him. Off the record, of course.

Travis didn't want tea and opted for bottled water instead. Deb sat quietly, satisfied that Travis had expressed her thoughts amicably and she had nothing more to add. However, she was tired and shocked by this turn of events and the next stage frightened her. Had Sam broken into her house? She was already entering into the grieving process.

It took the senior detective about fifteen minutes before he entered the room with a uniformed constable who took up a standing position against the wall.

"First, I would like to sincerely apologize for how my colleague handled your interview yesterday Mr. Sage. Furthermore, I will apologize for how today's interview has turned out. Please understand we make every effort to be discreet and efficient while we gather information and evidence, and it is paramount to the case that the evidence and information we have is not disclosed prematurely. Now, regarding the body found at the scene, I can tell you it was female. A young woman similar in age to the homeowner, maybe a little younger. It will be hard to determine the exact age due to the severity of the tissue damage. We issued a court order for the dental records of the homeowner. I'm sorry?" He was looking at Deb. "Would you prefer I use your name rather than be so clinical?" Deb shook her head, indicating she would not prefer him to use her name. She preferred the separation.

He continued. "As I was saying, when the pathologist checked the dental records, they didn't match. Therefore, we have to assume the possibility that a crime may have been committed. We ran a thorough background check on the homeowner and discovered you; I'm sorry, the homeowner had left the country about a week before the incident, bound for the United States. What we didn't know was, was there someone else living in your home with you, or do you have any knowledge of who the victim might be? Did anyone have access or keys to your property?"

"Yes, my close friend Mary O'Connell, has a spare set of keys. But she hasn't been to the house in almost two years since Christine died."

"Have you had contact with Mrs. O'Connell recently?"

"No my smartphone was damaged during my travels and I had no other means of getting in touch with her."

"I visited her the day before yesterday." Travis offered. "She advised me to come here." Deb looked at Travis, and Travis looked at Deb. They both knew what the other was thinking, but neither was sure if it was something they were comfortable verbalizing. Finally, realizing this, Travis took responsibility. "Detective, I have a reasonable suspicion of who the victim might be. If dental records are needed to confirm or deny the victim's identity, her mother is staying at the same hotel we are in Atherstone. God, I hope I'm wrong."

Deb reached over and took hold of Travis's hand as he relayed the story of Sam and provided all the information he feasibly could.

******

An innate sense of conviction took hold of his thoughts as Travis reflected on the events surrounding his relationship with Sam. A conviction enveloped in dissatisfaction with something neither of them understood. A set of seemingly random circumstances had brought them together and maneuvered a series of actions that he now felt, were calculated. But by what force? His conclusion that life is unpredictable and death holds many mysteries provided no answers. It was in the thought that the fear of both holds each person hostage, was where the answers lay and to understand life, he must first accept that life was temporary.

******

While Deb was taking a shower Travis decided to check up on Helen before getting dressed for dinner. The knock on her door was acknowledged by John, who upon seeing Travis, inched his way out of the room quietly and pulled the door closed behind him.

"Hi Travis."
"John. How is Helen?"
"Resting now; it's been a rough day for her."
"I understand. Look John, I think we got off on the wrong foot. Do you want to try again?"

"I would be delighted, but I think we need to talk privately."

"Okay, perhaps later tonight, after dinner. Let's see how everything develops."

"Sounds good."

******

During dinner, Travis looked around the table. Mac, Sis, and Deb. Each were important to his life in different ways and for just a moment, he felt overwhelmed with emotion. The love he held toward each one of them engulfed him. So this was his family, an American, a Brit, and an Aussie. What a rag-tag bunch they were, including himself and yet, such a perfect blend of everything you could ever wish for, and he felt blessed.

Continuing his observations, he realized Mac had never met Sam and was forced to wonder how little he knew about why they were all here, in this small English town? Most of the guests had left the dining room. A man and a woman were seated on the far side of the room when Travis announced, "Guys, we need to talk."

He waited for a few seconds before he continued. "I came here for a purpose with three main goals in mind, the first of which I'm pleased to say, has worked out amazingly," He smiled at Deb. "I have the woman I love back in my arms and I'm the happiest man in the world. So delighted in fact, that it would be far too easy for me to feel content and be satisfied in the achievement. But I haven't achieved anything. It was you Mac, who kept Deb safe where I let her down and failed to realize her importance in my life.

Sis, I could say I don't know where I'd be without your love and caring concern. But I have a pretty good idea and pretty or good would not be found in that image.

Deb, sometimes I feel like a fish out of water and I know I have some rough edges that you seem to see beyond. I'm grateful for that and every other quality you bring into my life. I love you Deb, and always have. I just didn't realize how much I loved you until I thought I'd lost you, and I ask for your forgiveness for that.

The three of you are my family. I arrived here not knowing what to expect or what trials I would face and like the great family we are, you all show up to let me know you have my back. It doesn't get any better than that. I love you all.

But as I said, I came here with three goals. Mac, you never met Sam and I'm still hoping that one day you might. She is this young, good-looking woman with strong instincts and crazy ideas. Who, by the very definition of charisma, you will develop affection toward. Sam has a good heart and a bold sense of adventure. I have to find her, and I need everyone's help."

Travis had not seen John walk into the dining room with Helen at his side several minutes earlier and pause to listen. Helen now quickly moved over beside Travis.

Surprised, he stood and as he did, Helen enfolded him in her arms and spoke.

"Thank you…. Thank you."

Chapter 46

Understandably, Helen wanted to see Deb's house and it didn't take long to convince Deb and Julie to accompany her. However, Deb did impose one restriction on Travis. He had to promise not to go near the arch. But, to quote John, 'It had been fortuitous that he and Helen, entered the dining room last night when they had, because it changed the depressive nature of Helen's perspective and gave her hope.' This in turn, allowed Julie and Deb to show their support toward Helen and leave Mac, Travis, and John, to enter into a serious discussion about the spirit phenomenon and the arch, and today, Travis had a new respect for John. The professor really knew his stuff, and Travis liked him.

They gathered around the painting in his room while Travis explained what he had seen emulating from the scene, and in the picture of the artwork on Sam's phone and how he sensed the presence of the buildings beyond the image of the arch. Mac looked confused, almost as if he wanted to scratch his head in disbelief. But he knew Travis and trusted his words, so he listened and watched. Travis convinced John that in order to know whose eyes were allowing him to visualize the phenomena, he first needed to date the redbrick structure to create a timeframe. They talked about the first meeting with Sam; the birthday party, discovering her in his home, and showing up on Deb's doorstep. The strange events at Deb's house and her cat Annie, and how Sam somehow was aware when he was in danger or had been hurt.

It relieved Travis to finally share so much information and his thoughts with someone who could actually interpret and communicate in a language he could understand. John's knowledge of the many different facets provided insight into aspects Travis had not even considered. And now, what remained was the test. John wanted them to go to the arch.

******

Helen suggested they stop at a florist's shop on their way to Deb's house. She had indicated no matter who the body belonged to; they should receive flowers. Julie knew Travis had not intended for Helen to hear his words last night and consider him the harbinger of Sam's safe return; it was a long shot, Travis was going with a gut feeling; if Sam could sense harm to him, surely the reverse would also be true. But after speaking with the detective yesterday, the odds were getting shorter. What if he had been cut off? Excommunicated in some way and the link had been severed? Perhaps he, Sam, or both of them had served their purpose? There was only one way to find out; he must return to the arch.

******

Mary, although shocked to hear Deb's voice over the phone and relieved once she was convinced it was not a horrible prank call, it was not enough. She wanted to see Deb in the flesh and be able to reach out and touch her. However, a promise made had to be kept and, because Helen needed the distraction and Deb wanted Mary to meet her sister-in-law-to-be (hopefully), she took the opportunity to drive over to Mary's house.

******

"Come on, Travis. What could possibly happen? I'll be there, and so will Mac, and you said last time it was just Deb with you, and she got you out safely."

"You're missing the point, John. I promised Deb I would stay away from the arch."

"But Travis, how would she find out? I won't say anything, how about you Mac?"

"Ya best back off professor, no one's gonna get between him and Deb, not while I'm breathin."

John looked at Mac and saw he was serious and held up his hands in submission. "Okay, I'm sorry."

Travis smiled; the professor had a lot to learn about Mac. "Hey John, how about we walk down the street to that sandwich shop? I think we need to take a break."

After they had eaten lunch, the professor decided to go in search of the courthouse, or a records office of some kind where he would be able to find out information about the redbrick building. Mac suggested he and Travis go walkabout, meet some of the natives and get the lay of the land. Travis thought that was much better than returning to the hotel room. The natives of Atherstone knew instantly, that men of a different breed were visiting them.

******

An extra chair was brought to the table, making seven places in all. Deb had invited Mary to dinner. In all the years' Mary had lived in Atherstone, she had never once stepped inside the Red Lion hotel and Deb decided to change that. But almost from the get-go, Travis became aware that Mary appeared to avoid making eye contact or engaging with him in any meaningful conversation. He didn't mind, Mary and Helen were of a similar age and they seemed to find plenty to talk about. But Travis couldn't help but wonder what he said the other day while at Mary's house that had changed the dynamic of their conversation.

Something Deb mentioned kind of stuck with him when she told him Mary had suggested she could live with her, in her house until Deb got herself sorted. That made him stop and think for a moment. Travis had not considered he and Deb would lead separate lives any longer. But they hadn't talked about it either, and on the opposite end of that spectrum, Julie was talking about going to Australia with Mac.

Travis was starting to feel like a fish out of water. He was already thinking about contracting new assignments. Heck, he was already receiving email requests inquiring if he was ready to go back to work. But there was a priority to finding Sam, or at the very least draw a sad conclusion that he had done everything he could. This life above the surface of the water was proving to be far more complex than the organized simplicity of his life below; right there, he knew it was time to visit the arch.

Without further debate, he turned to Deb and said, "I'm going to the arch." But before Deb could object, Travis turned his attention to the professor and said, "It's time." The professor rose from his seat, as did Mac. Deb stood too, "Travis no, you promised!"

"I'm sorry Deb, I have to know?"

Everyone at the table had gone quiet; Helen rose from her seat and followed them out of the dining room. Julie stood and took Deb's hand, Mary did not understand, but was not going to sit there alone, so the three women followed in the same direction the others had gone.

Deb's eyes were teary; she was afraid as they walked swiftly to catch up with their group. She was upset that Travis would so defyingly break his promise, and hoped he did not have some kind of death wish. The man thing. The need to prove a point no matter the cost. She knew she had to be there and if needed, she would slug him again. But this time she felt like she would keep on bashing him until she had knocked some sense into him. It was a woman thing.

******

The night air was cool and damp; the pavement glistened as the moisture was reflected from the light of the streetlamps. Deb saw

Travis up ahead, standing near the arch, talking with Mac as she approached. John and Helen stood close by in spectator positions. The arch was darker by contrast, there were no lights and St. Mary's church loomed in a gloomy, foreboding eeriness that seemed to overshadow the scene.

"Travis!" Deb stood, and he turned to face her.

"Deb, I must do this; I need to know." He took her in his arms "I love you," and kissed her tenderly.

It felt and sounded so final; Deb trembled in confusion, trying hard not to let go. But Travis pulled back turning to his sister, he held her tightly and whispered something in her ear, kissed her cheek and smiled, before walking toward John.

"Okay John, let's do this?"

"Remember to breathe, relax, get your heart rate down and empty your thoughts. Your brainwaves have to be on a low threshold to communicate."

"Got it John, and by the way, thanks for your help."

"Any time, now go find Sam."

Travis looked at the faces of his friends and those he loved, smiled unconvincingly, and then turned to face the arch. It didn't look threatening. In fact, it looked uninteresting, plain, and somewhat ordinary. The lack of light defused the brickwork pattern which looked like a dark gray tube. One he knew he was getting ready to enter. He was calming himself, regulating his breathing and doing his best to clear his thoughts, getting ready to focus on a singular source and hopefully interact with it.

Internally, Deb was nearly panicking, mentally preparing to rush forward and do whatever was necessary to protect Travis. Mac leaned toward Julie and quietly instructed her, "Take hold of Deb's hand and do not allow her to go under the arch." No sooner than Julie had placed Deb's hand in hers, Mac took hold of Deb's other hand and put his arm around her shoulders. Mary still didn't understand, she had no idea what was supposed to happen. Travis continued to calm himself. John moved to the edge of the arch, no more than two feet from Travis and suggested that he calmy provide him with a running commentary once it began. Anxiously, Helen stood, breathing shallow, knowing this could be the most terrifying night of her life or give her reason to rejoice. She thought she could prepare, thought she understood, but her intellect and knowledge were found in textbooks and......... Travis took a step forward and paused. The next step would find him entering beneath the arch. Helen held her breath. Mac tested his readiness to secure Deb if necessary. Julie made a silent plea to God. John crouched down and pressed the video record symbol on his phone. Mary, confused, moved closer to Deb. Travis took the next step.

Chapter 47

He took the third step and then a fourth before looking back at all the faces looking at him.

"Do you see or feel anything, Travis?" John asked.

"Do you mean apart from feeling stupid? Travis thought for a moment. "I'm going to place my hand on the wall in approximately the same location I did before." Moving back toward the entrance he hesitated slightly before making contact with his hand. Nothing apart from feeling the damp cold brick. "Well. that was disappointing?"

He turned and moved forward, further under the arch touching the wall as he went. "Huh, maybe no one's home tonight?" Turning, he crossed to the other side of the arch and did the same thing as he slowly moved back in the direction he came. Nearing John, he paused to contemplate as he looked along the arch and followed the curvature of the inside structure. Maybe he thought he had been excommunicated; that wasn't a good thought, he needed to find Sam.

John, Helen, and Travis were feeling disappointed, on the other hand Deb, Julie, and Mac were feeling relieved. Mary didn't know what to think as Travis reemerged from beneath the Arch. Deb worked her hands free, moved over to where Travis stood, smiled, hugged him and stated, "Sage, you're a bloody wanker. If you ever break another promise to me, I will...."

"Wait a minute!" Travis cut her off in mid-sentence. He was thinking as he turned back toward the arch and stared; without saying another word he walked back under the arch and continued walking out along the street on the other side, then turned and stood facing everyone as they wondered what the hell he was doing? Well, Mac thought that and he was pretty sure Deb was thinking that also.

"Okay John, let's try this again. Mac, look after Deb for me."

Mac stepped forward, took hold of Deb's hand and led her back to a safe distance. A distance he could, if necessary, recapture her if she made a break for it. Dutifully, Julie took hold of Deb's other hand.

"John, I just remembered when I saw the painting for the first time it was an image on Sam's phone and as we all know the artist, Anne O'Connell painted that picture from the approximate spot I'm standing in now. In that image on Sam's phone, I visualized a door in the wall of the arch, over to the left side but the door was not shown in the actual painting. So that's got to mean something don't you think?"

"Possibly, I'm not sure."

Travis took a deep breath, exhaled and began moving forward toward the arch.

He was still a good ten steps away from the arch when something caught his attention: fuzzy at first, out of focus but enlarging and taking shape.

"John, are you getting this?"

"What's going on Travis?"

He stopped walking. Travis was just inside, under the curvature of the arch and over to his left, the shape of a door was forming.

"There is a door; I'm looking at it. Can you see it?"

Stealthily, John stood and moved across to the far wall, carefully keeping his phone trained on Travis. "No, I can't see anything, can you describe it to me?"

"It looks old, made of wood but ha, there's a clue. There is no metal hardware it has a kind of wooden stick-latch to open and secure it. Wait a minute; something else is happening."

"Keep talking to me Travis. What do you see?"

Enthralled, Travis had no words to express what his eyes were communicating to his brain. A three-dimensional image of a young girl had transported herself through the closed door and was standing in front of him. He tried gathered his thoughts quickly.

"A young girl is standing in front of me. It's like looking at the negative imprint of an old black and white photograph. I figure, preteen maybe?"

"What is she doing? Are you in any danger?"

"I don't think so."

She was a lovely young girl and she seemed curious in the way she was watching him. She blinked her eyes and offered a sweet smile. Travis knelt on one knee to bring his eyes to her level.

"Travis. What are you doing?"

"We are introducing ourselves to each other."

Thoughtfully the girl slowly raised her arm and extended it until her hand touched his cheek.

John sees something. It's as if the silhouette of Travis has been edged with a faint light. "Talk to me, Travis. I can see something is changing."

"She is touching my face; she seems curious." And somehow he knew her name? "Her name is Sarah; she just let me know her name is Sarah."

"She's speaking?"

"No, I think it might be telepathic?"

Travis closed his eyes and tried to communicate his name by thought, then he opened his eyes again and was amazed at the familiar responsiveness of her facial gesture. She understood.

John stopped breathing when he saw the light emulating around the silhouettes of Travis and a young girl's figure and could only imagine there had been a connection of souls. They all saw it. Mary gasped. Helen tried to hold back tears; it was so beautiful. The features of the young girl were getting clearer.

Carefully, Travis opened his arms to invite Sarah in for a hug and she responded immediately by laid her head against his shoulder although he could not feel her physically, he sensed the affection.

Julie was crying; her hand covered her mouth, afraid that any sound might steal this moment away.

Travis had a question and although, in one sense, he felt in no hurry to ask, in another, he knew he didn't know how much time he had and so through thought, he posed his question.

Sarah smiled and stepped back a little, he felt the disconnect as a huge surge of information raced through his mind.

******

In a dark dank room below ground, as weak as Sam was, the unnerving experience was just another reminder she was not dead. It had been a desire she had nurtured many times during the past several weeks of repeated abuse which even now paled in comparison to the nightmare she had unwantedly managed to live through. Travis was in trouble; she sensed it but had long since given up on him coming to her rescue. Why would he? He didn't care about her and she hated him for it. There was just no way out, she had tried to escape and been severely beaten; her two captives were merciless and menacing in their efforts to contain and abuse her. She was hurt, cold, and hungry. She just wanted to die.

******

Several minutes passed before Travis regained consciousness and became aware of his surroundings. He felt crowded as the faces of Mac, Julie, and Deb blocked his vision, all talking simultaneously.

"What happened?"

"Damn mate, ya were thrown across the bloody road. Ya took off like a rocket and slammed into the wall. How'd ya feel?"

"I've had better days Mac."

"Thank God you are alive Sage; I haven't got life insurance on you yet and by the way, you're still a bloody wanker." Deb wrapped her arms around Travis and hugged him.

"Do ya think ya can stand?"

"Won't know until I try Mac. Here, give me a hand."

Mac helped Travis to his feet, he was a bit shaky at first but Mac stayed close.

John and Helen were looking at the screen of his phone. Julie and Deb stood next to him on the opposite side from Mac.

"Where's Mary?" Travis inquired, but no one appeared to know and concluded she might have gone home. It was getting late.

Helen came over and looked directly at Travis but didn't say a word, her eyes spoke for her, the uncertainty was pleading for the right answer and he was happy to deliver it.

"Sam is alive."

She laid her head on his chest and burst into tears. Julie maneuvered her away from Travis and wrapped Helen in her arms.

"Let's get ya back to the hotel; I need a damn drink."

Still all amazed by what had taken place, the conversation was limited during the walk back to the hotel. Nevertheless there was a reverence to what they had seen which bore thinking about. There would be time enough to talk later.

******

In the hotel bar Travis watched the replay on the John's phone. The image of Sarah wasn't as clear as he remembered her and although it lacked the depth of the emotional connection he had experienced he had to admit it was remarkable, especially the part where he was launched into the wall on the far side of the arch. That was impressive.

They all had questions but no one seemed to know how to present them, and the few questions that were asked were fielded by John; he was the expert. Travis sat quietly next to Deb; he had received so much information that he needed time to unpack and figure it out. The priority was still Sam; he sensed she was not safe and had to locate her.

******

"Travis, why did you not want me to go into the arch?"

They were lying in bed together; it was late and this would not be his idea of pillow talk. Pillow talk involved sweet little desires, fears, hopes, and dreams. Nonsensical stuff where you smile, laugh, play, and even tease, coax and inspire. But this had been on his mind for quite some time and her not knowing could have cost Deb her life had the situation been just a little different. Even so, it was not going to be easy.

"Honey, this will be tough for me to tell you and hard for you to hear but I swear it will be the truth. But first, I would like you to share the details about the last few minutes you spent with Christine, then I'll take it from there."

******

Professor Tanner paced excitedly back and forth in his room. He held something in his hands that had never been captured before. The interaction between a human and a spirit, and oh boy, was his reputation going to hit the big league. He would never have believed it possible if he had not witnessed the event himself. But stop! He had to reroll that thought; he needed eyewitness accounts. Authenticated eyewitness accounts to back up the digital video recording and he should duplicate the recording just to be safe. He continued to pace back and forth.

"Travis, you already know what happened. You and Mac sat beside me when I gave my statement to the police. You held me when I cried, took care of me when I was afraid and gave me reasons to continue living. I loved Christine, and there are still times when I think about her and miss her. So why do you want me to relive that tragic day?"

"Deb, honey, I love you and the last thing I want to do is to upset you, but I have some insight into what happened that day that conflicts with your belief. I have kept it from you because I love you and in doing that, it could have got you killed. I thought it had killed you a week ago and I was forced to carry the burden of leaving you vulnerable and unaware of the truth. So let me come at it differently and hope you will want to ask me the questions to help you understand. I mean you no harm.

Christine did not lash out and punch you in the face to push you away and save your life. She lashed out in an attempt to seal your fates and end both of your lives together. Christine did not want to die alone."

"Travis, why would you say something like that? It's not true. Christine would never try to hurt me. We were in love, she loved me and I loved her, why are you being so mean?"

"Deb, remember what happened in the arch? You saw what was happening to me, sensed it, slugged me, and probably saved my life. Remember later you asked me what I thought had happened and I said death happened. I saw images and flashbacks through someone else's eyes. I believe those images belonged to Christine; she was angry and jealous, and she wanted you to join her. Her spirit refuses to pass over to the other side because of something that remains unresolved. I think that is what this has all been about. Think about it, I met Sam and in turn, led her to you. Think about the painting?

Christine's great-grandmother painted it. Christine had that painting in her bedroom all the time she was growing up; then suddenly, it showed up in the States and Sam purchased it. I can't explain how Sam, or I saw things in that painting but again, everything brought us to the arch and you. Mary said that as a young girl, Christine would spend hours standing in that arch looking out at a woman smiling at her and think about the inexplicable things that happened in your house when I stayed with you. The house itself was everything Christine; it was a shrine, and you had turned her into a saint. But the truth is, that day inside the wreck, deep in the ocean Christine tried to end your life. She could not bear the thought of dying alone and you living a life without her and if I couldn't deliver you to her, she had Sam to use as an alternate source. That's why I couldn't let you come into the arch and why Sam is still in the UK. We are pawns in a game we have limited control over and you are the prize."

Chapter 48

Only in his self-deluded mind could Travis find humor and think he had now scored a twofer? Two for two. It was the second time Deb had walked out and left him hanging. But at least this time, she had told him where she was going.

'I'm going to stay with Mary, but that is not an invitation for you to visit me, and if I come by to visit with Mac and Julie, that is not an invitation for you to speak to me either. Travis, you need help!'

And Travis thought she might be right, because things were different last night under the arch. Where was Christine, or whatever it was that had been so threatening, and where does this young girl Sarah fit into the picture? Sarah had been a beautiful experience; one he knew he would never forget but the rest of it was like a nightmare that kept biting him in the ass. Deb was safe, for the moment at least and he was thankful for that, but the conflict between them was infected by Christine and might be a determining tactic outside of his control.

It had to conclude somewhere; if he were to believe in the grand scheme of things where destiny plays her hand, and right now, he felt like it was his move.

******

"Helen, it looks like you've been abandoned?" She was sitting alone at their usual table in the dining room when Travis walked in. "Good morning Travis; yes, John has returned to the arch to continue his investigation and I received a call requesting my presence at the police station in Hinckley. Will Deb be joining us for breakfast? I want to ask her to drive me over there."

"Deb has already left to spend the day with Mary, but I will be happy to go with you if you like? What exactly is John hoping to find?"

"I have no idea, but after last night who would blame any of us for wanting to understand and learn more. It circumvents most of what the naysayers have preached for generations. I'm intrigued myself, but now I know there's a good chance Sam is still alive I cannot allow myself to get distracted. I can't thank you enough for everything you have done and continue to do to find her."

"Helen, you're a good mom; Sam's a lucky girl. Have you seen anything of Mac and my sister?"

"They were leaving as I came downstairs. Said they were going for a walk-something-or-other?"

"Walkabout?"

"Yes, that was it, walkabout. Julie said the canal system in this area offers a diverse landscape that they were going to explore and they should be back by lunchtime, I believe. Have you had any more thoughts as to where Sam might be?"

Travis sat back in his chair for a moment to gather his thoughts. "Helen, that's a tricky question to answer but I'll try. You see, Sam nor I have control of that; it appears that when I've been in trouble Sam has felt it and so either Sam has not experienced a life and death situation, or I've just not picked up on it if she has. I'm hoping the former is true, especially after last night. I feel confident she is alive and I will find her given a chance. She understands how it works better than I do, so I need her to reach out to me. Anyway, if you're about ready I'll ask the front desk to call a cab?"

******

Travis could only guess that he was the last person detective Myers had expected to walk into his office when he arrived with Helen; the look on his face was evidence of that, but Travis was calm; this wasn't about him, and he already knew he didn't want any tea, pretty policewoman or not and it was no surprise that their meeting was brief; they were out of there in less than fifteen minutes. Detective Myers had acknowledged receipt of Sam's dental records by international overnight express delivery. The pathologist examined them and concluded Sam was not the victim they were trying to identify. So, it was official and Helen was relieved.

"Well, I must say Helen, they were efficient. Did you even finish your tea?"

With time on their hands and no taxi in sight, Travis simply suggested they walk to the pedestrianized shopping center, play tourist for a while and then catch a cab from there. Helen agreed; it was a plan and the walk would do her good.

******

It was a nice change of pace, something she and Mac both needed, not to mention the alone time together away from the hotel. The sun appeared now and then between the heavily laden gray clouds and seemed to flirt with them. Was it going to rain or was it not? That question seemed to be on most walkers' minds as they briefly engaged Mac and Julie in passing.

"Mac, what do you think about what happened last night?"

"Honestly I'm not sure what ta think. I mean, we both saw it so we can't unsee it. Was it a good thing, or will it mean trouble? After listening to ya brother and that professor talkin yesterday, I can't help thinkin nothin good will come of any of this stuff. Travis needs to go home and get on with is life."

"I kind of agree with you Mac, but I know Travis, and he's not going to abandon Sam as long as there is some hope of finding her. But last night, I'm like you; it was incredible to witness, but I remember what Travis told me about his previous encounter that almost cost him his life. So I agree that Travis needs to scoop Deb up in his arms and go home as quickly as possible."

"Is that what I need to do Julie, scoop ya up in my arms and carry ya off to Brisbane with me?"

Julie smiled. "Mac, open your arms and I'll jump right in. I know you are the man I love and I feel how much love you have to share with me. I'm yours Mac; wherever you go, I will go also."

"Well, I don't wanna leave Travis in the lurch, but I do have a business to run so I think it best I have a talk with him and find out where things stand. Fancy a drink? It looks like there's a pub up ahead.

******

Walking along, talking about the differences between the American way of life and the British; not paying much attention to anything, Travis suddenly had a feeling and stopped. Helen realized that she was alone two or three steps further along, so she turned to see where he was. "Travis?"

He was looking around while in deep thought and did not respond. So Helen walked back toward him. "Travis, are you okay?"

"Helen, I walked past here the other day and right in this very spot, I felt something and now I feel it again."

"What do you feel? Are you ill?"

"No, it's not that kind of feeling. It's a feeling of knowing something but I'm not sure what I'm supposed to know." He continued to survey the area around him, and he kept coming back to the vacant house. Fixing his stare, the feeling seemed to draw his thoughts toward it. "Helen, wait here. I'm going to take a quick look around this property, if anybody asks, say we are interested in buying it, okay?"

He didn't wait for an answer. Instead moving quickly he checked the door and the boarded-up windows on the front of the house;

they were tight, so he moved around the side, doing the same thing as he worked his way toward the back of the house. Along the back of the yard was a wooden fence with some of the boards missing, and he noticed a trail through the overgrown weeds leading from the fence to the backdoor of the house. Whoever used this property was either careless or stupid; it was a dead giveaway.

******

Saying goodbye to Mac on the platform at the train station in Nuneaton seemed oddly final. Of course, Travis knew they would meet again; he wouldn't consider missing out on the wedding. But a change had come and a shift in the dynamic of their relationship had taken place. Travis felt it and he sensed Mac felt it also. It was an unfamiliar moment as they stood awkwardly trying to figure out what to say to each other, knowing things would never be the same again. The brotherly fellowship had seen many adventures, faced dangers and endured some pain. Together they had ridden on the back of challenges, overcome adversity and sometimes beat the odds. In just a few short years they had built a lifetime of memories and an unbreakable bond of trust. Two men, bold and fearless in stature, warriors for what they believed in and protectors of those they loved, clasped in a handshake of iron grip, shared a knowing smile.

Looking at his sister, the older sibling, it was hard to believe he was in front of the same person. He loved her, and even in times of disagreement that love had always shone through. Her steadying force had influenced many of his choices and he thought he had known her so well.

Sam was safe, and once Helen's husband Richard arrived from the States she was transported to a private medical facility in London to await the necessary paperwork allowing her to fly home. The Professor? Travis didn't know what he was doing. However, he sometimes caught sight of him in the dining room and if push came to shove, he could make a pretty good guess.

The radiant smile on Julie's face told the story of the flower that had finally bloomed and gave proof of fate's ingenuity across all the rhythms of our lives. Travis stood in awe of her transformation and was reassured she was in safe hands. He loved Julie, he loved Mac, and he loved Deb, and at this moment he thought, two-out-of-three ain't bad.

Chapter 49

His focus had shifted and his handwritten note to Detective Myers anonymously dropped off should by now have served its purpose. The two fools who had confronted him in the vacant house didn't know what hit them and once subdued, presented no threat. Discovering Sam, he had removed her shackles and given the men a taste of their own medicine and after two days of no food and water, determined they were ready to be rescued. Sam was safe.

Sam was safe and in time. He had to think about that; would he ever see her again? He could learn to miss her; her crazy antics, but was that who she really was? He had no idea but she was cute and he smiled when the shower scene came to mind. Yes, she definitely was a cutie.

******

The hesitation before he knocked on Mary's front door belied the purpose for his visit, and depending upon who opened the door, and the reception he received would determine the transactional nature of his conversation.

"Hi, Mary. How are you?"
"If you're looking for Deb, she doesn't want to see you."
"No actually Mary, I came to see you."
"Wait a minute."

She closed the door leaving Travis on the stoop. It could have been worse, he thought. She could have slammed the door in his face.

The door reopened a minute or so later and Travis was allowed to enter. Although, he sensed the welcome mat had been taken away.

"Mary, I understand the situation and realize this is a bit of an imposition for you, but I'm getting ready to fly home. I want to thank you for your friendship and hospitality and for sending me the historical paperwork I requested. And as you requested, I have brought the painting to you."

As Travis intended, it was a psychological slap across Mary's face. First, she would have heard, 'imposition,' and thought, *it certainly is.* Second, she would have heard, 'he's leaving' and thought, *finally, great.* Then she heard, *'friendship,'* and thought, *'hum, I did enjoy meeting you.'* Followed by 'hospitality,' and thought, *'where are my manners?'* And then the kicker, 'I have a gift for you,' and inside, Mary would cringe at her own bad behavior. And that's the kind of thing you learn when you hang out with Helen for a while.

"I'm sorry Travis, would you like a cup of tea?"

******

Removing the painting from its box, Travis held it up in front of Mary.

"Mary, look at the painting. Something has been bothering me and I believe you know the answer? Christine's great grandmother Anne O'Connell was the artist; we've established that. Christine visited the arch frequently as a child and as you said, she was looking at the smiling lady. I have reason to believe it was Christine who interacted with me during my first visit to the arch, and something I said during my last visit with you reminded you of something unpleasant. And then, that night at the arch when you came with us something frightened you and you left. Everything appears to revolve around members of your family. Mary, I believe you know who Sarah is?"

Her reaction was instant; the color drained from her face. She cupped her hand over her mouth and although she wasn't crying, tears were visibly running down her cheeks.

Travis sat quietly, still holding the painting in front of her and waited. It took several minutes to compose herself and find the words.

"Sarah was Anne's younger sister. I... I don't know all the details the only information I have ever known is Sarah disappeared when she was young. No one wanted to talk about it but the other night at the arch, hearing her name and seeing the image of her has haunted me ever since. I can't get her out of my thoughts, something terrible happened, didn't it? I feel it deep in my heart.

******

Reduced to two, as they had become, John and Travis elected to sit at a smaller table for dinner. The camaraderie of their larger group had vanished and left them speaking in hushed tones in an almost empty room. Travis's bags were all but packed and he would be on his way tomorrow, and Deb had not made contact.

"Do you have any idea how many pubs there are in this town Travis?"

Travis shrugged his shoulders; he hadn't got a clue and wondered for a moment what kind of research John was doing.

"I was chatting with a couple of locals the other night, and they told me if you start at one end of Long Street; drink a half-pint of beer in each pub as you work your way along the street, they would almost guarantee no one has ever made it to the other end of the street. How's that for a great tourist attraction?"

He didn't even want to waste time thinking about that scenario. "John, how would you feel about accompanying me to the arch again?"

"Do you even have to ask? Of course I will, what's the plan?"

"I want to say goodbye to Sarah."

Travis had a hunch and believed now he knew whose eyes had allowed him to see the buildings beyond the arch.

******

Not entirely happy about the outcome but satisfied he had done everything he could, Travis boarded the train bound for London. It was time to go home and put his life back in order. There was little consolation to be found in trying to fix something that might be unfixable. Deb had her beliefs and he had his, so it is what it is, and Christine was a jealous mistress. Then, hit by a strange thought, the cat. Deb had not picked up Annie from her caretaker while he was there? Huh. It was just something else he didn't have the answer to, but rarely in life does anyone have all the answers because the deeper you dig, the more questions you uncover.

******

"Hi, Helen. How is she?"

"Travis. You might be in luck; she's awake, I'll let her know you're here."

Awake was a significant improvement from the way he had found her. Malnourished, battered, bruised, and he wasn't sure if she had been given drugs. Her limp body had felt weightless when he picked her up and carried her from the vacant house.

"Yes but be gentle; she tires very quickly. I'll take you to her room."

The thing was, as terrible as she looked physically, Sam would get better. The unknown psychological impact of all the trauma she had sustained was of more concern. He held her hand, kissed her forehead and waited a few moments before removing his sunglasses. The connection was still there, but in a very weakened state as he gently delivered his thoughts to her. Sam smiled before closing her eyes.

"So, when are you flying out?"

"In about four hours. How are you and Richard holding up?"

"We're doing well, but I'll be happy when we finally get her home."

"Any idea about when that might be?"

"Two, maybe three more days. Richard is at the American Embassy now."

"Well, Helen, I'll say goodbye and get to the airport. It's been an adventure and I'm glad we got the time to get to know each other better, you have an amazing daughter.

"Travis, you're family now, so don't be a stranger. Have a safe journey home and give my regards to Julie and Mac next time you get in touch.

******

Travis had already accepted two assignments, one in the Red Sea and one off the coast of Costa Rica. It was time to get home, get organized and get going. Do what he does best and let each new day unfold as it may. Life's an adventure and……? He didn't finish that thought; he was tired of all the drama topside living demanded and needed a break.

******

"What the hell?" He was sitting in the Atlanta airport waiting for his connecting flight to Pensacola when he received an email from John.

Travis, you are not going to believe this; I ran into Mary shopping in the market today. She told me the police had identified the body and took Deb in for questioning two days ago and she is still being held. It's Christine. They identified the victim as Christine.

He rose and began pacing the floor out of frustration; it was a ridiculous conclusion and he didn't want to go back. He couldn't go back. Damn Christine, she was a jealous mistress.

For now, he decided he had to sit this one out and hope the situation resolved itself. Deb had made her choice; she wasn't in any immediate danger as far as he could tell and surely someone would realize the impossibility of the circumstance.

******

Three weeks later, through a joint agreement with the Israeli and Egyptian governments, Travis was on assignment in the Red Sea, offshore from Taba. He had been there for a week and was really getting his stride back. It had been slow at first; the boat captain and his mate didn't speak English. But, once he found a diving companion who could speak several languages, including English, everything began to run smoothly. But he sure missed Mac; it just wasn't the same without him. But, of course he knew it wouldn't be, but thinking about it and actually experiencing it were two different things.

And Deb, he missed her too, and having not heard any more from the professor or her, he was left to assume everything must have worked out. Although initially, his imagination had played the devil's advocate and invented a grand conspiracy theory. How would anyone know that Christine had died in that wreck at the bottom of the ocean? He didn't go back to check and neither did Mac. Their priority was Deb, and they were unaware of Christine's existence until they were well on their way back to shore to have Deb checked out at the medical facility. And looking around Deb's house, there were just so many signs that Christine still lived there. And whose cat was Annie, Christine's, or Deb's? He never did get the answer to that question. But imaginary theories aside, how could, or why would Christine be in hiding for two years. There was no logical conclusion to be had and so he dismissed the whole concept. It was more likely to be a case of mistaken identity. But he thought it would make an excellent spine-chilling movie.

Chapter 50

Travis was not a fan of celebrity status, but it appeared his reputation had preceded him when he arrived in Brisbane for the wedding. He wondered if he had Julie or Mac to thank for that? A group of journalists and photographers rushed him at the airport, asking questions and offering invitations for exclusive interviews about his work for National Geographic and climate change. Mac tried to assure him it had as much to do with the high society of Brisbane, the pending wedding, and the Adams family name although he was not convinced there was no plot.

But he had arrived; it was great to see Mac and his sister again and not wanting to break with tradition, that night was set to be one helluva humdinger. It went from there, two weeks filled with family gatherings, social events, dinner parties, and luncheon engagements.

It all became a blur as Travis estimated he had been introduced and shook hands with about a thousand people in his role as the best man. And there were moments when he was thankful that he only had one sister, feeling he couldn't survive going through all that again.

But there was a reprieve found in a three-day dive off the Great Barrier Reef. Just Travis and Mac together in the element they loved. And then……

******

Travis, I'm sure after all the trouble I've caused you will think about disregarding this email, but I implore you to reconsider. I need to talk with you and get some answers; I love my mom and dad, but they are smothering me. You would think I was a fourteen-year-old who they needed to monitor twenty-four-seven and it is driving me crazy. So please come and visit; I will wear gloves and sunglasses if you require them. I desperately need your help to put the past behind me and move forward with my life; you are the only person who would understand. Sam.

******

Why in the world he would agree to travel back into the land of country music begged the question as to his sensibility, or would that be sanity? His truck done broke down, he lost his old dog, or the woman had the good sense to leave him. The, he hadn't taken a bath in a month and his horse couldn't stand the stench any longer type melodies that dribble out of the jukebox, accompanied by the same-ole twangy sound. Lawdy, Lawdy, heaven help him?

But, if it would help Sam, he felt obliged to risk it. So, knowing once he returned home from Australia, he had a couple of weeks before his next assignment in Costa Rica and her parents would provide the additional safety net, and to kill two birds with one stone, he could drive Julie's vehicle back to his house if he flew there. He didn't need it but as Julie had stressed, she wanted him to have it because she'd be damned before offering it to Steve. He responded positively.

******

The day had finally arrived, and he had never seen Mac look so nervous. He was anxiously waiting to hear the sound of 'Here Comes the Bride' from the string quartet who had fallen silent not more than a minute ago. "Where's Julie? Ain't she comin?" spoken in a concerned whisper into Travis's ear. "Relax Mac. It would take an act from God to keep her away." "What o ya mean, as somthin happened?" "No, Mac. It's a lady's prerogative to be late. You might as well start out right, so you can get used to it." "Do I look alright?"

"You look fine Mac…." Just at that moment the string quartet burst into action. Travis breathed a sigh of relief and caught his first glimpse of his sister.

******

Travis had to laugh. Sam, as promised was wearing sunglasses. But that was not the funny part. She was wearing white socks on her hands. But, apart from the socks she looked good in her little cotton dress, cowgirl boots and cowgirl hat. And she certainly looked the part of at least a thousand country and western songs about the cowboy who done lost his mind over an untouchable, smart country girl.

Helen was the first to step forward and greet him with a hug and kiss on his cheek.

"Hello Travis, it's good of you to come, Sam has been excited all week. Haven't you Sam? And, once you get settled I want to hear all about Julie and Mac, their wedding and what it was like in Australia."

"Helen, give the boy some breathing room. He's just got off the plane. Hi Travis, welcome."

"Thanks Richard; it's good to see you again and judging by the look of Sam, you've done some fine doctoring. Hi Sam."

Sam wrapped her arms around him and hugged tight with her head against his chest.

"Thank you." She whispered.

He was almost disappointed there was no attempt at a kiss, he might have enjoyed that.

"How are you doing Sam?"

"Maybe I'll let you be the judge of that." That statement was delivered with a coy smile as she linked her arm around his and led the way toward the exit. Followed by Helen and Richard.

******

After dinner, as requested, Travis shared news about his sister and Mac, their wedding and his thoughts about Australia. Later he retired to the guest suite, took a hot shower, and climbed into bed. The following morning he awoke as the bedroom door was flung wide open and Sam waltzed in wearing a short cotton nightie complete with matching white socks on her hands and sunglasses covering her eyes. She climbed on the bed, sat cross-legged, and used her hand to pat down the nightie between her legs.

"Sam, what are you doing? What will your parents think?"

"Travis, I'm a twenty-five-year-old woman, my dad's already left for his office. My mom's downstairs in the kitchen, fixing coffee for you, and besides they think you walk on water, and if there were a man in this world they'd trust with their precious daughter, it would be you. The door is wide open and I might add, you've already seen me naked, so what's the big deal?"

Travis smiled; he had no come back for that lengthy assessment; she was resilient and had bounced back nicely, but he thought, she hasn't seen me naked. He resisted the urge to throw back his bedcovers. "Sam, although I appreciate the gesture, the socks are a little over-dressy don't you think?"

"Good morning. How do you like your coffee? Sam? I hope you're not being a nuisance; if she is Travis, just ask her to leave your room. Of course, you would leave if asked to, won't you Sam?"

"Yes, mommy."

Helen chose to ignore the little girl's tone in Sam's reply.

******

Sam volunteered to drive Travis to Steve's house to pick up Julie's vehicle.

"Sam, so that you know, I'm ready to listen whenever you feel ready to talk."

"Well, we could start now, but you will be driving in a different vehicle in about ten minutes. So how about we drop Julie's vehicle off back at my house, then you and me, we go somewhere? I can't talk about this with anyone else it's complicated, and I'm grateful you agreed to come. I don't understand most of it, even now and I was there."

He glanced in her direction and saw her discreetly try to wipe a tear away with her fingers.

******

There was no perfect place for this; it just had to happen. "I remember being inside the arch, there was a door and I pressed my hand against it, wondering if it would open. It didn't, but I felt something whirling around on the other side. I don't know what happened but then I realized that my hand was pressed against Deb's door, and I pulled away. I sensed I had transported something from one place to another and I was afraid. Nothing made sense; I don't know what happened next or how I got back to the hotel. I was suddenly there, crying, and sad in my room."

"Wait a minute Sam. What did the door look like? Can you describe it?"

"Just pieces of wood joined together; it looked old. There was nothing special about it, it was just a door leading somewhere, I guess?"

"And you felt something on the other side of the door with your hand?"

"Yes"

"What happened next?"

"As I said, my hand was held against Deb's door. I pulled it away and stepped back sensing I had somehow delivered whatever that thing was to Deb's house."

"Do you remember when that was?"

"Do you mean what day?"

"Yes, which day was it?"

"It was the day after you and Deb took me to the train station. I'm not sure now what day that was but I got off the train, made my way to Atherstone and checked into the hotel. So it was the next day."

Travis thought about that for a couple of minutes. Was that the day Deb drove them to Coventry? On the same day they went to visit Mary. Was it that night in the early hours of the next morning when all those strange things happened in the house? He couldn't be sure, but it damn sure seemed like it would all make sense if it were. "I'm sorry Sam, I had to think about that. What happened next?"

"The next day; I don't know what made me go back, but I did the following day. I didn't understand and I needed some answers I guess. Standing under the arch looking out, I saw a woman with an artist's easel, painting a picture maybe. She was smiling at me and I felt myself almost floating toward her but, when I came out of the arch the sunlight caused my eyes to squint and then, she was gone. Quickly I looked around and there, under the arch, was a young girl. Travis, it was me; I was standing there looking at a younger version of myself, I was terrified and I ran."

"Sam! The lady you saw, I believe was Anne O'Connell, the woman who painted the picture of the arch. The little girl is different; at first I thought she might be Christine because of something her mother told me."

"No, Travis, you're wrong it was me, she spoke to me. She said her name was Anne."

"Christine also liked to be called Anne when she was younger, but I'll have to think this through because that was the morning after you felt like you had transported something to Deb's house. Trust me Sam, when I tell you about the things I've experienced you'll begin to understand how some of the pieces fit together, and together we will find some peace. What happened next?"

Sam looked at Travis, hoping to see some of the reassurance. The peace he spoke about finding and the understanding she craved before she continued.....

"Breaking into Deb's house. It was something I was not consciously aware of doing. I remember returning to the hotel to collect my things and taking them back there. I had a key then and let myself in; she was there, Travis, waiting for me. Christine was there and she wouldn't let me leave. She controlled my mind and used my body, sometimes angry and sometimes affectionately. Christine manipulated me into doing what she wanted to do.

How I escaped, I thought was a miracle, but I fled so instantly that I had nothing: no coat, change of clothes, money, credit cards, or my passport. I literally got out of the house with just the clothes I was wearing. I went back the next day still unsure how I would collect my things, but the house had burned to the ground."

"When you say Christine was in the house, could you see her?"

"No, but I could feel her. When she was angry she threw things, broke things, locked me in the bathroom or made me hurt myself. Then, at night when she wanted to be affectionate, I could feel her touching me, doing things to me, trying to make me want her to do more.

She was there Travis. I didn't imagine her; you have to believe me."

Through the tears Travis could sense her fear, Sam was afraid he would think she was crazy.

Carefully he removed her sunglasses, drew her into his arms and held her close. "Sam, I have felt her presence, I know exactly how dangerous she was, she almost took my life."

"You believe me? You believe me, Travis, it's been such a nightmare. It is a nightmare. How? Why did all this happen to me, to us? I don't understand?"

Fear, anger, and relief, the emotional barriers were released. Sam cried unabashedly and uncontrollably in Travis's arms knowing for the first time in perhaps a long time that she was not going insane. Later she told Travis that after a couple of nights of sleeping rough, out in the cold, two guys said they would get her some food and help her and she fell into their trap.

Chapter 51

In some ways, Travis thought Sam had behaved like an impetuous lovesick fool but now he knew better. To love is the most potent force of the spirit and to demand love is the corruption of all that is good. But on the other hand, to love and offer love without expectation is to be nourished in the purity of our soul. Travis understood the power he now had, the gift that Sarah had given him.

******

Sam was ready now to tell her story while Professor Tanner attentively took notes. Travis sat quietly in the adjoining room and waited, thinking about Sarah and everything she had accomplished. He thought about Anne O'Connell the artist, and wondered when she first knew?

It had seemed complicated through the conceptions and misconceptions of the mind including his and the similarities and irregularities of each person's interpretation of the events. A puzzle where some pieces just didn't fit and some are still missing. Of course, Christine was not the main story and that's what kept throwing him off, but now Travis understands.

The door opened and the John stuck his head out. "Travis, you can come in now."

Sam smiled as he walked in.

"How did it go, John?"

"Well. Sam was very thorough. Just a few points to clarify but first, let me ask you Travis, is Sam aware of the conversations you and I have shared?"

"No John. I felt it best, Sam tells you her story first."

"Good, I couldn't agree more. Would either of you like a cup of tea before we get started?"

"Didn't you get enough of that stuff while you were in England?"

"Travis. I like it; it grows on you, maybe it's an acquired taste?"

"Do you have coffee?"

"What would you like Sam?"

The refreshments were prepared and served.

"Would anyone care for a biscuit?"

"Okay, John, enough with the English patter."

Sam, we; Travis, and I have concluded that there were three entities which we can recognize as the young girl, the woman, and the old lady, and have determined that one of those entities did not belong in the overall objective of the other two. She was an intruder and a disruptive force; a relative newcomer to the group who we appear to agree was called Christine, so now I will piece the story together.

"Anne O'Connell had a younger sibling by the name of Sarah.

"No, her name was Anne."

"Bear with me Sam, you identified with her as Anne, and I understand how that came about.

Sarah disappeared when she was still a young girl and I should interject here that it is believed the young child has a much stronger recognition of their spirit and a greater ability to connect with other spirits. We as adults have outgrown the need to create what is referred to as 'imaginary friends.' But I can assure you that they are not imaginary to a child. We are now aware that Sarah met with a tragic death. What we are not aware of is, at what point Anne O'Connell became aware of her young siblings' tragic end. But supposition would suggest Anne knew her sister was dead while she was alive, which was why she created the painting depicting the arch. She knew something about that scene; it held deep meaning for her.

Sarah's spirit was strong, but she had not developed an understanding to control her senses enough to project, utilizing inanimate objects. And when Anne died, her spirit was weak but she held the artistic vision to project. So when Anne and Sarah came together in death, they were the perfect team. Using Sarah's strong spirit, Anne could project her thoughts animatedly utilizing the inanimate object she had created, the painting.

Sam, you wrote in your journal when you were eleven years old, Anne, my name is Anne, correct?"

Sam acknowledged with an affirmative nod.

"Your spirit was still quite strong then, so a direct transmission into your mind was possible. I'm just unsure about the identity of the entity you were communicating with at that time. It could be just a coincidence, I'm still working on that but from the moment you discovered the painting of the arch and felt an attachment toward it, you were directly connected to the strength of the spirit of Sarah, but receiving messages directly transmitted by Anne O'Connell.

Many people out in the world believe they can communicate with spirits, and there are just as many, if not more who have the same ability but are unaware they have it. And there are people whose spirit has the wherewithal to communicate with another living person's spirit.

Travis is such a person although, until he met you Sam, he was unaware of his ability and when you two met his spirit communicated with Anne through you. So, Sam, your spirit continued the projected link Anne had established with you and Travis called you Anne, which you subconsciously associated with. John took note of the confused look on Sam's face. Let's take a twenty-minute break. It's a lot of information to absorb."

Sam stood, took Travis by his hand and they walked outside the building together.

"So, I've been interacting with spirits since I was a baby and it's only as I age that the connection gets weaker? And what about you Travis, with your special ability, how does that work?"

Travis knew by Sam's tone, that she was agitated. "Sam, every person on this planet has a spirit and John is correct in his belief that our spirits are capable of interacting. Where he is incorrect is where he believes our spirits get weaker, they don't. We just learn to block them out and ignore the fact that we have that ability. Ask any person who is near death; for some reason, when we are dying, we as people desire communication with other spirits and we all have the remarkable ability to reconnect."

"How do you know that Travis? How can you possibly know that?"

Placing his hand under her chin, Travis gently turned her face toward him and said, "look at me." Their eyes locked instantly and Travis allowed Sam to see, feel, and know him. The penetration of his thoughts filled her with reassurance and desire. Then, two seconds later he severed the link. Sam's heart raced and she was breathless, Travis held her steady in place. Mesmerized in the moment, she could not have anticipated his kiss.

There was no reason for John to continue. As far as Travis was concerned, Christine's spirit was just a bad actor. A jealous dominating spirit who invaded the communication links that Anne and Sarah had established and used them for her own purpose to manipulate situations as she saw fit.

******

Travis packed his bag the following day and placed it inside Julie's vehicle before eating breakfast.

"Thanks Helen." She had placed a plate of food in front of him.

"Where are you traveling to next?"

"I'll be flying to Costa Rica in eight days. So I need to get my gear ready to ship."

"Sounds lovely. How long will you be there?"

"Two, maybe three weeks at the most, a lot depends on the weather."

"What a glorious life you lead."

"Yes, I guess it could be if you discount all the work. Have you seen Sam this morning?"

"Her bedroom door is still closed. I can't imagine what's she's doing. Let me go...."

"Hold up Helen, let me go."

Travis went upstairs to Sam's room and opened the door. Her bed was made and her room was tidy. So, he walked over to the bathroom and opened that door. As she said, he had already seen her naked, so what would be the big deal if he saw her naked again? Travis walked back downstairs and continued eating breakfast.

"Was she still sleeping?"

"No, Sam's not in her room. Is her car still here?"

Helen went to check. "Her car is in the garage."

"Well, Helen, that only leaves one other place. Sam is probably hiding somewhere in Julie's vehicle."

******

Looking for changes in the migratory habits of the Great White Shark and Blue Whale, Travis was working with a team of biologists, oceanic meteorologists, and scientists off the Costa Rican coast. Easy money really. When they spotted a shark, he just had to jump into the water, snap a photograph and then get the hell out before it snapped him. Yep, life's an adventure and Sam was right, there was only one man in this world they'd trust with their precious daughter and he was it. Still apprehensive about letting Sam go dig in the dirt in Mexico, Helen and Richard seemed fine allowing Sam to swim with the sharks off the Costa Rican coast. Who knew dirt was so dangerous?

******

John had mentioned in a previous conversation that he would like to make another trip over to England and take a couple of college students, slash Science Engineers with him. Travis wondered if he would have them run the pub challenge, or maybe it would be to stock up on more tea and biscuits. Who knows? And that was what surprised him about the email he received this morning.

Travis. Great news. Using a modified version of GPR: Ground Penetrating Radar and subsurface radar along the wall of the arch; approximately where the door was located, I have discovered skeletal remains. The authorities are now involved; I will contact you with any further developments. And, by the way, the pathologist in Hinckley still believes the body was Christine, and when I inquired about the cause of the fire, one professional to another. It had been determined; spontaneous combustion was the cause. Christine's body had burst into flames and that caused the house to burn down. No news on Deb or Mary; I haven't seen either of them.

"So, Travis thought. Anne O'Connell did have a purpose when she created the painting. It would come as no surprise to him if the skeletal remains were identified as that of a young girl. As for Christine, if you're going to die twice, you may as well go out with a bang the second time just to be sure. And he still didn't know what happened to Annie, the cat?

****** ******

Chapter 29, first paragraph. Unrequited* (not returned) is now an obsolete word according to the Webster's Dictionary, and quite rightly so, in my opinion. Unreturned love is emotional and hurts, and the now obsolete word unrequited bore a sharp edge which lacked the heart wrenching feelings needed to express such an emotional state of mind. Whereas, my word, unrequented, spoken softly and with awareness of the deep anguish, offers a subtle understanding of what has taken place. Hopefully Webester's will adopt it. Unrequented love.

More often than not, the correct answer lies at the end of the right question.

I hope you enjoyed getting acquainted with the characters in this story and felt entertained. If you have questions or comments, don't hesitate to contact me directly at https://www.jtbaxter.com

Also, please consider leaving positive feedback at your favorite online bookstore to benefit your fellow readers. Thank you.

******

Life after death theories.

The never-ending life theory

Claims that when you die, you are immediately reborn into your life again without any memory of the life you had just led before.

Opinion: The spirit does not immediately enter a new life form. A time to rejuvenate is called for, to replenish, and reflect on past experiences, good and bad. Time to understand what was learned and what lessons still need to be experienced to reach our full potential. Leaning more into Plato's Theory.

Plato's theory

Plato believed that the physical world limited our knowledge and that when a person dies, they move on to a new, more fulfilling life. His theory was that death gives souls a chance to find their true existence.

The many worlds theory

The many worlds theory claims that when we die, we are only dying in this one, current universe. There are other universes out there for us to move on to.

Opinion: There are other worlds alien to human existence, but the spirit is not exclusive to human coexistence and can choose to experience different forms of life. As is stated in the Hindu theory.

The Hindu theory

Hinduism also holds the belief of reincarnation. This is because their actions determine a person's status or form in the next life during this current life.

Opinion: Holds some threads of possibility per the Christian theory.

The Christian theory

Our soul is either going to a place called Heaven; or Hell and we, as individuals, have some control over that destiny.

Opinion: This is counter-intuitive to the biblical teaching that our lives are preordained. Our path through life was determined before birth, indicating our destination has been preselected.

******

Can there be life after death? What reason is there in mere mortality if nothing is left in its wake? Is not the soul divine, supercilious to the frailty of human form, and transcendent to a universal force far greater than life itself? But, if so, where does it go? What sustains it? Can it return? And in what state will it reappear?

Life is unpredictable and death mysterious. The fear of either holds us hostage, and we can neither live nor die well. So, to understand life as we perceive it, we must first accept it is temporary.

JT Baxter

The odyssey continues with part two ***Déjà vu Spirit Vision*** where Travis struggles to understand this seemingly limitless gift and the fallibility of human nature. Available in Paperback and eBook formats, from your favorite online bookstore or retailer.

Don't miss out!

Visit the website below and you can sign up to receive emails whenever JT Baxter publishes a new book. There's no charge and no obligation.

https://books2read.com/r/B-A-BOLT-XGCYB

BOOKS 2 READ

Connecting independent readers to independent writers.

Did you love *Déjà vu*? Then you should read *Unspoken Truth Never Rests*[1] by JT Baxter!

Intelligent, quirky, adorable Simon opens the door to truth and decries the falsehoods placed on every woman by man's hand. Unspoken truth never rests, although its silence must be endured. Baxter delivers another serious and oftentimes humorous insight into human behavior in his usual style. What the mind can conceive the body can achieve. There has been no greater truth. Seek out the adventure and embark upon a journey where no man has ever been. What are you waiting for?

Jennifer Thompson

I laughed, I cried. I fell in love with Simon, can I take him home with me? Emmy, Sarah, and Sally would make great friends.

---

1. https://books2read.com/u/bQPPGv

2. https://books2read.com/u/bQPPGv

Megan should spend more time with them. I loved the story, loved the characters, fast action. I was breathless at times, keeping pace. Beautifully written, not a dull moment. I was entertained, which is the reason I buy books.

Toni Danzia

Unspoken Truth is long overdue and ahead of its time. Great story, I could not put it down. Simon is adorable, and you portrayed several women of strong character. I will recommend Unspoken Truth to all my friends. Very enjoyable and well worth reading.

Also by JT Baxter

Déjà vu
Déjà vu Spirit Vision
Déjà vu

Unspoken Truth
Unspoken Truth Never Rests
Unspoken Truth Perfect Moments

Standalone
Abigale Hunt
Circles
Red is Random
One Man's Journey

About the Author

Born and raised in a small town in England, he stepped out into the world and became a world traveler. They say my unique writing style has proven to be exciting and compassionate, with an intuitive understanding of women's emotional desires and what they look for in men. So don't believe everything you read, I get surprised all the time.

Milton Keynes UK
Ingram Content Group UK Ltd.
UKHW020610121223
434223UK00011B/430